NOBLE INTENT

WILLIAM MILLER

NOBLE INTENT

Copyright © 2018 by William Miller.

This book is a work of fiction. Names, characters, businesses, organizations, places, events and incidents either are the product of the author's imagination or are used fictitiously. Any resemblance to actual persons, living or dead, events, or locales is entirely coincidental.

Book and Cover design by www.LiteraryRebel.com

First Edition: Feb 2018

Dedication and special thanks:
This book is dedicated to my father, who taught me to do the right thing.

I'd also like to thank John D. Patten, Natasha Lanckriet, and "Gunny" for their insight and feedback, my editor for laboring to catch all my grammar and spelling mistakes, and LiteraryRebel.com for the amazing cover and formatting.

Rescue the weak and the needy; deliver them from the hand of the wicked.

Psalm 82:4

CHAPTER ONE

A SMALL CRAFT CUT THROUGH CHOPPY BLACK WAVES under the cover of darkness. The forty-foot SeaVee humped over a swell and back down into a trough. Saltwater lashed the open deck while the outboard engines churned water into white foam. Clouds blotted out the stars and icy rain fell in sideways sheets, cutting visibility to zero.

Sacha Duval sheltered in the pilothouse, his collar turned up against the wind and driving rain. Thinning white hair was plastered to his skull and, combined with a hatchet face, gave him the appearance of a drowned rat. He didn't like boats, of any kind, and he didn't like the ocean either. He brought an inhaler from his coat pocket, took a deep hit, held it, and let it out slow. His English was laced with a French accent. He asked, "How much longer?"

The pilot, a wiry Englishman, shrugged. His face was a road map of deep-set wrinkles from a lifetime on the open sea. He had learned his craft in the British Royal Navy and now made a living smuggling people and contraband across the Channel. "Fifteen, maybe twenty minutes, assuming we don't run into any patrols."

Duval crossed his arms over his chest and tucked his chin against the cold. His stomach was a mass of writhing snakes. Every swell threatened to bring up his dinner. His imagination insisted on showing him images of black helicopters with searchlights. After ten minutes of pacing, he peered through the rain streaked glass and now saw tiny pinpricks of light in the darkness. "Is that the mainland?"

The pilot nodded. "You're home, mate."

"I have no home," Duval told him. "Not anymore."

A pair of mercenaries stood in the bow, bundled against the rain in slickers and watch caps. Duval had hired them through back channels on the Dark Web. They were members of an organization called *Le Milieu*, which specialized in money laundering, extortion, drug trafficking, intimidation and, for the right price, murder. Protection was a bit out of their wheelhouse, but if they could kill people for money, Duval figured, they could just as easily protect people.

One of the mercenaries, a swarthy man who went by the name Mateen, moved along the gunwale to the pilothouse and stuck his head around the partition. His thick black brows came together over a crooked nose. He said, "We'll be docking shortly. Gather your gear."

Duval gave a jerky nod. "Thank you for this."

"Don't thank me until the job is done, *bon homme*," Mateen said and then rejoined his partner in the bow.

The pilot dropped his voice. "You sure you trust these blokes?"

"They came highly recommended," Duval said by way

of explanation, as if that settled the matter. Reality was, his options were limited. He needed someone who could get him safely across the mainland and *Le Milieu* was the only group he felt reasonably sure hadn't been compromised.

He shouldered a careworn duffel bag, then clutched the handle on a large suitcase stuffed with all his earthly belongings. *Not long now*, Duval told himself. He just had to make it across France to Italy and from there to Montenegro where he could finally live as a free man.

The pilot cursed, throttled down, and spun the wheel. The sound of the engines dropped to a gentle rumble. The boat swung to port and drifted over a swell. Waves lapped against the hull while freezing rain made a steady tattoo on the fiberglass deck.

"What's happened?" Duval asked. His stomach gave an uncomfortable lurch. "Why are we stopping?"

"Look." The pilot pointed.

Duval followed his finger and saw nothing but darkness. He started to say as much when his eyes picked out a shadow moving against the deeper black of the English Channel.

"Oh my God, we're caught." His dinner started to make its way north. He wrung his hands together. "*Mon Dieu! Mon Dieu!*"

The mercenaries crowded into the pilot house. Mateen asked, "What is it?"

"*Gendarmerie Maritime.*" The pilot directed their attention.

A French *Géranium* class patrol boat slowly materialized out of the darkness. The ship took shape as the sound of the engines reached their ears. The large craft cut through the black waters at a steady fifteen knots. She was running with minimal lights, trying to stay invisible in the darkness.

Duval paced faster, wringing his hands and repeating, "*Mon Dieu! Mon Dieu! Mon Dieu!*"

"Have they spotted us?" Mateen asked.

"Don't think so." The pilot thrust his chin at Duval. "Bit nervous, isn't he?"

Mateen glanced in Duval's direction. "You would be too if you spent the last decade living in exile."

The French coast guard continued to bear down on them. It would pass within fifteen meters of the starboard bow. The pilot kept the engines running as long as he dared, trying to increase the distance.

Mateen said, "Can you outrun them?

"Sure thing. Only they'll radio a helicopter and then where'll we be?"

"Haven't they got radar?" the other mercenary wanted to know.

"I'm throttled all the way down," the pilot assured him. "Not giving off much signature."

"We're caught," Duval told them.

The pilot said, "Try to relax, mate. I've not been caught yet."

When the patrol boat was fifty meters out, the pilot cut the engines completely and let the SeaVee bob in the water. The engines died with a cough and the only noise came from lapping waves. Duval went on pacing and now he was muttering to himself as well. The others watched in silence.

A shaft of light shot out from the patrol boat. Drops of rain looked like diamonds flashing in the brilliant radiance.

The search light played across the choppy surface of the Channel.

"They spotted us," Duval nearly shrieked.

"No, they haven't," the pilot hissed. "They're just searching. Stay quiet."

Duval hunkered in the boat, rocking on his heels. He wanted to run, but where would he go? He was in the middle of the ocean. *This was a stupid idea*, he told himself. *A stupid, stupid, stupid idea!* He was going to be caught and he'd spend the rest of his life in prison. He never should have left the embassy.

Then you'd be dead, he thought.

The beam moved back and forth over the water. It came within a few meters of their prow. Duval gasped. Mateen cursed in French. Then the light was moving away. The pilot let out a shaking breath and spoke in a whisper, "That was a near thing."

The French patrol boat held her course, twenty meters off their starboard side. The noise from the twin screws grew to a throaty rumble as she passed by and the little SeaVee rocked in the cruiser's wake.

Duval chanced a peek over the gunwale and nearly laughed out loud. "I thought we were dead."

Mateen said, "They must know we're out here. Why else would they use the search light?"

"Probably picked up a blip on the radar," the pilot said.

"Won't they circle around and come back?" The other mercenary, a Frenchman named Jacques, wanted to know.

The pilot shook his head. "They can't be sure it was a boat."

"How do you know?" Mateen asked.

"If they had a good signature, they would cut their engines and search until they found us." He crossed his arms over his chest and leaned his hips against the wheel. "We'll just float here a while until they're out of range. Everybody relax. Like I said, I've not been caught yet."

For Duval, the next five minutes were the longest of the whole operation. Rain continued to hammer the deck and icy little spears attacked his bare head. The boat rocked side to side, making his stomach twist. He was sure he would vomit and was fighting to keep it down when the pilot finally pressed the starter and the outboard engines roared to life. Relief flooded his belly like a swallow of good strong cognac. He let out a trembling breath and mopped wisps of white-blond hair from his forehead.

CHAPTER TWO

TEN MINUTES LATER, THE SMALL CRAFT NOSED UP TO A stone jetty in the harbor town of Honfleur. Nestled on the south bank estuary of the Seine River, Honfleur is a picturesque port town of narrow lanes and closely packed buildings. It is home to medieval fortresses and the Sainte-Catherine church, built entirely of wood in the 15th century. The cafés and cobblestone streets have inspired Claude Monet and countless painters since. Rain was still falling, but now it was coming straight down. Sailboats bobbed on the water, sheltered from the worst of the storm by seawalls to the north and south. The fiberglass hull of the SeaVee bumped rotting wood pylons.

Duval tried to convince the pilot to take him down the Seine, all the way to Paris, but the old seaman only shook his head and cut the engines. The mercenaries leapt out and went to work securing the mooring lines.

The pilot said, "Good luck to you, Mr. Duval."

"Thank you." Duval paused to shake his hand.

While Jacques finished tying off the lines, Mateen went a little way down the jetty and checked their surroundings. The harbor faced a quaint little row of seaside shops, all closed at the moment. Street lamps glowed like fairy lights through the steady drizzle. A few boathouses lined the seawall and a row of cars were parked on the boulevard, but the town itself was asleep. Mateen nodded, satisfied, and returned to the ship. "All clear. Get your luggage."

Duval grabbed the oversized suitcase and heaved it over the gunwale onto the dock. He grunted with the effort. Butterflies were zipping around inside his belly. He felt totally exposed. He didn't like being on the boat in the middle of the ocean, but he didn't like being out in the open either. He wanted to ditch his luggage and run to the waiting Renault. He would feel safer once they were in the car, headed south. He clambered over the gunwale, slipped on the clammy stone and went down on top of his suitcase.

Mateen said, "We need to hurry."

Duval pushed himself up. "You could help."

Mateen glanced around the empty harbor, sighed, and reached for Duval's overstuffed suitcase. The moment he did, a sharp *thwip-thwip-thwip* split the air. Jacques made a sound like a seal giving birth, bent over at the waist and staggered. One foot slipped between the pier and the boat. He hit the side of the vessel and went into the water with a splash.

Duval's heart climbed up into his throat. He hunkered down, looking for the source of the noise. A black-clad phantom appeared through the rain, wearing a ski mask and pointing a small automatic machinegun capped with a sound suppressor. Duval didn't know much about guns, but he knew enough to recognize professional hardware.

Mateen dropped the suitcase and shoved a hand into his jacket. He didn't even get his gun out before another short burst of muffled claps ripped through the pouring rain. *Pthut-pthut-pthut.* Duval was close enough to hear the impacts and see wet droplets explode off Mateen's rain slicker.

The mercenary danced a jig. His hand came out of his coat with his gun. The assassin fired again. *Thwap-thwap.* Mateen's head snapped back. He let go of the weapon and pitched over onto the dock. The gun bounced over the stones and came to rest a few inches from Duval's feet.

His first instinct was to dive back into the boat, but his legs refused to obey. He felt rooted to the spot. His bladder surrendered the fight right then and there. He was standing up straight, leaning back away from the assassin. The weight of his duffel bag almost toppled him over.

The assassin moved along the dock, kicked Mateen's handgun into the water and then turned the stubby automatic on the pilot. The Englishman's hands went into the air and all the color drained from his face. He started to stammer out words. It might have been "Don't shoot," but it sounded like, "*Donchuma!*"

A woman's voice, muffled by the rain-soaked ski mask, said, "Do you want to live?"

The pilot nodded. "I've got two little girls at home."

"Get on the deck. Put your face down and count to one hundred, slowly."

He threw one terrified glance at Duval, muttered an apology, and then sank to the deck of the ship.

Fear turned Duval's arms and legs to rubber. A tortured sob escaped his throat. He screwed his eyes shut and waited to hear the *pthut-pthut-pthut* and feel the bullets punch through his chest.

Instead, the assassin grabbed his collar and hauled him along the deck. His toes caught on uneven paving stones and his knees threatened to give out. Air exploded from his lungs in panicked little gasps. He tried to beg for his life, but fear so powerful it was a physical force shorted out the circuits between his brain and mouth.

At the end of the jetty, the assassin steered him along the sidewalk toward an unmarked van with tinted windows. *This is it,* Duval told himself. He would be forced into the back of the van, duct taped, and driven to a black site where they would torture him. When they had wrung out every last bit of useful information, they would put a bullet in the back of his head. No one would ever find his body.

That thought finally tripped something in his brain. Survival instinct overruled his fear. In desperation, he drove an elbow over his shoulder, catching the assassin off guard. Her head snapped back. She made a noise that was more surprise than pain, but it was enough to throw her off balance. She lost her grip on Duval's collar and he ran for his life. He didn't know where he was going, only that he needed to put as much distance between him and the assassin as possible. Fear coursed through his veins, turning to blind panic, urging his legs to move faster.

CHAPTER THREE

MATEEN CAME AWAKE AND PAIN FLOODED HIS BODY IN crushing waves. He groaned, coughed, and gasped for air. His jaw felt like someone had hit him with a sledge hammer. One side of his body was numb. He rolled onto his stomach and spit blood all over the damp stone jetty along with several chipped and broken teeth.

His gun was gone. Duval was gone. And that meant the money was gone as well. Two months of careful planning shot to hell. The boat still bobbed in the harbor though. Mateen cranked himself up on one elbow and fought down a wave of nausea. The pilot was face down on the deck, counting.

"Seventy-eight, seventy-nine..."

Mateen probed at his aching jaw and knew it was broken. It felt like a sack of loose marbles. He moaned. Nerve endings screamed at the slightest touch. Another wave of nausea hit. He gripped the ground and waited for it to pass. *Don't throw up*, he told himself. *Do* not *throw up!*

The pilot finished counting to one hundred and rose up for a look. He spotted Mateen stretched out on the jetty, and hurried to release the mooring lines.

With his broken jaw hanging at a grotesque angle, Mateen managed to croak out, "Wait! 'elp me!"

The pilot ignored him, threw off the lines and started the engines. The SeaVee burped to life. Water frothed around the stern as the craft reversed away from the dock.

Mateen growled a curse, reached into his pocket and brought out a cell. He dialed, put the phone to his ear and waited for someone to pick up.

"Have you secured the package?"

It only took two tries to make himself understood. He said, "Da package is... in da... open."

"How in the hell did that happen?"

"Sum hashole... show up... oudda nowhere..."

"Get after them!"

"Can't..." Mateen groaned. "Been shot."

The line went dead. Mateen laid back down and reached a hand under his shirt. There was no blood, but his ribs felt mushy. Touching them was utter agony. He let out another long groan. He was going to find the guy who shot him and make him pay, but first he needed a hospital.

CHAPTER FOUR

Duval darted between parked cars and took off running along the line of shops fronting Quai de la Quarantaine. The duffel bag humped against his back as he ran. He was surprisingly quick for a paunchy, middle-aged man. Fear and adrenaline, mixed into a potent cocktail to give him a burst of speed. He turned down Rue des Logettes and then mounted the steps to Église Sainte-Catherine. He raced along the narrow corridor behind the old church that let out onto Rue du Puits. Fear carried him two more blocks before poor cardiovascular fitness took its toll. His tired legs started to slow and his feet grew heavier with every step. The muscles in his thighs burned with the effort.

He shot a glance over his shoulder, saw his pursuer and let out a terrified squeak. The assassin, built like a runner, was quickly closing the gap. Duval pumped his arms for speed. His head was on a swivel, like a rat looking for a bolthole to slip through. His eyes locked onto the glowing blue and white sign for the tram. A train car was pulling into the station. The long white shuttle slowed to a stop. Air brakes hissed and wires rattled. There were only two people waiting on the platform at this time of night. Fluorescent lights bathed them in a sickly artificial glow. Pneumatic doors sighed open. Duval was almost at the platform. If he could just make it onto the train...

The assassin stopped, shouldered the MP5, aimed low and triggered a three-round burst. The bolt carriage sounded out a rapid *clack-clack-clack*.

Pain, like he had never felt before, lanced Duval's right butt cheek. He clapped both hands over his bottom, gave a shout and went face down on the paving stones. The initial sting turned to a crushing throb that threatened to send him tumbling down a dark abyss. He fought the urge to pass out. He had to stay awake, had to escape. But all he managed to do was roll around on the ground, holding his bottom and moaning. Fear wrote itself on his face in large capital letters.

The train doors hissed shut and the gleaming white shuttle moved away from the station, slowly at first, then picking up speed. Duval made one feeble attempt to gain his feet but the exquisite hurt in his bottom convinced him running was, for the moment, out of the question. "Please, for the love of God, don't kill me."

The assassin closed the last few yards, knelt, and pulled off the ski mask. A long curtain of jet black hair fell around her shoulders. She was Asian, with high cheek bones and eyes that gave away mixed parentage. "I'm not going to kill you," she said. "My name is Samantha Gunn. I'm trying to save your life."

He spluttered. Rain flew from his lips. He heard the words coming out of her mouth, but they didn't make any sense. He took one hand away from his butt, inspected his palm and was surprised when he didn't see any blood. His face wrinkled in confusion.

"It was a rubber bullet," Samantha explained. "It'll sting, but it doesn't penetrate."

"Rubber bullet?" Duval muttered. His hand went back to his butt. The pain made him want to vomit. He had to fight down a wave of bile trying to climb his esophagus.

Samantha Gunn mopped rain water from her face. "Listen to me. We don't have much time. Those mobsters weren't your friends. They were going to sell you out."

Duval's brain was starting to catch up with events. He said, "Mateen? Jacques? They were going to turn me over?"

"I don't have time to explain it all," she said. "You're going to have to trust me. There's a CIA wetwork team on their way right now. We need to get you out of here. Can you stand?"

She gripped his elbow and helped him up. He put weight on his right leg and gasped. His eyes opened wide. "I can't." He shook his head, trying to lower himself back down. "You shot me. It hurts."

She hauled him back up. "They're going to do a lot worse if they catch you."

A pitiful whimper escaped his throat, but the threat had the desired effect. His legs started to move. His bottom still hurt. Putting weight on his right leg was utter agony, but once the shock wore off, he managed an ungainly trot. His rescuer urged him to go faster. Duval could hear his own pulse pounding in his ears. Every beat came with a stabbing pain.

CHAPTER FIVE

Sᴀᴍ Gᴜɴɴ ʀᴏᴜɴᴅᴇᴅ ᴛʜᴇ ᴄᴏʀɴᴇʀ ɪɴ ᴛɪᴍᴇ ᴛᴏ sᴇᴇ ᴀ silver Audi slide to a stop in front of the stone jetty. The rain was finally letting up, falling in a steady drizzle. The Audi's tires locked and the front end dipped. Frank Bonner, the CIA Chief of Station in France and Sam's boss, was behind the wheel. Three others were in the car. Sam couldn't make out their faces from this distance but she didn't have to. It would be Grey, Preston, and LeBeau.

She drew a sharp breath through clenched teeth and jerked Duval's collar like she was tugging a dog's leash. He whimpered and pulled his shoulders up around his ears. Sam tried to backpedal around the corner, dragging Duval with her, but she was too late. The car doors flew open and all four men piled out. Bonner's head swiveled in her direction and he pointed. "There!"

A scant fifteen meters separated Sam from Bonner and his crew. She took a step to her right, shielding Duval with her own body, and brought the MP5 halfway up. Bonner and his men reached into their raincoats for their weapons. Sam's heart was a jack rabbit, bouncing around inside her chest.

Bonner took a few cautious steps in her direction. He was older and balding with a salt and pepper beard. He could have passed for someone's kindly grandfather or a literature professor. He kept his gun down by his leg and shouted. "What's this all about, Sam?"

"You tell me," she said.

"We just want Duval," he said. "You can walk away. I'll forget you were ever here."

Sam shook her head. "That's not going to happen, Frank."

The muscles in his jaw cramped. "Sam, I'm ordering you to walk away. This is your last chance."

"You know I can't do that."

Bonner looked from Sam to the three hard cases on the other side of the car. Rain dripped from his gold-rimmed spectacles. Sam could see the battle taking place just below the surface. Frank had been her mentor for five months now, working side by side, teaching her the finer details of tradecraft. Sam thought of him as a friend. Just last month, she had helped him pick out a gift for his twentieth wedding anniversary. Frank hesitated, caught between their friendship and the mission. His face turned down in a scowl and Sam knew she had lost the battle.

Bonner heaved a sigh. "Have it your way."

His weapon came up. He gripped a Sig Sauer P225 with both hands, straight out in front of him, in the classic isosceles stance.

Sam pulled the trigger. The Heckler & Koch burped

out a three-round burst muffled by the sound suppressor. Shell casings leapt from the breech in a tidy little arc and jingled over the paving stones. Frank's head snapped back. One of the rubber bullets had hit him between the eyes, shattering his glasses. He sank to the ground like a trap door had opened beneath his feet. Sam knew right away he was dead. Her heart squeezed inside her chest. She had been aiming center mass, but bullets don't always go where you point them, and accidents happen.

The rest of the team returned fire. Thunderclaps split the air. Bullets whined off the wall to Sam's right and blew out a shop window. An alarm started to peal from inside.

She walked backwards, triggering two more bursts, and then fled around the corner. The MP5's bolt had fell on an empty chamber with a distinctive click. Sam dropped the weapon and ran. Sacha Duval was one step ahead of her, blowing hard.

"Get to the tram," Sam yelled.

He didn't need convincing. He ran flat out, pumping his flabby arms and legs in a desperate race to reach the station.

Sam pulled even with him, grabbed his elbow and hauled him along. His breath came out in tortured gasps. He started to slow. Sam felt precious seconds ticking away. She risked a look over her shoulder in time to see Grey and LeBeau round the corner.

A giddy rush of panic sent speed to her legs. She urged Duval to move faster. He tried, but he couldn't keep up and Sam was forced to slow down or leave him behind.

Grey stopped at the corner and took aim. He was about to pull the trigger when a gleaming white shuttle hurtled around the tracks. He checked the movement, lowered his weapon, and glanced around for witnesses.

The tram slowed to a stop at the station. The doors hissed open. Sam pushed Duval into the rear carriage and then drew a Springfield XD-S from her tactical vest. This one was loaded with 9mm hollow-points. Sam levelled the weapon at Grey and LeBeau, and they scattered, taking cover behind parked vehicles. She didn't fire. She was just trying to hold them at bay long enough for the tram to pull away from the station. It seemed to take forever. She backed up to the door and waited. When she heard the pneumatic sigh, she stepped backwards into the car. The doors slid shut. A moment later the tram was picking up speed.

CHAPTER SIX

GREY WATCHED THE SHUTTLE PULL AWAY AND SHOUTED a curse. His profanity echoed along the empty boulevards. Six months of careful planning. Everything had gone off without a hitch until Sam Gunn showed up and blew the op. Now Duval was in the wind and Frank Bonner was lying on the street. He turned to LeBeau and pointed at the retreating train. "Where does it stop?"

LeBeau hitched up his shoulders. He was a squat man with stubby legs. A long leather coat made him look even shorter. He said, "*Je ne sais pas.*"

"Find out," Grey barked.

LeBeau used his smartphone to bring up a map of the Honfleur tramway stations.

"We need to get out of here," Preston said. He had a long face and sad eyes, bearing a striking resemblance to a basset hound. "The police will be here any minute."

Grey agreed with a nod. They hurried back to the waiting Audi. Frank Bonner still lay on the wet asphalt with his eyes rolled up. A large purple welt had formed on his forehead. Preston pressed two fingers to his throat. "He's dead."

"Take his gun and ID," Grey ordered.

"We can't leave him," Preston said.

"We can't take him with us," Grey shot back.

LeBeau looked up from his phone. "The next stop is *le Garde de Grande*. Two miles!"

"Let's go," Grey said and slid into the driver's seat while the other two rifled the dead man's pockets. He had the car in gear by the time they piled into the back seat. The Audi leapt forward. Grey steered around a corner, in pursuit of the tram. The automatic transmission screamed through second and into third, then fourth.

CHAPTER SEVEN

Sam put her back to the carriage door, closed her eyes, and breathed out a long sigh. A simple snatch and grab had gone completely off the wire. *Why did you take off the mask?* Sam asked herself. *What were you thinking? They were never supposed to see your face!* Now she was exposed. *What am I going to do?* she wondered. She couldn't go back to the safe house tomorrow morning and act like nothing had happened.

Time enough to worry about that latter, Sam decided. Right now, she had to finish what she started. If Grey and his crew caught up with them, they'd kill her and Duval would disappear forever. She opened her eyes.

The tram car was lit by the anemic glow of fluorescents. The tracks made a soft hum. Sacha Duval had collapsed onto a bench. He dug out his inhaler and took a deep hit. Pink blossomed in his pale cheeks. He held his breath and let it out slow. "I thought I was dead."

Sam holstered her weapon, grabbed Duval's sleeve and

jerked him out of the seat. "Don't get comfortable." She dragged him toward the back of the car. "We aren't out of the woods yet."

"What?" He jogged to keep up. "What are you talking about?"

"It's not going to take them long to figure out the next stop," Sam told him.

Panic flooded back into Duval's voice. "What are we going to do?"

She led him to the rear of the car and Duval's eyes went to the emergency exit door. His steps faltered. "*That's* your plan?"

"You got a better one?" Sam asked.

Duval pulled free of her grasp. "That's insane."

Sam rounded on him. "I didn't have to save you. I could have let those mercenaries turn you over to the CIA. Now they've seen my face. They know I'm a part of this. I stuck my neck out for you."

"I'm not jumping off the back of a moving train!"

"Then you'll die."

His mouth worked soundlessly.

Sam pointed. "Those men back there? They'll be waiting at the next stop. They'll catch you and when they do, they will *make* you talk. You want to be tortured?"

Duval glanced around at the empty seats, looking for help that wasn't there. They were all alone on a train hurtling through the heart of Honfleur. Florescent lights turned his skin a sickly shade of yellow and his chin trembled. A shaking breath escaped his lips. "I'm scared."

"You should have thought about that before you leaked classified intel," Sam told him and moved toward the exit door. "I'm getting off this train, Duval. Come with me or take your chances."

"This is insane," Duval muttered.

Buildings flashed past the windows on either side. The tracks unspooled behind the car, dwindling in the distance. Every second brought them closer to the next stop. Grey and his team were probably there already, waiting. At this time of night, with no traffic on the streets, they could push eighty miles an hour the whole way.

Sam gripped the emergency exit handle—a sign warned her an alarm would sound—and yanked. The ear-splitting siren drove needles into her brain. The door popped open with a metallic *clunk*. Air rushed in to fill the cabin. Sam heard a honk, barely audible over the siren, and then had to grope for the door frame as the train started to slow.

She peered through the windows separating the carriages. In the lead car, the driver was out of his booth, checking on the alarm. He saw Sam at the same time. The tram was slowing down, the sound of the tracks changing pitch. Sam turned to Duval. "Jump!"

He shook his head. "I'm not sure I..."

Sam took hold of his duffel bag, spun him around and pushed him backwards out the door. Gravity did the rest. Duval's eyes shot open. A scream ripped from his throat. He pin-wheeled his arms for balance like a cartoon character climbing on air and then landed on top the duffel with a heavy thump.

Sam stepped to the edge, bent her knees, tucked her chin, and bunny hopped like she was stepping out of an airplane. The sound of the tram died away and Sam had the feeling of weightlessness for a brief second before gravity reasserted itself. The CIA requires all recruits to complete basic jump school, but that's a long way from mastery. The idea, according to her instructors, was to hit the ground with soft knees and let the momentum carry you. Sam had all of three training jumps under her belt and figured the skills were transferable.

The ground came up to meet her. She landed on her heels and momentum knocked her flat, rolling her over several times. The world spun end over end. Her shoulders and hips took a beating. She finally tumbled to a stop and lay there for several seconds, breathing the cold air. Silver clouds steamed from her open mouth.

Duval had rolled onto his side. His face was stretched in terror. Blond hair hung in limp, wet tangles. He clutched at his throat and gasped for air.

"Use your inhaler," Sam told him. She tried to stand. Her right ankle gave out with a shot of pain that forced her to sit down. She had landed on it wrong and twisted it. No time to think about that. She crawled over and patted Duval's pockets. His heels beat out a panicked tattoo on the wet blacktop. Sam found his inhaler and forced him to close his mouth on it. He squeezed three shots, coughed and managed to croak out, "You trying to save me or kill me?"

She struggled to her feet. Her ankle was swelling up like a balloon. "Can you walk? We need to get moving."

Duval sat for several seconds, filling his lungs with oxygen. Some of the color came back into his face. Then he remembered something, shrugged off his pack and ripped open the zipper. Socks and underwear went into the gutter, followed by a tin of biscuits and a package of Earl Grey. "No, no, no!" Duval muttered to himself. From the depths of the bag, he dug out a MacBook with a dented lid. A tortured moan rattled up from his throat. He opened the computer and tried to power it on. The machine refused to boot. "You destroyed my laptop," he said. "All of my files. Everything. Gone!"

Sam grabbed his collar and hauled him to his feet. "That's what you're worried about? Your computer? We have to move. They'll figure we jumped from the train when they get to the next stop and don't see us. They're probably on their way back here right now."

Duval started to repack his bag.

"Leave it," Sam ordered.

They were in a corridor formed by low rise apartments. Sam led the way between buildings back to the main boulevard. Every step sent lances of pain up through her leg. She needed to deal with the ankle before it swelled so bad she couldn't walk. Duval was no better. The rubber bullet had given him an identical limp. They hobbled along like a couple of eighty-year-olds helping each other down the corridors of a nursing home.

CHAPTER EIGHT

Ezra Cook and Gwendolyn Witwicky slouched in swivel chairs, facing opposite computers. They haunted a small work station on the first floor of Langley these days. The cubical was wedged in a corner, next to the bathrooms. The carpet was worn straight through in places and an air return at their feet made a constant rattling hum. The previous occupant must have been a cat lover; the stench of cat urine lingered and nothing they had tried managed to banish the smell.

Neither analyst had seen much of the sun since Mexico and the fallout had left them radioactive. The last five months had them handling menial tasks. No department wanted to touch them after the firing of Deputy Director Foster. Currently, they were debugging lines of code from Langley's surprisingly complex fire alarm and sprinkler system. It was thankless grunt work and not why they had joined the CIA, but they still had jobs and considered themselves lucky. Together, they had taken to calling themselves Team Pleb.

There was one upside to being radioactive in Ezra's mind; it had given him plenty of time with Gwen. They ate lunch together in the cafeteria and went for drinks after work most days. He hadn't made a move yet but figured, sooner or later, it would sort of happen naturally, saving him the uncomfortable task of actually asking her out. And besides, he was counting drinks after work as dates and by that reckoning, they were practically going steady.

Gwen stood up, stretched, arched her back. Her mousy brown hair was pulled back in a ponytail. Ill-fitting slacks rode low on skinny hips. Long hours working on code had carved ten pounds from her already slender frame.

Ezra, meanwhile, had gained a paunch and soft jowls. He had made a half-hearted attempt at a workout regimen in January, but that was already over. Now, a bag of Gummy Bears lay open on his desk next to a twelve-ounce bottle of Mountain Dew. He dug a mushy orange bear from the bag, popped it in his mouth and chewed. "I compiled the latest build. I think we're ready for a test run."

"Let's do it." Gwen plopped back down into her chair.

They initiated the debugged code and ran it through a virtual sequencer. While the sequencer looked for errors, they discussed the finer points of the latest Star Wars movie. Gwendolyn held to the view that the newest installment was simply a rehash of the first episode, while Ezra was convinced it was the best of the series. They had moved on to debating the recent trailer for the second movie when Timothy Coughlin appeared in their cubical. They both turned to their computers and tried to look busy.

Gwen wanted to scream. Higher-ups always manage to catch computer techs waiting on code and it led to the assumption that techs didn't do any real work.

"First of all," Coughlin said, "The new movie looks freaking amazing."

He held out a fist.

Ezra bumped it. "Right on."

Coughlin was the acting head of Clandestine Operations while the Company looked for Foster's replacement. A twitchy eye precluded him from field work, but he had a reputation for laying in successful missions and the field guys had a lot of respect for him. He was in his mid-forties and fit, with close-cropped hair. He'd be handsome without the facial tick. He leaned an elbow on the cubical wall and his left eye jerked. He said, "Second, what are you two computer ninjas up to?"

"We're waiting on some code, sir." Gwen's words came out in a nervous rush. "It's takes a little while for the information to propagate through the system and it hogs down processing power, so there's not much we can do but wait."

"Uh huh." He obviously had no idea what she was talking about and didn't care. "I heard you two were topnotch. I also heard you've been languishing down here since Mexico."

Ezra ducked his head. "That about sums it up."

Gwen pushed the glasses up the bridge of her nose. "It's not so bad. It's important work. Happy to be doing our part and all."

"How would you two like a chance to work on something a little more mission-critical?"

"Sounds great."

"Absolutely, sir."

They both nodded in unison.

He brought a pair of badges out of his pocket. "Put whatever this is on hold and follow me."

The new badges had their names and LEVEL B3 in large capitals at the bottom. Ezra and Gwen exchanged eager glances. They followed Coughlin to the elevator. He punched the button for the third-floor basement. For tech nerds, going down meant moving up. The bowels of Langley house some of the most secure databases and processors in the world.

The elevator dinged and they stepped into a long room with a low ceiling lit by fluorescents. The smell of recycled air and overworked motherboards greeted them. Instead of cheap government carpeting, the floors here were linoleum with anti-static rubber mats under foot to prevent accidental discharges of electricity. Thick bundles of cables hung down from the ceiling, providing power to dozens of work terminals. Fake windows let in artificial light to make the denizens of the basement corridors feel less confined, not that it mattered to the computer ninjas working on B3. They preferred being indoors. The dress code down here was more relaxed. Half the people wore denim and T-shirts emblazoned with superheroes. The cubicles were decorated with plastic figurines and posters. Some wit had printed out a long banner that read, *We Are Groot* and hung it on the wall next to the elevator.

Coughlin led the way to an unused work station in the back corner. "This will be your new home for the next few days."

Gwen looked around the terminals and nodded. They

had six computers all to themselves and the smell of over-worked processors was better than cat pee. She asked, "What are we working on, sir?"

Coughlin sat in one of the unused chairs, propped his elbows on his knees and made a steeple with his fingertips. "This is a pilot program of sorts. Several weeks ago, we laid in a dummy operation codenamed MEDUSA. Now we want to know if it's possible to break into the system and erase all evidence the operation ever took place. That's where you two come in."

Gwen said, "What was the operation, sir?"

He waved a hand in the air. "Nothing. Just a dummy operation that our guys upstairs invented so you would have something to root out of the computer."

"Why?" Ezra asked.

"Think of the ramifications," Coughlin said. "If you can break in and erase an operation from our databanks, what's to stop someone else from doing the exact same thing? Destroying all of our records even. Hell, we haven't kept hard copies of our case logs in decades. Or worse, what if someone added logs for an operation that never took place?"

Ezra was nodding. "They could make the CIA look guilty of anything they wanted. Like overthrowing a democratically elected government or a nuclear meltdown."

Gwen said, "So the test is to see if we can erase all evidence of operation MEDUSA?"

"Make it like it never existed," Coughlin said. "Is it possible?"

Ezra took a seat, thought it over, nodded. "With enough time anything is possible."

"Then get started." Coughlin stood up. "Remember,

this is highly classified. You report only to me. Let me know if you run into any snags."

"Yes, sir." They chorused.

He started to leave, stopped, turned back. "I almost forgot. Crank this one out of the park and I'll see what I can do about moving you down here on a more permanent basis."

CHAPTER NINE

The Sail Pavilion is an open-air bar just south of the convention center in downtown Tampa. It's the Bay's only 360-degree waterfront bar, located smack in the middle of a large pedestrian concourse with a view of the causeway. Several ships coursed silently along the channel, churning up the water in their wake. The sun was a fiery disk hanging low on the horizon and a cool breeze came off the water. It was early February and Florida natives were bundled against the chill like it was the start of another Ice Age.

Jake Noble sat at the bar, nursing a beer and watching highlights from last night's hockey game—the Bolts had lost to the Bruins, three to zero. He was dressed in denims, a rumpled sports coat, and scuffed deck shoes, despite being a Florida native. A decade in Army Special Forces had taught him the real meaning of cold, and fifty-eight degrees didn't qualify. He had been here two and a half hours already. His butt was numb. He was on beer number two and it was only half empty—no sense getting hammered. He pawed through a basket of cold shrimp tails, found one with a little meat left on it, and nibbled. With rebelliously long hair and a lean frame, he blended in nicely with the beach crowd.

Foot traffic around the convention center was light. Two guys tossed a Frisbee back and forth, and a pair of lovers sat on a park bench near the bar. The bartender, a twenty-something blonde in a thick sweater and frilly pink earmuffs, favored Noble with a smile on her way past. "Anything I can get you, sweetie?"

"Just a check," Noble told her.

She went to her register and came back with the bill. Noble dropped several greenbacks on the bar top and told her to keep the change. She thanked him with another bright smile.

He was getting up to leave when Howard Lamb sauntered up from the direction of Channelside Drive. He was an aging hipster in his late forties, wearing skinny jeans, a top knot, and a wispy beard. He flashed a smile that showed off a mouth full of crooked teeth. "You leaving? I just got here."

"You were supposed to be here two hours ago," Noble pointed out.

"Yeah, man, sorry about that. I got hung up. You know how it goes." Lamb plunked himself down on the stool next to Noble.

"Sure," said Noble.

The waitress reappeared but Lamb waved her away. He leaned in and dropped his voice to a whisper. "You got something for me?"

Noble took a plain white sheet of folded paper from his

jacket pocket and laid it on the beer-stained bar. "User-names and passwords for the entire staff at United Credit. You can access their entire customer database. Every customer's private information at your fingertips."

Lamb reached for the page, but Noble kept his hand on it. "Let's see the money first."

Lamb gave him a rueful grin and reached inside his coat. He pulled out a thick envelope stuffed with cash. "Fifty thousand. It's all there."

"It better be," Noble told him. "I spent six months collecting those passcodes."

"Count it if you don't trust me," said Lamb.

Noble took the envelope, peeked inside, then slowly and deliberately ran a hand through his long hair. He said, "I trust you."

Lamb took the sheet of paper, unfolded it, and scanned the list of names and passcodes. A grin spread over his face. He nodded to himself. "This is beautiful, man. Really good work."

The moment Noble's hand went to his hair, the Frisbee players let the blue disk drop in the grass and started over. At the same time, the lovers on the bench got up. The woman peeled back her coat to reveal a badge hooked on her belt. "TPD," she announced. "Both of you keep your hands where we can see 'em."

Howard Lamb sprang up from his stool so fast he turned it over. All eyes turned in their direction. The bartender put a hand to her mouth. Howard turned to run. He made it three whole strides before one of the Frisbee players tackled him. They landed with a heavy thud and the air went out of Lamb's bird chest in a loud whoop. The officer pinned Lamb's head to the ground and twisted one arm behind his back. "You're under arrest."

Lamb sucked air and shouted, "Police brutality! Police brutality! Anyone getting this on video? Hey, I got rights, man."

Several people were, in fact, getting it on video. Everybody at the pavilion had their cellphones out, recording.

Noble put his hands in the air. One of the undercover officers forced him face down on the bar top and said, "Get your head down, dirt bag, and don't make a move."

Noble sat there, his face in sticky beer stain, while the officer wrenched his arms behind his back. He felt the metal cuffs lock onto his wrists and then the officer jerked him off the stool and started him across the park to an unmarked sedan. The other three cops were on Lamb. The woman read him Miranda rights while the other two hauled him up off the concrete. "Howard Lamb," she said, "You're under arrest for conspiracy to commit fraud and identity theft. You have the right to remain silent..."

Her voice trailed away as Noble reached the car. The officer leading him opened the back door and told him, "Watch your head."

CHAPTER TEN

Two hours later, Jake was sitting in the downtown office of the Florida Deputy District Attorney. His eyes wandered over the room. A pair of diplomas graced the wall along with a photo of the Deputy shaking hands with the Governor. Picture windows looked out across the glittering lights of Tampa Bay.

"You handled yourself incredibly well today, Mr. Noble," the Deputy said as he sorted stacks of papers piled on his desk. Benjamin Paulson was a stout, middle-aged man, with a bad dye job trying to hide early grey. He wore a suit that probably fit impeccably well several years ago. Gold cufflinks flashed from an expensive blue silk oxford. He said, "With your help, we shut down a major identity theft ring. Lamb is already spilling his guts. With his info, the feds will be able to round up a long list of wanted fugitives. Not bad for a few days' work."

Noble nodded. "Happy to be of service."

I'll be more happy to deposit the check, Noble thought.

His bank account needed a cash infusion pronto. It had been nearly two months since his last job. After paying for Mom's assisted living facility, Noble's funds were depleted. Devastated would be a better description. He'd be dining on ramen noodles until the check cleared.

Deputy Paulson picked up a sheaf of papers, scanned them, and then leaned back and inspected Noble with the tired, appraising eyes of an experienced trial lawyer. Noble had the feeling another bit of work was coming his way and sat patiently while Paulson made up his mind. The Deputy District Attorney explored a molar with his tongue before saying, "I've taken the liberty of reaching out to our personnel department to inquire about job openings. The Attorney General is on board. We'd like to offer you a full-time position. The AG's office can always use experienced investigators. We feel that with your... skills, you would make an excellent addition to our team. It wouldn't be quite what you did in Special Forces. Mostly running down leads and checking on people's alibis, but there's a steady paycheck in it."

Noble sat in stunned silence. Chasing leads for the district attorney would be boring as hell, but a darn site better than babysitting celebrities who got a death threat in the mail. Plus, it would keep him in the area, closer to Mom.

"It's not much," Paulson went on, "We can start you at fifty-two thousand dollars a year, with benefits of course, and two week's vacation time. What do you say, Mr. Noble?"

"Where do I sign?"

Paulson grinned and passed over the sheaf of papers. "In about twenty places, plus initials, a non-disclosure agreement, routine background check, then a four-week training that starts Monday morning. Can you handle it?"

"Yes, sir." Noble felt like he was walking on air. He had come in hoping for a quick payday and maybe a few more off-the-record jobs. Now he was looking at a full-time position, steady paychecks, plus medical insurance. The background check would expose him as a former CIA field officer, but that would only make his new position inside the District Attorney's office more secure. If he could handle secrets for the Company, he could keep his lips tight for the criminal lawyers handling high-profile organized crime.

He borrowed a pen from Paulson's desk and flipped through the pages, signing and initialing on the X's. When he finished, he passed the documents back and Paulson scrawled his signature on the last page. The sheaf of papers went into a desk drawer.

Paulson stood up and stuck out his hand. "Welcome aboard, Mr. Noble."

Noble pumped it.

"Be here Monday morning at 8 a.m. sharp."

CHAPTER ELEVEN

Noble's 1967 Ford Fastback was parallel parked on East Kennedy. He climbed behind the steering wheel and turned the key. The engine came to life with an energetic rumble. The sun was down and the sky over Tampa Bay had turned a mottled blue shot with deep purples. Traffic in the business district on a Saturday evening is nonexistent, but the sounds of music and life came from the direction of Amalie Arena only a few blocks south. Noble checked his watch. If he hurried, he could make it back across the bridge to the Wyndham Arms before lights out.

He shifted the hotrod into gear and swung out of the spot, headed west, following the signs for the Howard Franklin. The temperature this far south rarely dips below fifty degrees, even in February. Noble cranked the window down and enjoyed the feeling of the wind in his hair. The fresh scent of saltwater from the Bay filled his lungs. *Fifty-two paychecks a year*, he thought with a smile.

Things were finally looking up. He put on some gas and

made it across the bridge in record time, slowing down only when he got to Fourth Street and had to fight his way through Saint Pete traffic. He found a spot across from the assisted living facility, shifted into park and killed the engine.

The double doors of the Wyndham Arms whooshed open with a gentle push of warm air. A solidly built woman behind a desk reminded Noble that lights out was in thirty minutes. He jotted his name in the registry and found Mary Elise Noble in the second-floor rec area. A group was gathered around a television watching the evening news at volumes that shook plaster from the ceiling. Noble wove his way through a roadblock of walkers and made the mistake of calling out, "Mom!"

All of the ladies turned their heads. A few of them narrowed their eyes, trying to decide if he was that long-lost son finally come to visit. Only one of the women lit up with recognition. His mother smiled and levered herself off the sofa with some difficulty. She had thinning white hair and parchment skin, but her eyes had a spark that not even cancer could extinguish.

Noble stepped carefully over the end of a cane and put one strong arm around her. She patted his back. A few wiry chin hairs scratched his neck.

"How you feeling today, Ma?"

"Every day with the Lord is a blessing," she assured him.

Noble was in such a good mood he let that one slide. He and mom had differing opinions on the nature of God. Mary Elise Noble was a firm believer, but Jake had seen too many good people killed and evil people walking free to subscribe to the notion of an all-loving creator. If God existed at all, Noble had a bone to pick. He said, "Let's get away from the TV."

"I've been learning Karate," his mother told him as he led her across the room. He was trying to get far enough from the television to actually hear.

He raised his voice. "You're taking karate lessons?"

"Well, chair karate, actually. After that business at the bank, I thought I should learn to protect myself," she said. "You can't be too sure nowadays."

"I pity anyone who tries to take your poker money," Noble said.

She rewarded him an elbow to the ribs and asked, "What's your good news?"

"How do you know it's good news?"

They sat down at an empty table. Noble kept one hand on her elbow while she lowered herself into the seat.

"I'm your mother," she told him. "I always know."

He tried and failed to hide a grin. It broke through and turned into a full-on smile.

"Must be *very* good," she said. "I haven't seen you smile like that in years."

"I got a job," Noble told her.

"Oh, Jake, that's wonderful. See? God is good."

Instead of *God had nothing to do with it*, Jake said, "I'm going to be working for the Attorney General's office. Fifty-two paychecks a year, plus benefits."

She reached over and patted his hand with fingers that felt like brittle paper. "I've been praying God would open a door for you."

To humor her, he said, "Well, He did."

Her intentions were good even if her method had all the finesse of a baseball bat to the side of the head. It had always been that way. Faith seemed to permeate every part of her life. Bible verses sprang from her lips like wildflowers along a highway. Noble had known guys in the service who could quote that dusty tome every bit as well as his mother. They had read it every day and carried it with them into battle. Noble could never get past all the *thee*'s and *thou*'s. His idea of good reading was a Mike Hammer novel. He took mom's hand and gave it a squeeze, told her about the deputy District Attorney and the kind of work he would be doing. "Safe stuff," Noble assured her. "No need to worry. And the best part is, I won't need to travel so often."

A staff nurse came through, reminding residents that it was time for bed. She was tall with short cropped hair. A full sleeve tattoo peeked out from seafoam-green scrubs. She stopped by their table and put an arm around Mary Elise's shoulders. "Hey there, Mary. Who's your friend?"

"Cathy, this is my son, Jake."

Cathy offered a hand and Noble shook it. She had a good strong grip. Lifting old people in and out of tubs all day long must build hand strength. Noble gave her a tight smile.

"Mary is one of our favorite residents," Cathy told him. "She's a real spitfire."

"Try growing up with her," Noble said.

Mary Elise reached across and gave his cheek a playful pinch. Noble took it with a smile and winked.

Cathy laughed. "The apple doesn't fall far from the tree."

His mother said, "Jake just came by to tell me about his new job. Go on, Jake. Tell her."

Noble waved it away. "She's not interested, Ma."

"Jake just got a job working for the District Attorney's office."

So much for non-disclosure agreements.

Cathy managed to look impressed. "Are you a lawyer?"

"No," he said. "A janitor."

Mary Elise flapped a hand at him. "Jake's an investigator."

"Wow." Cathy's interest went from polite to intrigued. "Like Sherlock Holmes."

"Only without the heroin addiction," Noble told her.

"Well, congratulations on your new job. I just came by to remind Mary bedtime is in ten minutes and visiting hours are officially over, but I'll give you two a few extra minutes. Okay?"

"I'd better shuffle off," Mom said. "I don't want the warden locking me in solitary."

Cathy laughed and went to roust the rest of the old timers, but the room had mostly cleared out by now. Only the genuine night owls were still up at eight. Most of the patients put themselves to bed shortly after supper at four-thirty.

Mary Elise turned to Jake and said, "She's single you know. Just broke up with her boyfriend."

Noble groaned. "Not this."

"You've got a good job now. You're young."

"Young*ish*," Noble corrected.

"Any girl would be lucky to have you."

"I'm not looking for a relationship."

That wasn't exactly true, but Noble let the statement stand.

"I worry about you, Jake. Living out there on that boat all by yourself. It's not healthy. You need someone in your life."

For Mary Elise Noble, getting Jake hitched was second only to saving his soul. She wanted grandkids before she died and Jake couldn't blame her for that, but he wasn't exactly marriage material. He stood up, kissed her on the forehead and said, "I'm not alone. I've got you."

Before she could argue, he said, "I'd better scoot before Cathy throws me out."

CHAPTER TWELVE

Noble stopped through Publix on Fourth Street for rice, black beans, eggs, and coffee before heading to the marina. Home was a forty-foot wooden schooner christened *the Yeoman*. Noble had inherited the ship after his father passed away. When his career with the CIA went belly-up, Noble lost his apartment and moved onto the boat. It was that or sell her, and Noble would never willingly let go of *the Yeoman*. Strings of lights decorated the trees of Straub Park in downtown Saint Pete. The Saturday night crowd was out and Ocean Boulevard was alive with the sound of music and laughter.

Noble swung into the lot, shifted into park, gathered his groceries and spotted Duc Hwang with his back to a palm tree. Duc had been a cold weather SEAL, specializing in arctic warfare before making the leap to Special Operations Group. Sweat beaded on his forehead despite the chill. He spent plenty of time at the weight rack and it showed. Cannon ball shoulders threatened to split the seams on his polo shirt and a wiry black beard stuck out from his chin like a steel bristle brush.

If Duc were here to kill him, Noble never would have seen it coming. The big Korean had chosen a spot right out in the open, where Noble couldn't miss him. That was a good sign. On the other hand, Duc might be the distraction. Noble ignored a tickle of fear, got out of the car and nodded.

Duc nodded back. "Just here to talk, brother. No one wants a fight."

"Okay," Noble said. "Let's talk."

Duc thrust his chin at the *Yeoman*. "Inside."

They walked down the jetty, side by side. Noble had to shift the grocery bag to make room for Duc's bulk. He said, "How you like this heat?"

Duc snorted. "Man, if I wanted this kind of weather, I'd have stayed in Busan."

"See any action lately?" Noble asked.

"Did a sneak-and-peek into Venezuela a while back."

"Yeah?" Noble said. "What's it like down there?"

"Whole damn country is collapsing under socialism." Duc shook his head. "They haven't even got toilet paper, forget about food. Imagine that. A whole country without toilet paper."

Noble gave a low whistle.

Duke stopped at *the Yeoman*, crossed his arms over his chest and turned his attention to the park.

Noble took that as his queue to board. There was a light chop on the bay and a cool wind blowing in from the Gulf. The polished wood deck rolled on the waves. Noble mounted the gangplank and the sweet odor of cigar smoke hit him as he ducked inside the cabin.

"Hello, Mr. Noble."

A blonde was seated at the galley table, wearing a pinstriped suit with a knee-length skirt and her hair in a plastic clip. The skirt rode up, showing off a pair of toned thighs. She was over forty, under fifty, and took good care of herself, but crow's feet betrayed her age. Noble recognized her right away. Her name was Jaqueline Armstrong. The newly elected president had recently appointed her head of CIA, making her the first female director in the history of the Company. She gazed out the port windows toward the parking lot. She had the kind of throaty tenor that came from years of smoke and bourbon. She said, "It's a beautiful car."

"Thanks." Noble set his groceries on the counter. "I picked her up at an estate sale."

"I heard about that sale. I think half the intelligence community heard about it." Her lips turned up in a half smile and she said, "Do you know who I am, Mr. Noble?"

"I watch the news."

She re-crossed her legs and took a thin cigar from her coat pocket. "Mind if I smoke?"

"Actually, I do."

Armstrong flicked a butane lighter and puffed, quietly establishing her place. She was Director of the CIA. He was a burned spy. A lazy cloud of blue smoke formed in front of her face. She waved it away.

Noble put his eggs in the fridge, crossed his arms over his chest, and leaned his hips against the counter. "What can I do for you, Mrs. Armstrong?"

"Miss," she corrected him. "Are you still connected with anyone in the intelligence community, Mr. Noble?"

He shook his head. "Not really."

"Care to elaborate?"

"Not really."

She grinned around the cigar. "Burke told me you didn't go in for idle chit-chat."

Noble let the statement speak for itself.

"You know who I am," said Armstrong, "so you probably have a good idea why the president appointed me."

Noble had done his homework on Armstrong. Call it professional curiosity. He wanted to know who was minding the store, and what he found impressed him. Armstrong had graduated Brown, risen to the rank of Major in the United States Air Force, and made a name for herself in the Defense Industry Research Department before taking the job with the Company.

Noble said, "Diversity in the workplace?"

Armstrong didn't rise to the bait. "He hired me to clean up shop. Put the Company back on the straight and narrow. The president needs to know who he can trust and right now there are factions inside the CIA actively working against him. Burke says you're a good soldier and I believe him."

Noble waited her out. She wasn't here to size him up. Newly appointed CIA directors had better things to do than go around interviewing former spies.

She puffed on the cigar. The glowing end flared and dimmed. She fixed him with a steady gaze. "I've got a problem, Noble. I've got a dead Chief of Station and a field officer on the run. I need to know how it happened and why."

"Not sure how I can help you with that." He started putting the groceries into the cupboards.

"A team at Langley is working to track down the rogue officer," Armstrong told him. "But I need answers and I'm afraid the officer will end up dead before I can get them. Your former co-workers can be incredibly clannish. They get a little testy when a team member starts murdering their own."

Noble finished putting away the groceries, wadded the sack and stuffed it in a garbage can under the galley sink. "I'm not interested, but thanks for stopping by."

"I'm offering an olive branch, Noble. Track down my rogue officer and there might be more work for you in the future. Play your cards right," she shrugged. "Who knows?"

A bitter smile turned up one side of Noble's face. "You have to be kidding me. First you burn me. Then you abandon my friend in Mexico and send Gregory Hunt to kill me. Now you're asking me for favors?"

"I'm not here to dig up the past, Jake." Armstrong puffed her cigar. "A CIA officer was shot dead on the streets of France and I want to know why. I need someone with the skills to operate under the radar. There's no one in the Company I can trust, and Burke say you're the best man for the job."

Noble crossed his arms over his chest. They had come to him for help, again, after hanging him out to dry. Two years ago, the CIA had come to him with their hand out and Noble took the job because mom had needed the money. That was then. He was done grasping at every dollar dangled in front of him like a dolphin jumping through hoops for fish. Forty-eight hours ago he probably would have said yes. Strike that, he definitely would have said yes. But starting Monday morning, he had a job and a steady pay check. A nice *normal* job. He'd put some money in savings, get an apartment. Who knows? Maybe he would surprise Mom and ask Cathy out on a date.

He shook his head. "I'm finished working for the Company, Miss Armstrong. You burned me once and you'll do it again next time you need a fall guy. I've got a job now. A real job. Steady paychecks. Health insurance. I'm sorry for your problems, but I have problems of my own."

Armstrong took a long drag, tipped her head back and shot smoke up to the ceiling where it gathered in a slowly eddying cloud. "Your mind's made up?"

Noble motioned to the galley door. "See yourself out."

Armstrong didn't bother to get up. "What if I told you the rogue officer was Samantha Gunn?"

CHAPTER THIRTEEN

A COLD WEIGHT DROPPED INTO HIS BELLY LIKE A SLAB of ice calved by a glacier. Noble had recently lost a friend to Mexican drug dealers. He had killed the man responsible and left the cartel in tatters, but the wound was still raw. Torres had been sold out by a politician more interested in votes than national security and a careerist CIA officer riding her coattails. The thought of losing Sam made his chest tight.

Armstrong said, "I understand you two have history."

Noble nodded slowly, went to the galley table and sat.

"I only know what I read," Armstrong was saying. "Seems she was instrumental in helping us expose that bit of business with Secretary Rhodes. Burke says she's good people."

"The best," Noble said. He felt disconnected from his body, as if this were happening to someone else and he was only a spectator. His brain raced to make since of what he was hearing.

"Last night, she shot the Paris COS dead in the street and then disappeared."

The block of ice turned into a cold hand gripping Noble's heart. He chewed the inside of his cheek and stared at coffee rings on the tabletop. He knew Sam and cold-blooded murder didn't jibe. Hell, when he first met her, she had been running a shelter for abused women in the Philippines. She was a devout Christian who didn't believe in sex before marriage. Murder? It didn't make any sense.

"How did that happen?" Noble asked.

Armstrong leaned back. The leather creaked. She fixed him with a steely glance. "In or out, Noble?"

When he didn't answer, Armstrong said, "Jake, I've been on the job less than two months and I've already got a dead CIA officer. I want answers. The ground team is a trio of freelancers we use for illegal snatch-and-grabs, unwarranted wire taps, and a host of other activities Congress doesn't need to know about. They're guns for hire with itchy trigger fingers. Now, are you in or out?"

If he walked through this door now, there was no going back. He would be giving up his new job with the DA's office and the steady paychecks. The District Attorney represented security. More importantly it would keep him close to Mom and she needed him. Maybe he needed her. Walking away from that meant going back to the odd jobs and scraping to get by. It meant having to tell Mom goodbye every few weeks and climbing aboard a plane.

But the thought of Sam on the run for murder made up his mind for him. He set his jaw and spoke through clenched teeth. "In."

Armstrong folded her arms across her breasts. The cigar

pointed straight up, trailing smoke. Noble caught a subtle whiff of rose-scented perfume. "Down to business. Gunn transferred to Paris shortly after the dustup in Mexico. She had a black mark on her record, but Frank Bonner, the Station Chief running Paris Branch, said she was a good kid, doing good work. Everybody liked her."

"How did it go sideways?"

"That's what I want you to find out," Armstrong said. "Here's what I know so far. Bonner picked up intel that a French mercenary group contacted a British smuggler about an early morning trip across the Channel. We're talking low priority stuff. No red flags. The French group is called *Le Milieu*."

Noble shook his head. "Never heard of them."

"That doesn't surprise me," she said. "They're a French organized crime outfit. They were suspects in a witness intimidation case a few years back, a few disappearances, but nothing major. French police never managed to indict them. This is the first time they've even come to the attention of American intelligence agencies."

"Stepping up their game," Noble commented.

Armstrong nodded. "Bonner put together a surveillance team of independent contractors and went to check out the boat, tail the French group, see what they were bringing into the country. Routine surveillance. Samantha Gunn, who was not even a part of the operation, showed up and started shooting. She hit Frank in the head, he died on the scene. Sam escaped."

"What do we know about the contractors?"

"Three of our best agents. Two Americans. One French. The leader's name is David Grey. All three have been on the Company payroll for ten years or more. They're top-notch when it comes to covert surveillance, clandestine entry, and intelligence gathering. They've spent most of their time in the European theater, but all three have some time in the Middle East as well. These guys know their way around a fight."

"They're the ones who called it in?" Noble asked.

"Right. They represent our boots on the ground."

"You buy their version of events?" Noble asked.

Armstrong paused to consider that and shook her head. "I don't know what to believe. Grey is either telling the truth or making the whole thing up, and Gunn isn't talking to anybody. Either way, Bonner is dead, the French are asking questions and the president wants answers. I'm afraid if Grey and his team catch up to her first, Gunn will be dead before she has a chance to tell her side of the story. That's why I came to you. I figure you'll give her the benefit of the doubt."

Noble leaned back in the seat and crossed his arms. "Why am I not hearing this from Burke?"

"He's part of the team at Langley tracking her down. This is the second time one of his recruits went off the reservation. First you, now Sam. It doesn't look good. The only way to prove he didn't have a hand in this is to help bring her in. Maybe I'm a complete fool, but I figure with Burke on one side of the search and you on the other, Sam has a better than average chance of coming home alive."

"Where's Wizard in all of this?"

"Laid up in the hospital," Armstrong said. "Needed to have a valve stint replaced. Coughlin is running the Directorate of Operations."

"He going to pull through?" Noble asked.

"I don't know," Armstrong admitted. "I think so."

Noble closed his eyes and exhaled. Burke was a good man, even if he did look the other way when the CIA hung Noble out to dry. He'd also helped Noble track down Torres' killer. He didn't deserve to get blacklisted and he was too old to do anything else.

Armstrong cleared her throat, pulling Noble out of his reverie. She said, "I need an answer, Noble. Can you find Sam and bring her in before Grey and his team get to her?"

"I can try."

"Then pack a bag."

"When does my plane leave?"

"Soon as we get to the airport," Armstrong told him. "I've got a private jet fueled and waiting."

"I'll need equipment..."

"Duc put together all the gear he thought you might find useful. All you need are clothes."

Noble glanced out the window at the former Navy SEAL. He stood on the dock, arms crossed over his barrel chest, looking at nothing but seeing everything.

"Any chance I could take Duc?"

Armstrong grinned and shook her head.

CHAPTER FOURTEEN

Half an hour later, Noble stood on the tarmac at Clearwater International Airport. He had changed into a dark gray windbreaker with plenty of pockets, a good pair of hiking boots, and added a Kimber Ultra Carry chambered in .45 ACP. A Cessna Citation X waited on the runway. Twin Rolls-Royce AE 3007C1 engines sucked wind, screaming out one long song. Runway lights reflected in the sleek white fuselage. The Citation is one of the world's fastest planes and would get him to Paris in a little over four hours. A lifetime, Noble thought. This thing might be over in four hours. Sam had the entire strength of the Central Intelligence Agency hunting her. He frowned. *Hang in there, Sam.*

Behind him, a black Lincoln Town Car idled. Duc had buzzed several yellow lights and ran two reds while Armstrong briefed Noble on the situation. They stood with him on the runway. Armstrong handed him a thick file held together with a rubber band and an iPhone. "It's unlisted and untraceable, preprogramed with my direct number. Keep in mind, I won't know who's listening in on my end, so use it sparingly. Once you land in Paris, there won't be much, if anything, I can do for you. From here on out, consider yourself full dark."

Noble pocketed the phone and nodded. He knew the drill. He was off the reservation, a pilgrim in unholy land. If he got into trouble, there would be no rescue party. That part didn't bother him. He had been doing it so long now it felt natural. He was worried about what came after. Assuming he got to Sam first, then what? She was a wanted fugitive with a murder hanging around her neck. Finding her was the easy part. If he wanted to clear her name, assuming she was innocent, he'd have to unravel what happened in France over the last forty-eight hours.

Armstrong stuck out a hand and Noble took it. She had a surprisingly firm grip. Her mouth worked into a tight smile. "Good luck."

Duc handed him a simple leather messenger bag. "Stay frosty."

Noble slung the bag over his shoulder and climbed the steps to the waiting aircraft. The pilot met him at the hatch. He was dressed in khakis and a leather bomber jacket, looking like a character in a post WWII adventure film. He even had the five o'clock shadow. "Where to, buddy?"

"Charles De Gaulle and step on it," Noble told him.

"Buckle up." The pilot worked the door controls and the stairs started up with a mechanical whir. "There's a bar at the back. Water, booze, snacks. It's self-serve."

The interior was all calfskin leather and blonde wood. Tiny lamps illuminated the tables. Noble collected two bottles of water from the minibar, then settled into a seat and pulled the rubber band off the folder. A thin red stripe on the cover indicated it was EYES ONLY. The stairs closed with a soft sucking noise. The pilot gave Noble a thumbs-up and then disappeared into the cockpit. There was more than enough room to stretch out and get some sleep, but Noble chose to study the file instead. He couldn't get through it all before Paris, but he could familiarize himself with the key players and maybe get some insight into what happened.

As he thumbed through the pages, the Cessna taxied onto the runway and the engines built to a fevered pitch. The gleaming white missile started forward, slow and hoggish at first, then picking up speed. Noble felt himself pushed into the leather seatback, then the jet left the runway and the sound of the tires fell away. Only the sound of the twin engines remained as the craft climbed and leveled out.

The file was packed with mission logs dating back six months. It was four and a half inches of tiny, single spaced, reading. The dead officer, Frank Bonner, had been, by all accounts, a straight shooter. He played by the rules and kept his nose clean. He had made his bones in Iraq and Afghanistan during the troop withdraw. Afterwards he took over Paris Branch. Nothing in his file raised any red flags.

Grey and his crew were freelancers. It would surprise a lot of people to know most of the actual spy work being done for the CIA these days was third party. The Company hired mercenaries and private intelligence outfits. They paid through shell companies so the American government could deny any involvement. Most were guys just like

Noble; military experience, no family to speak of, no connections, no jobs, no direction in life. They were efficient and, more importantly, expendable. That was bad news for Sam. These guys had no allegiance to the Company, or the United States for that matter.

Noble spread their pictures out on the table in front of him, three black and white head shots. He picked up the photo of Grey, the ring leader. Noble chewed the inside of one cheek. None of these guys worked directly for the Company, so their jackets weren't complete, but they weren't raising any red flags either. In fact, the only person with a blemish on her record was Sam.

She had been running an illegal intel gathering op against Helen Rhodes during the presidential campaign. Noble didn't need the after action report to know who laid in that operation. He had lived the other side of it. He picked up Sam's black and white. With his other hand, he twisted the cap off a water bottle and took a swig. Beyond the rain streaked windows lay an unbroken field of utter black. Noble gazed at her picture and said, "What did you get yourself into, Sam?"

————

Armstrong stood on the edge of the tarmac and watched the Cessna lift off. The jet screamed as it left the runway, leaving behind twin streaks of nebulous gray streamers. The landing gear folded up and the running lights dwindled to tiny red blips in the dark sky. The roar faded away to a tiny hiss on the edge of hearing. Armstrong reached in her breast pocket for a thin cigar. Duc flicked a lighter and held it out for her. His eyes followed the jet's trail. When it was out of sight to his younger, sharper eyes, he turned and opened the back door. Armstrong clamped the smoke between her teeth and dialed a number on her cell before climbing into the back seat.

Burke picked up on the first ring. "Is our boy in?"

"He's on board," Armstrong spoke around the cigar. "Now let's hope he can find Sam before anyone else."

Duc shut the door and circled the front bumper. He got the car started and motored across the tarmac to a runway on the other side of the airport where a second jet waited to ferry them back to Virginia.

"The only way we're going to untangle this mess is throw a wild card into the mix," Burke said.

Armstrong buzzed down her window and tapped ash. "That's a pretty good description for Noble. Can we trust him to bring her in?"

There was a pause on the other end and then Burke said, "We're about to find out."

CHAPTER FIFTEEN

DAVID GREY AND HIS TEAM WORKED OUT OF THE TOP floor of a nondescript apartment on the northwest corner of Pont Neuf. Arched windows looked out across the steel gray waters of the Seine. The Company owned the building and the floors below were kept empty, used occasionally as safe houses or black sites. It gave Paris branch the ability to work without worrying about who might be underneath, listening in on their conversations.

The seventh-floor command post trapped a whiff of the ever-present smell of sewage which dominates Paris. It wasn't so bad in winter. Summer was unbearable. With no central heat, all three men were bundled in thick sweaters. Mugs of coffee sat cooling on their work stations. Computers clustered around a large server in the center of the room, along with a communications array bristling with antennae. From here, they could tap into the video feed of any traffic camera in France but they still hadn't managed to locate Sam or Duval.

LeBeau, a native Frenchman, sat with headphones covering one ear, listening in on the various police and emergency channels. He puffed on one cigarette and had another tucked behind his ear. Preston muttered to himself while he worked. Grey was hunched over a terminal, checking hotel registries for any of Gunn's known cover identities and watching the surveillance feed in front of her Paris apartment in case she tried to go home.

Outside, the first quiet fingers of dawn were creeping over the rooftops of Paris while panic gathered in Grey's gut. It felt like an angry rodent gnawing at the lining of his stomach, an ulcer in the making. Frank Bonner was dead and Duval was in the wind. If they didn't locate him soon, all hell was going to break loose. It was only a matter of time before Langley learned Duval was in play.

"He could be half way to Montenegro by now," Grey said, more to himself than anyone else. "Has anyone got anything?"

"Give me another minute or two," Preston said. He was hammering keys with his brow bunched in concentration. His wide-set eyes were fixed on the screen in front of him. He nodded to himself. "Okay. Yeah. Take a look at this."

Grey and LeBeau crowded around his terminal. He brought up video feed from Honfleur. Six surveillance cams were grouped on his screen. He pointed at a tramway stop that Grey recognized. "This is where they got on." He pointed at another square in the bottom corner. "This is six blocks away. Watch as the train goes by. The back door has already been opened. If you look at this angle," Preston pointed to another square, "you can see in the windows. The cars are all empty. So they had already jumped off by this point." He brought up a street map and highlighted a section of track in red. "They got off the train somewhere between here and here. If we focus our search of surveillance feeds around this neighborhood, we should be able to pick them up and follow them to wherever they are now."

"Good work." Grey clapped his hands. He felt the vicious little rodent relax, but not completely. It wouldn't let go entirely until Grey had Duval in his hands and Sam was on a slab at the morgue. "Get on it."

His phone vibrated in his pocket. Grey looked at the number and groaned. He answered brusquely. "We're working on it."

"Are you any closer?"

"Preston narrowed down the section of track where they jumped from the train," Grey said. "From there we should be able to follow them on traffic cams. It won't be long now."

"Well, you had better work fast."

Grey said. "We're doing everything we can."

"Do more," came the reply. "I just found out Armstrong sent a private contractor to Paris. He's going to be landing in a few hours."

The rodent went back, savaging his stomach lining in earnest. He switched the phone to his other ear and said, "Why would she do that?"

"I have no idea."

"Do you think she knows?"

"She's got a dead officer, another on the run, and a French mercenary group tied into the whole affair. She probably suspects you have more information than you're sharing. She's understandably suspicious."

Grey cursed. He could practically feel the acid eating a hole through his belly. He'd need to have a doctor look at it, but that was a problem for another day. He said, "How do you want to proceed?"

"I want you to put *Le Milieu* onto the freelancer. This whole thing is their mess. They should help clean it up. He's coming in on a private jet. Have them pick him up at the airport and find out what he knows."

"Isn't that going to look suspicious?"

"I think we're a bit beyond that, don't you? If that next Cipher Punk vault gets released, we are *all* going to burn. Put *Le Milieu* on the freelancer. They can put the screws to him and find out how much Armstrong knows, or suspects. When they're done, make sure they dispose of the body. I want you to find Duval and make sure no one hears from Sam Gunn ever again. Maybe we can hang this whole affair around her neck and divert attention from us."

Grey hung up the phone. Preston and LeBeau were watching him with raised eyebrows and questioning faces. He said, "We just got a whole new set of problems."

CHAPTER SIXTEEN

The sky over Normandy was a dull gray. Sunlight struggled through a thick blanket of steely clouds that threatened more cold and rain. Sam and Duval sat in a café called L'Abri Normand on Rue du General de Gaulle. It had taken them nearly two hours last night to find a car without modern GPS. Between Sam's twisted ankle and Duval's asthma, it was a slow, tedious search. The stabbing pain in her ankle got so bad she had been forced to lean on Duval for support and he complained every step of the way. Finally, they had stumbled on an '03 Passat, only to discover it had less than a quarter tank. Sam didn't dare stop for gas. Every filling station between France and Slovenia is wired with cameras and the Company would be checking every single one.

Over the past two decades, Western Europe had become a surveillance state. It's impossible to go anywhere in Britain or the mainland without your face on camera.

By 9 a.m., a red fuel light forced them off the highway.

The needle had been pointing to E for half an hour. They ditched the stolen Passat on a side street in a little town called Gaillon, leaving Sam's tactical vest in the trunk.

The boulevards were a confusing tangle and the only thing exceptional about the village was a castle perched on a hilltop. Sam and Duval limped along until they found a secondhand shop, paid cash for a change of clothes, and then stopped for breakfast.

"You know the A13 would take us straight through Paris," Duval was saying. Half a dozen tables crowded a cozy space filled with the warm smell of fresh bread and strong coffee. The heat was cranked up so high it was making Sam sleepy. She had been awake nearly twenty-four hours now and her thoughts were edged with the fog of exhaustion.

"That's why we aren't on it," she told him. She picked up a shallow bowl filled with *café au lait* and sipped. The French take their morning coffee in bowls rather than mugs. Breakfast is toast, mostly used as a delivery system for sugary sweet jams.

Duval had a pub cap on and the collar of his coat turned up to obscure his face. He was on his second slice of brioche, slathered in butter and raspberry, and he kept shooting nervous glances at the wait staff. He spoke around a mouthful of food. "I don't like this. Someone could recognize me."

"Act like you belong here instead of on a wanted poster," Sam said. "And stop looking around. You already draw attention with that limp."

He leaned forward and hissed, "I can't help *somebody* shot me."

"Are you still mad about that?" Sam had traded her tactical vest and cargo pants for a pair of denims and a black fleece jacket. The coffee was starting to drive back the cloud of sleep and at the same time made the pain in her ankle worse. "You'd be dead right now if I hadn't beaned you."

"Are you looking for gratitude?"

"No," Sam told him. "I just want answers."

"Careful what you wish for."

"I stuck my neck out for you," Sam reminded him.

"So now I owe you?"

"Yes," she told him. "You've been held up inside the embassy for nearly a decade. You were safe there. Why did you decide to move? Why now? And what have you got on Frank Bonner? Why was he after you?"

Duval shook his head. "Never heard of any Frank Bonner."

"I don't believe that for a second." She put her coffee down and turned to him. "Come on, Duval. What's going on?"

"How do I know I can trust you?" Duval asked. He put his brioche down and licked crumbs from his fingertips. "You come out of nowhere, kill my bodyguards, shoot me, and then force me to jump from the back of a moving train. How do I know this isn't some twisted CIA scheme?"

Sam winced and glanced around. "Keep your voice down. I didn't kill anybody... or at least... I didn't mean to. I was using rubber bullets."

"Frank Bonner looked dead enough."

"Thought you didn't know who that is?"

Duval didn't bother to comment.

"It was an accident." Sam told him, and she felt a barb

dig into her heart. When she joined the CIA, she had taken a battery of tests. The interviewers wanted to know if her faith would prevent her from killing another human being. Sitting in the safety of the interview room, imaging herself working for the greater good, Sam had told them no. In her mind's eye the hypotheticals were always cut and dry. The bad guys wore black hats and twirled handlebar mustaches, but real life had proved very different. It was hard to tell the good guys from the bad. She told Duval, "I was aiming low. One of the bullets must have taken a bad skip and hit him in the head."

"And it killed him?" Duval asked. "A piece of rubber?"

"A piece of rubber fired at thirty-two hundred feet per second," Sam told him. "If it hits you in the head, it can jar the brain hard enough to kill you."

He whistled low. "Was he a friend?"

Sam shrugged. "He was my boss."

"But was he a friend?"

"Yeah," Sam said, a little irritated. "He was a friend."

"And you still tried to save me?" Duval asked.

"It was supposed to be a clean getaway. I had it all planned out. I was going to hit the bodyguards, snatch you, and disappear before Bonner and his crew showed up. They were never supposed to know it was me."

Duval turned his attention to the street. "I thought you were there to kill me. Why did you do it? Why did you save me?"

"I've got my reasons," she said. "Why did you leave the embassy and risk capture?"

"I've got my reasons," he said.

"Look, Duval, there are a lot of people who want you dead. I can't help if I don't know what the problem is."

He set his jaw and shook his head, intent on keeping his secrets. "We should be headed for Montenegro as fast as we can, not sitting around sipping coffee."

"That's exactly what they expect us to do," Sam told him.

"So what's your plan? A leisurely trip across Europe?" He thrust his chin at an old cathedral across the street. "Maybe we should do some sightseeing while we're at it?"

Sam leaned forward and spoke through clenched teeth. "First of all, we'd be in Switzerland by now if you hadn't tried to run. I had a clean, unmarked van with a tank full of gas waiting at the pier. Second, if you'd rather take your chances on your own, be my guest. I'm not stopping you."

Duval sat in sullen silence.

Sam arched her back, stretched her neck, and rolled her shoulders. Other than the sprained ankle, she had survived the jump from the back of the train but it wasn't something she wanted to try again. Every muscle in her body ached. Her limbs were covered in scrapes and bruises, and a whole bottle of Advil wouldn't cure the pounding in her skull. The sharp, unrelenting pain made Duval's constant complaining unbearable. She sighed and rubbed her temples. "Sorry. I lost my temper."

"I'm sorry too." He took a hit from his inhaler, held it, and asked, "What is our plan?"

Sam said, "You know anything about the chateau?"

He shrugged. "Like any of the other castles in France, I suppose."

"How long do you figure it would take someone to walk through and have a look?"

"An hour," he said. "Maybe two. Why?"

"Finish your breakfast," Sam said. "There is a clinic down the road and I need a blood pressure cuff."

He stuffed the last bit of bread and jam in his mouth before following Sam outside into the bracing cold. She stuffed her hands in the pockets of her fleece jacket and limped along the avenue to a small clinic, the French version of a CVS, where she bought a blood pressure cuff, aspirin, and several crushable ice packs.

"What are you going to do with all that?" Duval wanted to know.

Sam led the way up the hill to a flat parking lot for visitors to Gaillon's only tourist spot. The spires of the Norman castle reared up into the slate gray sky, an imposing reminder of the French monarchy that had competed with Great Britain for the New World. Now it was little more than an economically collapsing socialist state with tourist traps and expensive wine.

As they moved along the rows of cars, a beige SUV swung into a parking spot and a family of four piled out. The kids slammed the doors too hard and dad barked at them. Mom made sure the youngest had his shoes tied while Dad checked that the van was locked. Then they headed off toward the castle.

Sam watched them go, blew out her cheeks and muttered, "Thou shalt not steal."

"What?" Duval asked. He was looking around, making sure no one saw them.

"It's a verse," Sam told him. She stuffed the blood pressure cuff into the driver's side door and started squeezing.

"Huh?"

"From the Bible," she said.

"I know that," Duval said. He shrank against the side of the vehicle like an escaped convict hunkering next to a prison wall. "Why are you quoting it? Are you a Christian?"

"Is that a problem?"

The blood pressure cuff filled with air, pressing on the frame until the door popped open with a loud *clonk*.

Sam winced.

Duval put a hand to his chest, like he might be having a heart attack.

They both looked around to make sure no one was watching, then Sam climbed into the driver's seat, reached across and unlocked the passenger side.

Duval piled in next to her. "It's just that I never would have pegged you for a Christian."

"Thanks a lot." She pressed her lips together and reached under the dash. Using a pocket knife, she cut and twisted together a pair of wires. The engine roared to life.

Ten minutes later they were on the road. Sam had her ankle wrapped in ice packs. The cold was helping with the swelling and keeping her awake at the same time. They were half a kilometer from the castle when Duval muttered, "Thank you."

Sam, intent on the road, said, "For what?"

"Saving my life."

She looked across at him and then back at the road. "Why don't you stretch out? Get some sleep."

Duval crawled into the back, laid out across the seats and was asleep in minutes.

CHAPTER SEVENTEEN

For Matthew Burke, it had been a long night and it was looking like an even longer day. He couldn't remember the last time he ate. His stomach let him know about this unprecedented turn of events with frequent, loud rumbles. Burke had grown up in Georgia and played college football. He still had the shoulders of a defensive lineman, but years behind a desk had softened him up around the middle. He clutched a chipped mug emblazoned with the CIA logo in one giant black paw. His tie hung loose and the top button of his starched white collar was open.

A low-level buzz filled the situation room on the third floor of Langley. It reminded Burke of the quiet noise that filled a stadium before a big game, when the crowds are filing in, excited but not yet screaming. Someone in the room had bathed in cologne—Burke suspected Ben Jameson —and the stink mixed together with the odor of moldy carpet to form a lethal cocktail.

A dozen surveillance experts crowded around the array

of computers, sifting through every piece of security and traffic footage across France and half of Europe. The large center screen showed images from three separate drones orbiting the operation area. Full color images zoomed in on vehicles cruising the A13. The pilots snapped pictures of the drivers and computers filtered the images through facial recognition software. Every time they got a possible match, they had to reroute one of the drones for a low pass to get a better look. In the movies, facial recognition software is close to perfect. Reality is far different. Humans share facial characteristics. Computers can look for similarities, but the processors can't actually recognize an individual face. An hour ago, they had gotten a possible and done a low pass, only to find an Asian man with long hair behind the wheel. If Burke squinted, the guy kind of resembled Sam.

Burke had been doing this so long now he started to wonder if there were only so many faces to go around. If you lived long enough maybe you would see the same faces recycled. Maybe someone was walking around with Helen of Troy's face. Perhaps simple mathematical combinations reproduced exact replicas of humans dead and gone. Burke was reminded of all the time travel movies where a man finds his long-lost love reborn under a new name at some point in the future or distant past. Always played by the same actress of course.

The door cranked open and Dana came in, pushing a trolley piled with sandwiches from the cafeteria. Their eyes met. A half smile turned up one side of her mouth. She wore navy blue slacks that hugged her curves and a white button-down with a pale blue scarf. Her blonde hair was up in a ponytail. The frosted glass door sealed shut behind her with a soft sucking noise.

Analysts left their stations long enough to grab a sandwich from the trolley and pour coffee before returning to their vigil. Dana joined Burke, handed him a turkey on rye with mayo. The smell of her perfume enveloped him in a secret lover's embrace. "I saw Coughlin in the hall," she said under her breath. "He's right behind me. I think he was checking out my butt."

"Can't say I blame him." Burke set down his mug, tore open the white paper and took a bite.

The door opened and Coughlin came in. His tie was missing and his sleeves were rolled up to the elbows. His left eye winked in rapid fire. "Bring me up to speed."

"Nothing to report yet," Burke said around a mouthful of food. "It's like she dropped right off the face of the planet."

Coughlin stuck his fists on his hips. "She didn't just disappear. She's out there somewhere. We need to find her."

"We trained her," Dana pointed out. "She knows everything we know. She'll stay off the main roads."

Burke nodded. "She might even have her face disguised. Any idea what she's up to?"

Coughlin shook his head. "None."

Burke put his sandwich on a nearby desk and dusted crumbs from his fingertips. "Surely Grey has some idea why she killed Bonner? He was there. He's closer to this than anybody."

"Don't you think I asked him?" Coughlin's tick turned his face into a grimace.

"Noted," Burke said. He was pressing Coughlin's

buttons, looking for a reaction. There was more going on here, but Burke had no way of finding out unless they managed to make contact with Sam and that didn't seem likely. He picked up his sandwich. "Has Grey made any progress?"

"They're doing everything they can from their end," Coughlin said.

"He's our boots on the ground," Burke said.

"I'm aware of that."

"Stands the best chance of finding Gunn."

Coughlin took his eyes off the screens and turned to face Burke. "I run France. You run the surveillance. You do your job and I'll do mine."

Burke took a bite. "This'll be easier if we all share information."

"You'd like that, wouldn't you?"

"I would," Burke said.

Dana cautioned him with an elbow to the ribs.

An incredulous grin turned up one side of Coughlin's face. "Of course you would, Burke. Another recruit blew a gasket. Seems like every couple of months we have to run down one of your people. You have a history of recruiting officers who go off the reservation. Why is that?"

"We can't all spend our career safe behind a desk at Langley," Burke said. "Mistakes happen in the field. You'd know that if you'd ever been there."

"You son of a—"

"I have a possible," Ben Jameson said.

Burke and Coughlin both leaned over his shoulder. The cloying stink of Jameson's cologne filled Burke's nose. He tried not to breathe and said, "Let's see it."

"Eighty-seven percent," Jameson muttered. He was in his forties, balding and recently divorced. Burke suspected the overdose of cologne had something to do with his new status as a single man. He pulled up a video feed of a beige minivan. An Asian woman was behind the wheel. The distance and speed made it hard to be sure.

"Let's get a pass over," Burke said. "Where is this?"

Jameson consulted a map. "It's on the A13 southeast of Paris."

"Who's closest?" Burke wanted to know. His heart was tap dancing inside his chest.

"Able-6-1 is passing over Paris now," came the reply.

Burke looked around for a headset.

Dana was faster. She snatched up a set from a work station and passed them over.

"Patch me through." Burke put one of the headphones against his ear and adjusted the mic. "Able-6-1, this is Command. Do you copy?"

"Copy. This is 6-1-Able. Go ahead. Over."

"I need a low pass on the A13 southeast of Paris, headed east. You're looking for a beige Renault, license plate..."

He turned to Jameson.

Jameson consulted the still photos and read off the number.

Burke relayed.

All eyes turned to the main screens.

Burke said, "Bring that up."

Dana tapped a command into the console in front of her and Able-6-1's video feed filled the screen. They watched as the unmanned drone turned a tight arc over the French countryside and then swooped low over a parade of cars on the Autoroute. Thick cloud cover forced the pilot to go lower than usual and that meant the gleaming white fuselage was visible to any drivers who happened to look up. Fortunately, people rarely look at anything but the tail lights of the car in front. The camera singled out a beige Renault.

Burke said, "There. That's it. Give us a look at the driver."

The angle changed as the drone pulled even with the car and reduced airspeed. The pilot, a twenty-two-year-old kid working out of the 70th ISRW at Fort Meade, Maryland, maneuvered his craft so that they could see right in the driver's side window.

"Can you zoom in?" Burke asked.

The image jumped in size. It was an Asian woman, about Sam's age, but the chin was all wrong.

Burke shook his head. "That's not her."

"Are you sure?" Coughlin said. He was looking at the Company head shot of Sam on every monitor in the room.

"I'm sure." Burke instructed the drone pilot to resume course. The angle banked sharply and for a moment they were looking at sky, then more French countryside.

Coughlin cursed and stalked out of the situation room.

Burke waited until he was gone and turned to Dana. "Something doesn't add up. I want you to work with Jameson and see if you can bring up video of the pier at Honfleur. I want any angles he can come up with."

"Does it have to be Jameson?" Dana whispered. "He smells like he showered in Calvin Klein."

"And keep it quiet," Burke said.

She shielded her mouth with a mug of coffee and

dropped her voice. "What are you going to do if we actually locate Sam?"

"I'm not sure." Burke put his hands on his hips and grimaced, showing the gap between his teeth. "Let's hope we don't find out."

CHAPTER EIGHTEEN

NOBLE FELT THE TIRES TOUCH DOWN WITH A SHRIEK. The sudden friction gave him a gentle shove against the seat back. The flight across the Atlantic had taken nearly five hours; an eternity. If Sam had a reliable set of wheels, she could be in eastern Europe by now. She could be dead by now, whispered a little voice at the back of Noble's mind. He pushed that thought away. He couldn't allow himself to dwell on it. *Operate on the assumption she's still alive,* he told himself. Sam was tough and resourceful. She knew how to avoid detection and had the skills to drop off the radar, which would keep her alive but make Noble's job of finding her that much more difficult. His first stop would have to be her apartment. She might have left a clue about what she was doing, or at least where she was going.

While the jet taxied, Noble inspected the contents of Duc's care package. Inside the messenger bag, he found a titanium fountain pen, a handcuff key, half a dozen microdot transmitters small enough to fit in a pocket, and a ruggedized laptop. It wasn't much, but for Noble—who normally scrounged what he needed from local hardware stores—Christmas had come early. The handcuff key went under the padded insole of his hiking shoe and the titanium pen went into his breast pocket. The rest of the gear stayed in the bag.

The Cessna rolled into a private hangar where a Mercedes G63 AMG was parked. Beyond the hangar doors, the airfield was drab and overcast. Iron gray clouds spit icy rain.

Noble shrugged into his jacket and worked the zipper. The co-pilot emerged from the cabin, handed Noble a set of keys, and let the stairs down. A draft of chilly air spilled into the cabin. After balmy Saint Petersburg, it felt like stepping into a walk-in freezer.

The Mercedes was a four-wheel drive affair with dark tint on the windows. Not very inconspicuous, but good for wet, rainy streets and ramming other vehicles. Noble dropped the messenger bag in the passenger seat, turned up the heat, and pulled out of the hangar. Droplets of rain dotted the windshield and Noble inspected the dash for wiper controls, but rain sensors did the work for him. From Charles de Gaulle, he took the A1 southwest toward the heart of Paris.

He had been on the freeway five minutes when he glanced in his review and spotted a fire engine red Alfa Romeo on his tail. The sports coupe had left the airport at the same time. It could be coincidence, but Noble didn't believe in those. He eased up on the gas and let the Mercedes fall back several car lengths. The Alfa slowed, staying two car lengths behind. Warning bells in Noble's head started to jingle. He sped up again. The Alfa changed lanes and passed a slower moving Nissan to keep up. Rain streaked the back windshield, making it hard to see, but Noble counted at least two people in the red coupe.

He took out the cell Armstrong had given him, dialed, put the phone on speaker, and dropped it in the cup holder.

The Director picked up on the first ring. "I didn't expect to hear from you so soon. You must have just landed."

"I did," Noble told her. "And I've already made friends. A pair of bricks in a red Alfa Romeo are following me. Friends of yours?"

"They don't work for me," Armstrong assured him. "Where are you?"

"I'm on the A1, headed toward the city."

Armstrong was quiet, thinking through the implications.

Noble said, "You need to check your seals. You've got a leak."

"Duc?" Armstrong asked.

"Doubtful." Noble checked his rearview while he spoke. The Alfa Romeo was still hanging two car lengths back. He said, "I'd have a talk with the pilots. See who they talked to."

"I'll do that," Armstrong said. "Do you think you can ditch your new friends?"

"I should be able to lose them when I get to the city."

"See if you can get a picture for me."

"You're high maintenance," Noble said. "You know that?"

"I'm worth it," Armstrong said and hung up.

Noble stepped on the gas and jogged around a line of slower moving vehicles. The needle on the Mercedes inched toward eighty-five miles an hour. The Alfa Romeo gave chase. The smaller sports coupe had no trouble keeping up, but the gambit had forced the tail out into the open. There were no cars between them now. Noble swerved into the breakdown lane and stamped the brakes. Tires shrieked on wet asphalt. The back end started to fish-tail. He wrestled the wheel in an effort to keep the big Mercedes steady.

The Alfa Romeo shot past like a sleek red torpedo cutting through the chilly spray. Noble cramped the wheel and mashed the gas pedal to the floor. All-weather tires slipped on wet blacktop, then caught traction. The Mercedes leapt forward with an energetic growl. Noble barely avoided a panel truck. Horns blared. Noble swung out around the Alfa Romeo and pulled alongside.

A thug with a unibrow and his jaw wired shut glared at Noble from the passenger seat. He had a brace around his neck and both eyes were puffy purple slits. Noble smiled, raised his cellphone, and snapped a picture. The shot was blurry, but should be enough for Armstrong to work with. Unibrow twisted in his seat, buzzed down the window and produced a CZ61 Škorpion machine pistol.

CHAPTER NINETEEN

Mr. Neck Brace brought the automatic pistol up, with his elbows tucked tight, so the weapon wasn't hanging out the open window. Noble's heart jogged inside his chest. What he thought was a simple tail job was turning into a hit.

He tapped the brakes and cramped the wheel as the assassin squeezed the trigger. A short dull crack rose above the driving rain. Noble heard the angry buzz of bullets whipping past the windshield. He swerved behind the Alfa Romeo and closed the distance. The space between the bumpers shrank to a few feet. Noble was hoping the driver would get cute and lay on the brakes. The heavier Mercedes would smash the sports car like a snowplow through a drift. No such luck. The Alfa Romeo sped up. The chase slalomed through traffic. Try as he might, Noble couldn't keep pace. The Mercedes had the horsepower, but weighed too much and didn't handle like the Alfa. He let off the gas just in time. The driver of the Alfa pulled the same trick on him. The car swerved into the breakdown lane. Tail lights flared and rain made halos around the brake indicators.

Noble shot past. He pushed the gas pedal all the way to the floor. The needle crept up to ninety, edged past, then moved toward one-hundred. Noble barreled along the highway at reckless speeds with his heart ping-ponging off the walls of his chest. His knuckles turned white on the steering wheel. Sweat beaded on his forehead. He weaved around slower vehicles while the Alfa Romeo kept pace. At this speed, even the smallest mistake was a death sentence. A high-speed chase is not about who can drive the fastest. Anyone can redline an engine. It's about who makes the first mistake. When the other driver has a partner in the passenger seat with a gun, it tips the scales in their favor. Noble used the breakdown lane to pass a semi, mashed the horn and swerved back into traffic in an attempt to jack-knife the rig. Bumpers almost kissed. The driver braked and twisted the wheel, but managed to keep the big truck steady.

Noble bared his teeth in frustration.

The Alfa Romeo came shooting up the breakdown lane and Noble cramped the wheel in a half-hearted attempt to pin the Alfa against the concrete barrier. Mr. Neck-Brace raised the machine pistol and Noble had to swerve into the outside lane. The gun roared. Through the wind and driving rain it was just a distant *snap-snap-snap*.

Noble heard a loud *thwack* against the back door of the Mercedes, like deadly hail drilling through the panel. He veered left, into the outside breakdown lane, pressed his foot down, and willed the engine to give just a little bit more. The Alfa Romeo used the inside breakdown lane and they raced past lines of traffic. Slowing down wasn't an option. The Alfa could simply match speed. Noble stayed on the gas and looked for anything that might give him an edge. He had just made up his mind to veer back across traffic and use the bigger vehicle as a ramming device when he spotted an exit ramp ahead. The driver of the Alfa saw it too and started across the lanes of traffic, but he would never make it in time. They both knew it.

Noble waved goodbye and cut the wheel. The Mercedes glided along the exit ramp toward the junction that would put him on the N2. From there, it was a straight shot into Paris. He eased off the gas and watched his rearview as he sailed around the curve and back into the flow of traffic. His pulse rate matched the speedometer, slowly returning to normal.

He hadn't been in France twenty minutes and already someone wanted him dead. That was a record, even for Noble. Whoever was behind it had reach. They had an information source inside Armstrong's camp and deep enough pockets to put a hit on Noble before he had even landed.

Noble added up the facts; a dead CIA officer, another on the run, and someone who didn't want anyone putting all the pieces together, someone with enough money to hire a hit on short notice. Noble was left with an incomplete jigsaw puzzle and no one he could trust. He would have to pick and choose what information he shared. Anything

Armstrong knew, Noble had to assume, the bad guys knew as well. He let out a breath, reached for his phone and forwarded the picture of his would-be assassin to Armstrong. That much at least was safe.

CHAPTER TWENTY

GREY WAS STANDING IN FRONT OF THE TOILET. A clawfoot tub and a pedestal sink crowded the dingy bathroom on the top floor of the safe house. The overpowering stink of septic waste backed up through the pipes and made Grey wrinkle his nose. The vicious little rodent inside his belly was back at work, scurrying and biting and gnawing. He shook off, zipped up, and reached into the medicine cabinet for a roll of Tums. He popped two pink disks into his mouth and chewed. His face pinched at the bitter chalk taste. The medicine made it down to his stomach where it helped settle the angry rat.

Grey checked his watch. Time seemed to be racing by. Every minute brought them closer to another Cypher Punk release. If that happened, it would be Grey on the run. He would have to disappear. Where would he go? His face tightened and the rat in his belly lifted its nose for a sniff. Grey was usually the one tracking down fugitives. He was the guy who walked up behind them on a dark sidewalk and pumped a bullet into the back of their skull. He knew the score, and if that Cypher Punk release went public there was no place he could go they wouldn't find him. He would have to spend the rest of his life on the move. Eventually he'd get tired, get sloppy, slip up. Then he'd be the one with a bullet in the back of his head.

He turned on the sink. Water gurgled up through the pipes. Grey cupped his hands under the chilly spray and doused his face. The bracing cold helped drive out those fears and refocused him on the task at hand. *Find Duval*, he told himself. *Kill Sam*.

When he left the bathroom, Preston said, "Everything alright?"

"Fine," Grey muttered. "Anything new?"

"Nothing," Preston said.

LeBeau sat with one headphone pressed against his ear and shook his head. He was listening to the French police scanner. A cigarette dangled from the corner of his mouth, dropping ash onto his trousers. He said, "It may be time to cut our losses and disappear."

Preston seconded that sentiment.

"Nobody's going anywhere," Grey told them. He felt his phone vibrate, recognized Mateen's number, and put it to his ear. "Is it done?"

"*Non*." Mateen spoke through his wired jaw. "He spotted us and got away."

"How the—?" Grey started to ask and pinched the bridge of his nose. "You had *one* job. Pick him up and find out what he knows. How hard is that?"

"We were careful," Mateen said. "He must have known we were coming."

"He didn't know anything," Grey snarled. "You screwed up. Just like you screwed up at the docks. Now I've got another mess on my hands. I'm starting to think hiring you was a mistake."

"Duval was not my fault," Mateen said. "We had everything in hand until the *femme fatale* showed up and started shooting. I'll be eating dinner through a straw for the next three months because you can't control your people."

Grey wanted to reach through the phone and strangle the Frenchman. *Le Milieu* had been paid handsomely and couldn't even mange to kill one man. He said, "Sam Gunn is on me, but the new player is your problem."

"What do want us to do?" Mateen asked. "He's gone. I have no idea where he is."

Grey rubbed the back of his neck. *What would his first move be?* His eyes went to the computer screen where a feed showed the entrance to Gunn's apartment. He said, "Send a couple guys to Gunn's building. He'll probably go there first, looking for clues."

"And if he's not there?"

"You lost him. You find him," Grey nearly shouted. "You've got to have people on the street. Put the word out."

"I'll see what I can do."

Grey dropped his voice to a dangerous whisper. "Don't give me that crap. Find him, or I'll put *Le Milieu* on top of the CIA's terror watch list. How long do you bastards think you'll last with the entire United States government after you?"

"Alright," Mateen said. "We'll find him. But it's going to cost you."

"I don't care what it costs."

Grey put the phone in his pocket and shook his head. "They lost him. Can you believe it?"

LeBeau cursed under his breath. "This is getting out of hand."

"Tell me about it."

Preston said, "Well, I've got some good news."

He was pointing at surveillance footage of Sam in tactical gear and a terrified Duval hurrying along a side street in Honfleur. The image was dark and grainy, but there was no mistaking them. Sam was limping heavily and leaning on Duval for support. While they watched, she elbowed the back window out of a midsized hatchback.

"Yes!" Grey hissed. It felt like a lead weight had been lifted from his chest. "Finally. Good work. Pull up all the feeds from the surrounding area. Get the license plate number of the car. I want to know which direction they're headed."

Twenty minutes later the excitement had evaporated. Sam was good. They followed her on traffic cams along the A1 but she pulled off at a tiny hamlet called Gaillon, which was too small for France's extensive network of cameras.

Grey sat with his chin in his hand and a frown on his face. The mean little rodent had started gnawing again, ripping and tearing at the lining of his stomach. "She's clever," he said.

"They're not far from the German border," Preston pointed out.

"Would she risk it?" LeBeau questioned. "The Germans want Duval as bad as we do."

Grey considered it. Duval was wanted on two charges of rape in Germany. A pair of call girls claimed he had forced himself on them at a rave more than two decades ago, but there was some debate about the legitimacy of the girls' stories. Grey scrubbed his face with both hands. "I don't know. I don't even know what Sam's game is. She might try crossing into Germany and going south from there. Pull up the Gaillon police blotter."

LeBeau rapped the keys. "Bingo. Gaillon police are on the lookout for a beige Citroën SUV stolen from the parking lot of the Château de Gaillon."

"When was that?" Grey wanted to know.

"Two hours ago."

Grey let out a frustrated sigh. "They could be half way to Switzerland."

"They could already be across the border in Belgium," Preston said.

Grey felt the rat dig in with its claws. He cursed. "Get on the phone with French authorities," he said. "Give them the plate number of the stolen Citroën. Make sure they throw up road blocks and stop anyone who fits the description from crossing the border."

"This is France," LeBeau pointed out. "The border is like Swiss cheese."

"Just do it," Grey said. "Maybe we'll get lucky."

CHAPTER TWENTY-ONE

NOBLE CIRCLED THE BLOCK HALF A DOZEN TIMES. IF there was surveillance on Sam's apartment, he didn't see it. The freezing rain had finally let up, but a thick blanket of brooding clouds had plunged Paris into an early twilight. Shadows pooled around the overhangs, turning the dingy neighborhood bleak and depressing. When he didn't spot any watchers, Noble swung the big Mercedes into a spot against the curb and killed the engine.

Sam lived on the second floor of 14 Rue du Moulin Vert in a building with balconies so small they were barely deserving of the name. The front door was open to the public, saving Noble the trouble of picking the lock. He climbed a groaning flight of steps to the second-floor landing and found Sam's door hanging open.

The frame around the knob was splintered. Someone had kicked it in. There were no sounds coming from inside so Noble slipped the gun out of his waistband and nudged the door with his foot. It swung in on tired old hinges that sounded like a chorus of banshees in the stillness.

The place had been tossed. Sofa cushions were slit and the television lay dismantled on the floor. Stuffing covered every surface like snow drifts. In the bedroom, Noble walked over women's clothing and chips of broken glass. It looked like a Victoria's Secret sale on Black Friday. Drawers were turned out, the mattress was sliced open, and picture frames were smashed. Whoever had been here did a thorough job. The bathroom door was propped against the wall with the hinge plates removed. If Sam had hidden any information in the apartment, it was long gone.

In the bathroom, he picked up a bottle labelled *Coco Mademoiselle* and sprayed. The sweet smell of citrus mixed with jasmine reminded him of the first time they met. Sam had been staking out an apartment in Manila and the scent clung to the inside of her old Toyota like a faded memory. It was a complicated smell for a complicated woman.

A decapitated teddy bear lay on the bed with his tummy sunken in. Noble's mouth turned down at the sight. The teddy's head had landed in a corner. Sad button eyes stared up at him. Noble scooped stuffing back into the deflated bear, collected the head and wedged it in his jacket pocket.

Back in the living room, Noble surveyed the wreckage of Sam's life and asked, "What did you get yourself into?"

He had come looking for answers, hoping to find some clue that would tell him what Sam was doing or, at the very least, where she was going. But he was no closer to finding her now than when he landed. Instead he stood in the midst of the destruction, wondering who had ransacked Sam's home and why.

Standard procedure is to collect as much information on a target as possible, but the CIA doesn't smash up apartments. Field officers are trained to leave a residence exactly as they found it. Whoever tossed Sam's place either didn't work for the Company, or they had no time for subtlety. It could have been the same two thugs who tried to kill Noble on the highway, but Noble's money was on Grey and his buddies. This was probably their first stop after Sam dropped off the radar. Which meant it was the first place they would expect Noble to go.

A small tickle of fear walked up his spine. He turned in a circle, doing another sweep of Sam's apartment and found what he had been dreading. A small wireless camera sat atop a bookshelf, pointed at the door. He had missed it amidst all the chaos. Noble cursed under his breath.

He was turning to leave when he heard the stairs creak. His stomach muscles clenched at the sound of the boots creeping up the steps. Noble went to the window and pushed aside the curtain. A dark SUV was parked in front of the building, blocking the street. The driver sat behind the wheel, engine idling, headlamps blazing on cracked asphalt, and the back doors standing open.

CHAPTER TWENTY-TWO

THE ONLY WAY OUT OF SAM'S APARTMENT WAS THE front door, unless Noble wanted to leap from a second-floor window onto concrete. He could probably make the jump without breaking an ankle, but not without being seen. Instead, he crossed into the kitchen and picked up a frying pan from the stove. If he could get out of here without starting a firefight, all the better. He didn't want the French police to have a description of him or his vehicle.

He heard two pairs of boots on the stairs, one heavy, the other pair lighter. Overpowering one man is tricky. Overpowering two at the same time would require lightning reflexes. Noble would need to get in so close they couldn't use their weapons without fear of hitting each other. It would take precision timing and, if he screwed up, he wouldn't live long enough to regret his mistake. He stepped behind the kitchen door and waited.

Through paper thin walls, he heard a pair of hard cases

reach the top of the steps and pause outside the front door. A man whispered in French. "You check the bedroom."

"*Oui.*"

Adrenaline flooded Noble's limbs like the current through a high-tension wire. He could hear his own heartbeat pounding in his ears and his breath sounded like a hurricane. *Slow is smooth and smooth is fast,* he reminded himself.

As the first man started across the apartment for Sam's bedroom, the second man turned toward the kitchen with a handgun leading the way. Noble stepped around the doorframe and smashed the skillet down on the weapon. The pistol hit the hardwood floor and bounced under the sofa. The man reeled back with a bark of pain. Noble followed up with a backhand swing. Cast iron impacted the man's forehead with a resounding *bong*. He stumbled back a step and cradled his head in both hands.

The second man turned at the sound of the scuffle, saw Noble and brought his weapon up to fire. Noble swung the frying pan and managed to bat the gun aside. The skillet hit with enough force to torque the killer sideway and knock him off balance, buying Noble fractions of a second.

The first man was quickly recovering from the blow to the forehead. Noble hit him again. This time he brought the skillet straight down on the man's crown. The thug staggered. His eyes rolled up and his knees buckled.

Noble pivoted in time to swat the gun a second time. The hard case winced in pain as the skillet smashed his knuckles again. He retreated across the apartment, trying to get enough space to use the weapon but Noble closed the gap. He jabbed with the frying pan like a fencer, catching the man a blow to the teeth. Blood burst from split lips. The man staggered and spit chips of broken teeth out on the floor.

That was all the opening Noble needed. He drove a kick into the thug's kneecap. His heel connected with a meaty crunch and the man's leg bent the wrong way. The hard case gave a tortured gasp. Noble hit him in the face with the frying pan, driving him back against the wall and buckling the plaster. Before he could recover, Noble got his free hand around the gun and levered enough pressure on the slide to force it out of battery.

The killer spit French curses from bloody lips. Sweat sprang out on his forehead and the veins in his neck pulsed. He wasn't dying without a fight. He grabbed a fistful of Noble's hair and twisted.

Where the head goes, the body will follow and Noble felt his head twisting inexorably to the left. He dropped the frying pan, grabbed the titanium fountain pen from his pocket and rammed it through the big man's temple. The pen punched through skin and bone with a wet crunch. All the strength drained from the killer's arms and legs. His knees gave out and he slid to the floor. Blood ran down over his jacket and red bubbles formed around his nostrils.

The fight had taken less than two minutes but Noble felt like he'd just gone ten rounds with a heavyweight. He palmed sweat from his forehead and stuffed the dead man's gun into the pocket of his coat.

The first man gave a weak moan and put a hand to his forehead. Blood ran from a deep gash above his right eye and his face pinched in pain. By the time he opened his eyes, Noble was standing over him with a fileting knife.

"One wrong move and I stab this into your throat."

The thug managed to croak out, "I need an ambulance."

"You've probably got a fractured skull and some internal bleeding," Noble said. "I'd say you've got ten, maybe fifteen minutes before your brain swells up. That doesn't give us much time. I'll make you deal. You tell me everything I want to know, and I'll call an ambulance for you."

The man worked his face into a snarl and told Noble where he could get off.

Noble pressed the point of the knife against the man's throat.

"Alright!"

"Who do you work for?" Noble asked.

"*Le Milieu.*"

"Was it your boys who just tried to run me off the A1?"

"*Oui.*"

"Who put out the hit on me?"

"I don't know."

"You're disappointing me," Noble said and leaned on the knife. A spot of blood welled up around the tip.

"I can't tell you what I don't know," he said.

"Who calls the shots?" Noble asked.

"Mateen," the mercenary grumbled. "He runs *Le Milieu.* Gives all the orders."

Noble held the knife in one hand, took out his cellphone with the other and brought up the picture of Mr. Neckbrace. "That him?"

"*Oui.*"

"What happened to him?"

"Someone shot him with a rubber bullet," the mercenary said. "Broke his jaw."

"Bet that hurt," Noble commented. "Where do I find Mateen?"

The mercenary shook his head, just a small side to side movement so he didn't risk cutting his own throat. "I don't know where to find him. When he wants a face-to-face, he calls me. I don't even know if Mateen is his real name."

Noble pocketed his phone. "You wouldn't lie to me, would you?"

The mercenary shook his head.

"What are your orders?" Noble wanted to know.

"Find out what you know and then kill you," the mercenary said. His face had turned an alarming shade of blue and his pupils were different sizes. "Please, I need an ambulance."

Noble patted him down, found a phone in his pocket and said, "First you're going to call the driver downstairs. Tell him you got me, but you need help carrying me to the car. Convince him to come up. Get cute and I slit your throat."

The mercenary took the phone and dialed. In French he said, "Henri, we got him, but he's a fighter. Give us a hand getting him downstairs."

When he was done, Noble took the phone back, punched in three digits and put the phone on speaker, then laid it on the mercenary's chest. A French operator came on the line. "112, what is your emergency?"

While the mercenary spoke to the emergency operator, Noble put his back to the wall next to the open door and waited. He heard a car door open and feet on the stairs. Henri climbed the steps and saw his partner stretched out on the floor. He cursed.

As Henri stepped through the door, Noble stuck a foot out. It was a schoolyard trick, but it worked. The mercenary let out a yelp and crashed to the ground. Noble was on him before he could recover. He grabbed a fistful of Henri's hair and cracked his head against the hardwood floor three times. There was a crunch and blood drizzled from Henri's nose.

Noble wedged his knee into Henri's neck, keeping him pinned and did a quick pat-down. He found a 9mm CZ in Henri's waistband. Noble whistled and stuffed the gun in his belt. *Le Milieu* must pay well if their foot soldiers could afford hardware like that.

Henri recovered from the clobbering and moved straight to begging. It was easy to see why they had left him in the car. Noble pressed his knee down hard and said, "Shut up."

Henri's pleas cut off and he laid there breathing heavy, with his shaking hands out to either side.

Noble said, "If I see you come out this door in the next sixty seconds, I start shooting. Got that?"

Henri started to nod, realized it was too painful with Noble's knee against his neck, and grunted instead.

Noble went downstairs and found the Mercedes boxed in by the SUV. There was no time to move the SUV and come back for the Mercedes with emergency services on their way so Noble would have to make the room he needed. He climbed into the Mercedes, threw it in reverse, and eased back onto the bumper of the car in back. The vehicles met with a light tap. Noble put his foot down on the gas and the big V8 growled, pushing a four-door sedan backwards into a sport coupe. Bumpers buckled. Bleating sirens split the air. Headlamps flashed. Noble managed to accordion four vehicles before the engine redlined and the tires spun on the blacktop. He shifted into drive, shot forward and then reversed again, using the gap he had just created.

He reversed all the way to the end of the block and then spun the wheel. The big Mercedes swung around with a shriek of rubber in the middle of the intersection and Noble shifted into drive. From the corner of his eye, he caught sight of a black van barreling down on him. The vehicles met in a scream of twisting metal and shattering glass. Noble hadn't bothered with his seatbelt. The airbag saved him from smashing his face on the dash, but the impact threw him violently around. His skull bounced off something hard and the lights went out.

CHAPTER TWENTY-THREE

JAQUELINE ARMSTRONG HAD A PHONE TO HER EAR. HER fourteen-year-old daughter was on the other end, raising hell, the way only a fourteen-year-old can. Armstrong leaned forward in her chair, one elbow propped on the edge of a mahogany desk, pressing her aching feet against a massager.

Her office on the top floor at Langley came with its own private bathroom. A pair of leather sofas flanked a low table. The CIA emblem was emblazoned on deep-piled carpet. Track lighting illuminated a shelf full of thick leather-bound volumes, legal codes, and operations manuals. A small machine in the corner pulled in the smell of tobacco and filled the office with a steady electric hum.

"It's not fair," Nicki was saying. "Why do I have to stay with you when you're going to be working all weekend? At least Daddy is going to be around."

That one stung. Jaqueline's lips formed a strict line. She was in no danger of winning Mother of the Year, but she was making an effort. It didn't help that her ex used the job against her in their never-ending battle for possession of Nicki's affections.

"I agree," Jaqueline said, "It's not fair, and I'm sorry, but something really important came up."

"That's what you *always* say."

"Hang tight for a few more hours," Jaqueline told her. "I'll see if I can get out of here and then we can spend some time together."

"Whatever. I'll just sit here all night waiting. Like always. There's nothing to eat by the way."

Jaqueline winced. She had meant to stop through the supermarket last night but she forgot. "There's some cash in my dresser drawer. Why don't you order in some Chinese for us? You still like moo goo gai pan?"

"Gross. I'm a vegan. I've been a vegan, like, *forever!*"

"When did this happen?"

"I went vegan two years ago," Nicki said. "You'd know if you were ever around."

Jaqueline closed her eyes and massaged her temples. "Order whatever you like and when I get home we can go see that new musical. The one with Ryan Gosling."

"That's been out of theaters for months. I've seen it twice on Blu-ray. At *Dad's* house."

It was like arguing with a brick wall. Jaqueline leaned back in her office chair and swallowed a tight knot in her throat. "If you really want to go to your father's place for the weekend, then you can call him and tell him to pick you up."

"I'll take the tube."

"No," Jaqueline said. "Nicki, listen to me; I don't want you on the subway at this time of night."

The line was already dead. Jaqueline hung up. She loved the kid dearly, she would die for her, but sometimes she wanted to pick her up and shake her. *That would make a great news article*, Jaqueline thought. She could see the headline in her mind's eye: CIA Director Arrested on Child Abuse Charges.

She hung up the landline and picked up the pre-paid burner, dialed and listened to it ring a dozen times before going to voicemail. On her computer screen was a mugshot of Mateen Slevic culled from French law enforcement. The boys in IMINT had gone over Noble's freeway pic, run facial analysis and come up with a match. That was almost three hours ago. Since then, Armstrong had been trying to raise Noble on the cell with no luck. She was about to dial again when the intercom buzzed.

Her secretary, a legacy named Ginny Farnham who had worked for Clark Foster, came on the line. "Mr. Hwang here to see you."

Armstrong pushed the button. "Send him in."

Duc filled the doorframe. His beard stuck out like a wiry black brush. "You wanted to see me?"

"Close the door," Armstrong said.

Duc let the door swing shut, put his back to it and crossed his arms over his chest.

"I've lost contact with Noble," she said.

Duc frowned. "Dead?"

"Too early to say," Armstrong said. "There was a greeting party waiting for him at the airport. Noble suspects the pilots. The Cessna will be touching down in an hour. I want you there to meet it. One of those pilots talked. I want to know which one and who they've been talking too."

Duc nodded and put a hand on the door knob. "What about Noble?"

"Not much we can do for him until we know more," Armstrong said. She was hoping and praying he wasn't dead. As Director of the CIA it was only a matter of time before she made a decision that sent some pour soul to his death, but she didn't want it to be a private contractor on an undisclosed mission and she didn't want it to be now. Since Noble was a contractor, if he died, Congress would never have to know about it—Armstrong could sweep the whole thing under the rug and pretend it had never happened—but she would know, and she'd have to live with it. She told Duc, "Go have a talk with those pilots. If they so much as muttered in their sleep I want to know who was sleeping next to them."

"Understood," Duc said and let himself out.

Armstrong dialed again and got voicemail. She put the phone down with a sigh and shook her head.

CHAPTER TWENTY-FOUR

SAM KEPT PINCHING HER EARS TO STAY AWAKE. SHE needed sleep. Fatigue crowded her brain and gummed up her thoughts. She had been nursing a cup of coffee for the last hundred miles. It was cold now, but the caffeine still helped. Duval was stretched across the back seat, sleeping fitfully. Every few minutes, he grunted and flinched from unseen attackers plaguing his nightmares.

The sky had turned from a dull gray to a flat black. Icy rain came down in sporadic drizzles. The tires made a long droning song on the blacktop and the sound would hypnotize Sam if she let it.

She checked her rearview, stole a glance at the fugitive tossing in his sleep, and returned her attention to the road. The long stretch of wet asphalt continued spooling out behind her. She resisted the urge to check the sky. There could be a drone up there right now, a silent ghost gliding along overhead, watching every move she made.

Don't think like that, Sam told herself. That kind of

thinking would only make her paranoid. Endlessly sifting through all the what-ifs would drive her mad. She needed to stay focused on the next move, but her mind kept wandering and she would find herself thinking about the future. She had started imagining the word in all caps, bolded, in twenty-two-point font. THE FUTURE. What future? Her lips pressed together and a tight knot formed in her chest.

She could probably get Duval to Montenegro. Then what? Her plan to snatch him had gone completely off the wire. They had seen her face and there was no going back now. She thought about putting in a call to the new DCI. *Maybe Armstrong would listen*, the voice of reason tried to say. *Maybe she was in on it*, another voice insisted.

Call Jake. The idea came to her like an announcer's voice breaking through static on the radio. It was so strong, so sudden, that she had her phone out and was about to power it on. Jake would know what to do. She would call him up and... say what? *Hi Jake. I blew it. I went off the reservation. Now I'm wanted for treason. Any chance you want to run away with me to some forgotten corner of the globe and live like fugitives?*

Tears welled up in her eyes and her throat clamped shut. She held back a pathetic little sob.

"What are you doing?" Duval was sitting up and his eyes were wide. He leaned forward between the seats like he would snatch the phone from her grasp.

Sam realized her thumb was still hovering over the power button and she dropped the cell in the cup holder. "I don't know what I was thinking. Getting tired I guess."

Duval climbed into the passenger seat and gave her a

good hard look. The concern was clear on his face. "Need me to drive?"

"No." Sam wiped tears from her eyes. She tried to do it covertly, make it look like she was rubbing sleep from her eyes, but that never works. She said, "I'm good. Just a little punchy."

They rode in silence for several miles before Duval said, "You gave up your whole life for me. Why?"

"Don't flatter yourself," Sam told him. "They were never supposed to see my face."

"You didn't answer the question," Duval said. "Why did you rescue me? You could have let them have me and gone on with your life. What does it matter to you?"

Sam raked a hand through her raven locks. "I joined the CIA because I wanted to make the world a better place."

"Not everybody in your organization feels the same, I'm afraid."

A bitter laughed worked up from her chest. "Now you tell me."

"It's overwhelming when you realize just how deep the corruption goes." Duval stared out the passenger side window at the dark countryside rolling past. "When I got the first package of leaked documents, I was horrified at some of the things I was reading. I spent a week pacing my grubby flat in Paris, going over the material, hardly daring to believe some of the things in those files. I didn't want to believe it. I didn't *want* to believe the very same agencies that were supposed to be keeping us safe could be responsible for covering up such atrocities."

"Why *did* you release it?" Sam asked. "You had to know they would come after you."

"Why did you rescue me?" He looked over at her. "Because it was the right thing to do."

"Touché."

Flashing lights winked in the darkness up ahead and the first giddy rush of fear started in Sam's belly. She sat up a little straighter. Duval, noticing her sudden tension, peered through the rain-streaked windshield and the color drained from his face. "*Mon Dieu.* We're caught."

"Don't panic," she told him. "Could be a traffic accident."

CHAPTER TWENTY-FIVE

Sam's foot eased up on the gas pedal. Traffic was slowing down and stacking up. A line of cars crept toward the flashing lights. Duval clutched the dash with one white-knuckled hand and whispered under his breath, "No, no, no, no..."

Sam tried to calm him down, but her own gut was screaming a warning at her. They eased forward, stop and go, until the flashing lights came into view. French police had set up a roadblock and were checking cars.

Sam's stomach did a flip-flop. The line of cars suddenly seemed to be moving too fast. The Renault in front of her kept edging forward and Sam wished it would stop. She needed time to think.

It could be a routine drunk driving stop. France had started cracking down on drunk driving in recent years. Gone were the days when French drivers could enjoy an entire bottle of wine with dinner and then climb behind the wheel of a car. The government had set the legal limit at .05

and even passed a law requiring French motorists to have a breathalyzer in the vehicle, but supply problems essentially made the law unenforceable. Sam drummed the steering wheel. *A drunk driving stop or something more?*

"What are we going to do?" Duval wanted to know.

Sam took a deep breath, offered up a quick prayer and said, "Buckle up."

"*Mon Dieu.*" Duval fastened his seatbelt and gave it a tug to be sure it was secure.

When the Renault in front eased up, Sam cut the wheel hard and pushed the pedal down. The stolen Citroën swung out and crossed a grassy median toward the west-bound lane. The back tires threw up tuffs of wet sod. Horns bleated. Sam narrowly avoided a fast-moving Mazda as she joined the flow of traffic going the opposite direction.

"You trying to get us killed?" Duval pulled out his inhaler, gave it a shake and took a hit.

Sirens blared. Sam glanced in her rearview in time to see a pair of patrol cars break away from the checkpoint. They tore across the grass and bumped onto the black top, weaving through traffic. Their horns moved slower motorists out of the way.

Sam pushed the pedal down and watched the needle climb to eighty miles an hour. The engine let out a plaintive whine and the van started to rattle. She had to wrestle the wheel to keep them on the road.

Duval craned around for a look out the rear window. "You think you are going to outrun police cars in a stolen minivan?"

"Don't distract me while I'm driving." Sam jogged around the back of a slow-moving truck. She was hunched forward over the wheel with her shoulders drawn up, then remembered her training. "Sit back," she told herself. "Arms extended. Focus your eyes where you want the car to go."

"How long did you say you've been with the CIA?" Duval asked.

"About a year," said Sam. "Remember what I said about not distracting me?"

Duval took another look out the back window. "Well, I don't want to distract you, but they're gaining."

"It's not about who drives the fastest." Sam swung the wheel and the Citroën veered back across the grassy strip. "It's about who makes the first mistake."

Duval clutched the dash with both hands. His chest rose and fell in panicked gasps. "We're going to die."

"Stay positive," Sam said.

"I'm positive we're going to die."

The stolen Citroën crossed the breakdown lane and into oncoming traffic. Drivers mashed their horns and swerved. Tires shrieked on the blacktop. Duval screamed and threw one arm over his eyes. Sam had to jerk the wheel to avoid a head-on collision. The back end of the Citroën slipped on the wet macadam and the van started a slow, sideways drift. Her heart crawled up into her throat and her hands locked on the wheel. Her foot came off the gas and she was just about to slam on the brakes.

Remember your training! a voice screamed inside her head.

She resisted the urge to hit the brakes, tapped the gas instead, and steered into the slide. The tires caught traction and Sam managed to pull the vehicle out of the deadly drift in time to avoid a wreck. A panel van knocked off the passenger side mirror with a sharp *crack*. Duval shouted and crowded toward the center console. Sam took one hand off the wheel long enough to push him back into his seat.

"Stay!" she ordered. If they got hit, she wanted the airbag to catch him.

From behind, she heard the tell-tale crunch of metal and glass and one of the sirens fell silent.

Duval twisted around in his seat. "They crashed!"

"Both?"

"Just one."

A nervous grin tugged at Sam's lips, but she didn't let herself celebrate yet. One more to go. She spotted an exit ramp and said, "Hold on!"

She had to time it just right. She waited until she was even with the exit, let off the gas, pulled the emergency brake and spun the wheel. The Citroën went into a controlled slide. Rubber howled on the blacktop. Duval let out a long, high-pitched wail. The minivan humped up onto two wheels and the breath froze in Sam's lungs. For one terrifying moment, she thought she had over-steered. Then the vehicle crashed back down on all four. Sam released the parking brake and pressed the gas. The Citroën surged forward.

The remaining police cruiser tried the same stunt with different results. A pickup slammed into the passenger side as the officer tried to make the turn. There was a shriek of tires and a split second of silence before a rending crash. The siren cut out.

Sam glanced in her rearview and winced. "Hope he's alright."

They shot down the exit ramp toward a small French

village. Sam took corners at random and doubled back to make sure they weren't being followed. Duval slumped down in his seat like a limp doll and brought out his inhaler for another toke. He took a shot, shook it, and tried again before tossing the empty inhaler in the floorboard.

"Take it easy on those things," Sam told him. "How many more do you have?"

"Just one," Duval told her.

She gave him a worried glance.

He said, "I'll be alright."

CHAPTER TWENTY-SIX

Burke considered slipping down the hall to his office where he could sneak in a short nap. They were no closer to finding Sam than when they first got word Frank Bonner was dead. Burke checked his watch. Outside, the sun would be sinking toward the horizon. Being cooped up in a situation room all day under the artificial glow of fluorescents had screwed up his circadian rhythm. A yawn tried to split his jaw in half. He gave his head a shake to clear out the cobwebs. His feet were aching, but he didn't dare sit down for fear he would nod off in the situation room.

The cadre of analysts and surveillance experts crowding the computers weren't in much better shape. They were all younger, but hours watching traffic patterns took a toll. Burke would have to start rotating them, four hours on, sixty minutes off. And if this went on much longer, he would need to bring in fresh faces. That meant more people who knew what was going on and more opportunity for sensitive intel to leak. Burke reached for a cup of cold coffee.

Dana put her hand over the mug. "You need rest," she said. "We might be at this for hours yet. Stretch out. I'll let you know if anything pops."

"You're probably right."

"I'm always right," she whispered.

Before he could slip out, Ben Jameson turned on his swivel chair and gave Burke a barely perceptible nod.

Burke bent low over his shoulder, tried to hold his breath, and whispered, "What have you got?"

"Take a look."

Burke watched a grainy black and white image of a masked assassin with a Heckler & Koch MP5 marching a terrified man along an ocean boulevard toward an unmarked van.

"Who is that?" Burke wanted to know.

"Not sure," said Jameson. "But it gets better."

Burke was so focused on the video feed that he forgot to hold his breath. The smell of Jameson's cologne overwhelmed his senses and started a throbbing headache at the back of his skull.

On screen, the man elbowed his attacker and made a run for it. The assassin gave chase and they disappeared out of the frame.

"Is there another angle?" Burke asked.

Jameson held up a finger. "Wait for it."

Burke watched. It was a quiet seaside boulevard in the middle of the night. Only the patter of rain drops in puddles told him the video had not frozen. He said, "What are we waiting..."

A silver Audi roared onto the screen and slammed on the brakes. Rain made halos around the headlamps. The tires locked and the doors cranked open. Four men leapt out.

Burke said, "Is that...?"

"Bonner," Jameson said, "Along with Grey, Preston, and LeBeau."

"Why would Bonner take an entire covert action team to investigate a low-level smuggler?" Dana said. "And who was the other guy?"

"Don't miss this part," Jameson told them.

The assassin came back into view, just barely visible in the lower right corner of the frame. The mask was gone now but only the top of the head was visible. It was clear Bonner and the assassin were talking. Bonner took a few steps forward. He looked like he was yelling. Then he brought his gun up and backpedaled to the open car door for cover. Windows blew out of the vehicle. Grey and his team returned fire. Burke watched silent muzzle flashes. Frank Bonner got caught out in the open. His head snapped back and he dropped to the ground.

Dana cursed under her breath. "They had a shootout in the middle of the street."

"And it looked like everybody started shooting at the same time," Burke said.

Jameson asked, "You think that was Gunn they were trading bullets with?"

"The figure is right," Burke said.

Dana gave him a significant look.

He shrugged.

While they watched, Grey and his crew chased the shooter off-camera. They were gone maybe ten minutes and then came back. They rifled Frank Bonner's pockets, loaded into the car and took off.

Burke said, "Get still images over to the boys in IMINT. Have them compare it to photos of Sam and see if they can get a positive match. Any idea who was with her?"

Jameson shook his head. "I tried running his face, but they're at a bad angle. No close matches. One probable popped in the system, but it's impossible."

Burke questioned him with a look.

Jameson switched screens. "The software returned a forty-two point two percent match for Sacha Duval, but he's holed up in the Ecuadorian embassy in London."

Dana grabbed Burke's forearm. "The smuggler was bringing something over from England. How do we know it wasn't a person?"

"You think that's Sacha Duval?" Jameson asked.

"I don't know what to think," Burke said. "I know Grey lied about how Bonner got killed and we have only his word that Sam Gunn pulled the trigger." Burke turned to Dana. "Go back to my office. Use a secure line. Get on the phone with the Ecuadorian embassy in London. Find out if Duval is still a guest."

She nodded and hurried off.

He turned back to Jameson. "I want you to put a copy of this footage on a thumb drive."

"We aren't allowed to have thumb drives in here," Jameson pointed out.

Burke bared his teeth, revealing the gap between. "Close copy it to my company email. Eyes only."

Someone across the room said, "Sir?"

Burke looked up. "What do you got?"

"A stolen minivan just took French police on a high-speed chase along the A2. Witnesses say there were two occupants. One male. One female."

"Are they still in pursuit?"

The analyst shook her head. "This report is about an hour old. The minivan got away. Believed to be somewhere in the vicinity of Vesoul."

"Where in the hell is that?" Burke wanted to know.

"South east France," she said.

Someone else added, "It's near Lyon."

Burke put his hands on his hips and considered his next move. The report wasn't a positive ID. It might have been a couple of drug traffickers, but Burke didn't believe in coincidences. Grey and his team would get hold of the report soon, if they hadn't already. There was no way Burke could bury this and let Sam slip through. He said, "Reroute one of the drones. Give them the description of the minivan."

"Just one?"

"We don't know for sure it's them," Burke said. "Let's not put all our eggs in one basket."

CHAPTER TWENTY-SEVEN

NOBLE WOKE UP WITH HIS FACE SUBMERGED IN freezing water. Callous hands gripped his hair and held him under. His own hands were cuffed behind his back. Concrete bit into his knees. He tried to lever himself up, but his captors forced him back down into the icy depths and gave him a rough shake. His lips parted in a muffled scream. Bubbles boiled out of his mouth and raced to the surface. The cold attacked his eyes and rushed down his throat. His lungs screamed for oxygen. The contents of his stomach tried to escape. His body convulsed.

The next thing he knew they were hauling him up. Cold water exploded from his mouth and nose. His eyes burned from the freezing temperatures. Tears welled up, doubling his vision. He gasped for air, retched, and hacked out a series of coughs intermingled with curses.

Before he could get air back into his lungs, he was plunged forward again. Noble fought with all his strength, but two sets of hands forced him down and freezing water enveloped him. He clamped his lips shut, closed his eyes and tried to wait them out, but it was no use. Seconds ticked by and his chest cried out for air. The muscles in his back and legs tensed and he started to thrash. One of his captors gave him a knee to the ribs and Noble choked out a scream. His heart tried to hammer its way out of his chest. He strained at the cuffs. The metal cut into his wrists and he could hear his own garbled screams through the water. His lungs felt like they would burst.

Just as his mind started drifting toward oblivion and his struggles tapered off, they pulled him back up. This time they let him catch his breath. He coughed, sucked air, and blinked a few times.

They were dunking him in an old metal wash basin covered in rust. The building was an abandoned warehouse. Forgotten machinery stood like shadowy hulks in the darkness and a thick layer of dust covered the cracked concrete foundation. Grime-encrusted windows let in just enough light to see. Beyond the windows was a deserted industrial district, miles from the nearest inhabitants. His messenger bag, along with all his gear, laid in the corner near the door.

The accident victim with the neck brace and the unibrow stared down at him. He took a bottle of prescription strength pain relievers from his coat pocket, shook a pair into his palm and dry swallowed. Noble wracked his brain and came up with a name.

"Mateen," he choked out.

The French gangster didn't react but the pair of thugs holding Noble gave him another dunking. They didn't keep him under as long this time but he still came up coughing.

"What do you want?" Noble managed to say.

"*Moi?*" Mateen motioned to himself. "Nothing, *Monsieur*. I'm a business man providing a service. Nothing more."

"You must want something," Noble said. "Or I'd be dead already."

A half smile turned up Mateen's face. It looked like a painful grimace. "You have your employers," he said. "I have mine."

At a motion from Mateen, the two goons submerged Noble again. They held him down until his struggles ceased and then pulled him up and brought him around with a few slaps across the face. This went on for what felt like hours but was in reality probably only thirty minutes. Noble was starting to believe they would kill him by accident when he heard a car pull up outside.

David Grey entered through a side door, dressed in slacks, and a heavy overcoat. His dark hair was cut short and swept back from a high forehead. He had a business-like demeanor; cold, detached, professional. He wasn't here to waste time. He reached in his coat, handed Mateen an envelope stuffed with cash and Mateen passed over Noble's wallet.

"ID says he's John Comstock from Milwaukie," Mateen said.

Grey tossed the wallet aside, knowing everything in it was fake. "I'll take it from here."

Mateen pocketed the envelope and exited through the side door, leaving Noble with Grey and the two bruisers. A moment later they heard the sound of an engine and then tires on broken asphalt. Grey stuffed his hands in his coat pockets and sniffed. "So who are you really?"

"Benny Goodman," Noble told him.

One side of Grey's face hitched up in a smile. "We got a comedian."

One of the goons reached in his pocket and pulled out a switchblade. The knife opened with a sharp snap and steel flashed in the dim light. He said, "Comedians get their balls cut off."

"How original," Noble said.

The goon waved the knife under Noble's nose, but Grey held up a hand. He said, "You put one of their guys in the morgue and another in the hospital. They're looking for payback. Can't say I blame them. Here's how it's going down: You aren't leaving this basement alive, but if you tell me what I want to know, I'll convince them to kill you quick. If you dummy up then we start cutting off pieces until you talk. Make this easy on yourself. I already know you work for Armstrong. So how about you tell me your name?"

The bruiser held up the knife and light winked on the blade.

Noble was in a jam. Fear was a small, hard knot in his belly. He didn't have anything that was worth losing a finger over, but he didn't have anything that would convince them to keep him alive either. He had to bide his time and hope an opportunity presented itself.

He glanced at the knife and said, "My name is Jake Noble."

Grey nodded to himself. "Now we're getting somewhere. What are your orders?"

When he didn't answer right away, Grey examined the

side Noble's head where a dark knot was forming on his temple and said, "That's a nasty bruise you got there."

Grey jackhammered a fist into the knot. The impact threw Noble backwards into the pair of goons. A blinding pain tried to split his skull in two. He closed his eyes and breathed until the throbbing passed. His vision swam and sweat broke out on his forehead despite the cold.

Grey glanced at his knuckles and then wiped his hand on his coat. "Let's not play games, Noble. I know the Director sent you. How much does she know?"

Noble saw an opening and said, "I don't know how much she knows or what she suspects. I was hired to come over here and sort things out. Gunn is bent. I'm supposed to kill her. Does that answer your question?"

Grey's eyes narrowed. "And what did she tell you about me?"

"You're not my problem," Noble told him. "Far as the Company is concerned, Sam Gunn murdered Frank Bonner and she has to die. Now why don't you call off the dogs and we can all work together?"

Grey stuffed his hands in his coat pockets and stared down at Noble with a thoughtful frown on his face, like he was trying to decide what to do with a particularly naughty puppy. Before he reached a conclusion, his phone rang. He dug it out and said, "What have you got?" There was a pause. "When was this? ...Good work. Stay on it. I'm on my way."

"Seems your services won't be needed after all," Grey said after he had hung up. "My guys found her."

Grey went to the door, stopped and turned back. "Get rid of him."

CHAPTER TWENTY-EIGHT

Noble's stomach twisted in knots. As a Green Beret, he had operated deep behind enemy lines where death was an ever-present threat. Going to work for the CIA hadn't changed anything. He was still behind enemy lines, he had simply traded jungles and deserts for city streets. Death was still one wrong move away and nothing can prepare you for that. He had thought about it; every SF operator did. This was the life he had chosen and risk came with the territory. He knew one day his time would come, but thinking it and being ready for it were two different things.

The bruiser with the switchblade wrenched Noble's head back and put the knife to his throat. With his hands cuffed behind his back, there wasn't anything Noble could do, except maybe try to shoulder the goon, and that would only delay the inevitable. His heart shifted into overdrive and his stomach seemed to shrink in on itself. Air burst from his lips in panicked gasps.

Before the bruiser could slice open Noble's exposed throat, his partner said "Hold it! Not here. Take him downstairs first."

The killer stopped, one hand still clutching Noble's hair in a painful grip. "Why not kill him now?"

"Because I don't want to spend all night mopping up his blood," the other goon said. "Besides, you want to lug his dead body down the steps?"

Noble said, "He makes a good point."

"Shut up," the bruiser snarled.

Noble had started to think of these two as Frick and Frack.

Frick said, "On your feet."

"I'll go start the car," Frack said. "Weight the body before you dump him."

Frack walked outside while Frick pulled Noble to his feet. He waved the blade in front of Noble's face. The edge came dangerously close to his chin. "Try anything and I'll carve my name in your forehead."

Frick frog-marched Noble across the warehouse, their feet leaving tracks in a thick layer of dust, to a steep flight of steps in the back corner that led down to the basement. Frick stopped at the top and said, "Slowly. Don't get any ideas."

Noble looked at the risers and said, "With my hands behind my back?"

Frick took hold of his collar with his free hand and said, "Go on."

Noble started down the steps. He went slow, taking his time. He could hear a curious rushing sound, like running water from the shadowy basement. Frick was behind him on the stairs, one hand gripping Noble's collar, and he said, "Come on. Quit stalling."

Half way down, Noble made his move. He reached back with his cuffed hands, grabbed a fistful of Frick's puffy North Face jacket, and then twisted. It was a desperate gambit, and just as likely to end in a broken neck for Noble, but it might be his only chance to turn the tables.

Frick gave a yelp, stumbled into Noble and they both went down. Noble's heart seized inside his chest. The basement tipped on its head as he tumbled. Time slowed. A concrete riser bit into his shoulder and one knee spanged off the railing. He curled up in a ball in an effort to protect himself from the worst of the damage, but with his hands behind his back there was no way to protect his head. He could only hold his breath and wait for the world to right itself.

Frick was caught completely off guard. His hip bone crashed into the sharp edge of a riser and there was a sickening *pop,* then his head bounced hard against the ground.

Both men sprawled out on the floor at the base of the ladder. Frick's hips and legs were still on the bottom steps, like a drunk who had lost his balance and splayed out in a stupor. He arched his wounded spine, let out a strained croak that might have been a call for help, and clutched at his back.

Noble was curled into a fetal position, his feet on Frick's stomach and his hands still clutching the man's jacket. He let out a slow breath, surprised his neck was still in one piece. It felt like someone had done a tap dance on his shoulder, his knee wasn't any better, and his left thumb had twisted the wrong way in the fall. It wasn't broken, at least

Noble didn't *think* it was broken, but the digit felt two sizes too big. All in all, pretty lucky.

Frick twisted onto his side and searched around for the fallen knife. His face was a swollen purple beet with veins throbbing in his forehead. Blood dripped from a nasty cut on the back of his skull and his hands jerked like fish flopping around on a dock.

Noble rolled onto his knees, jackknifed himself to his feet and aimed a kick at Frick's face. His toe caught Frick on the chin and snapped his head back. A tooth flew from busted lips along with a gob of dark blood. Frick abandoned his search for the knife and tried to wrap both arms around Noble's legs.

Noble shuffled backwards and sent another kick at Frick's face. This time Frick's nose broke with a wet snap. Bright red drops sprayed over the concrete floor and Frick curled up, trying to protect himself.

Noble stomped the goon's head until he stopped moving. When Frick lay in a spreading puddle of blood, Noble staggered back to the stairs and collapsed on the bottom step. He gasped for breath. Sweat beaded on his forehead and his heart rate slowly returned to normal. Adrenaline was pumping through his limbs, dulling the pain, but his body promised him hell tomorrow.

He took a moment to get his bearings.

The floor of the dimly lit basement had a channel of brackish water running right down the middle. Two narrow footbridges passed over the foaming current. Noble suddenly understood the rushing sound he had heard. It was an underground river that entered through a barred aqueduct on one side of the basement and exited the other, only the bars had been cut away from the exit. This was a part of Paris's extensive sewage network; the same labyrinth network Victor Hugo had described as "fetid, wild and fierce." There was no telling where a body might turn up after being tossed in. One thing was sure, by the time the authorities found the bloated corpse, any forensic evidence would be long gone.

Noble thought about what he would look like after a few days in the silent depths and shivered. He twisted around for a look at the handcuffs. They were law enforcement grade with a single hinge, which would make getting his wrists down over his feet torture. Time was short. Frick was out of commission but Frack would get curious that his partner was taking so long. Noble bent over at the waist, worked the cuffs down the backs of his legs and, grunting with effort, passed one foot, then the other between his wrists. With that done, he quickly kicked off his shoe and dug under the insole for the handcuff key.

Once he was free of the cuffs, Noble grabbed Frick under the arms and lugged him across the floor to the aqueduct. Limp bodies weigh a ton and Frick was a big boy to begin with. Noble was blowing hard by the time he reached the open sewer. The stink of offal rolled off the muck in nauseous waves. Noble had to fight back a gag reflex that tried to empty his stomach. He rolled Frick over the side and the body hit the water with a heavy plop. The current was stronger than it looked; the body bobbed to the surface, passed quickly under a narrow stone footbridge and then disappeared through the open grate.

CHAPTER TWENTY-NINE

Two hours later, Jaqueline Armstrong was still at her desk and still hadn't heard from Noble, but she had gotten several stinging text messages from her daughter.

Duc was busy sweating the pilots at a safe house in Fort Washington. So far neither man would admit to anything. Both claimed they had flown straight to Charles de Gaulle and back. But the interrogation was just getting started. Right now, Duc would have each man in a separate room, asking polite questions, much like an after-action report. As the night wore on, the pilots would get hungry, thirsty, and tired. Then Duc would start turning the screws. They would find themselves locked inside their rooms for hours without access to toilets. They would not be allowed to call wives or girlfriends, and they had no idea when they'd be released. The mental stress of the situation was usually enough to loosen up even experienced field officers and if it didn't, there were other ways to make a man talk.

Meanwhile, Armstrong was meeting with Coughlin and

Burke. She directed them to a pair of seats in front of her desk. The two officers couldn't have been more different. Burke was powerfully built and black with gray around his temples and a gap between his teeth. His suit coat strained against his shoulders. Coughlin was tall and angular with frown lines in a pale face and carefully polished shoes. He could have passed for a Wall Street banker or a high-priced attorney. But looks weren't the only thing that set them apart. Burke had come up through Special Forces in the United States Army and earned his stripes in the field. Coughlin's only knowledge of field operations came from intel gathered after the fact.

"What's the latest?" Armstrong asked.

Coughlin said, "We've got a possible on a stolen van that led French police on a high-speed chase. Right now believed to be in the vicinity of Vesoul. I want to reroute all aerial reconnaissance. Burke doesn't seem to think that's necessary."

"I sent one of our drones to check it out," Burke said. "It's not likely enough to warrant moving all of our eyes in the sky."

"Visual ID on Gunn?" Armstrong asked.

Burke shook his head.

Coughlin said, "Come on, Burke. It's her and you know it."

"I'm trying to cover all of France with three drones," Burke said. "It's like looking for a needle in a haystack when the needle keeps moving. I'd like to know what's going on with Grey and his team. Are they any closer to figuring out why Frank Bonner was shot?"

"We've been over this," Coughlin said.

Burke said, "I keep asking myself what makes a good agent suddenly kill another officer and then go on the run. I think it's time we bring Grey in and sit him down for some questions."

"Sure, and give Gunn more time to disappear," Coughlin said.

"Anything is better than chasing our tails," said Burke. "We need to figure out what happed in Honfleur."

"We'll know what happened as soon as we locate Samantha Gunn."

"Assuming they bring her in alive. Grey and Bonner were close. I don't like the fact that he's heading the ground team," Burke said. "Suppose Sam gets killed before she can answer any questions. That would be very convenient."

"What the hell are you driving at, Burke? You think Grey is bent? Is that it?"

"I think the whole situation smells bad."

"Grey's been working for the Company twenty years," Coughlin said.

"Eighteen," Burke corrected.

"Close enough," said Coughlin. "Samantha Gunn has been playing the game less than a year and she's already got a black mark. We're going to take her word over Grey's?"

Burke shook his head. "I didn't say that. I'm trying to get a more complete picture. That's all."

Coughlin looked to Armstrong. "Gunn killed one of my people in Paris. She's on the run. She's needs to be caught and Grey's team is the closest. I told him to bring her in alive. He'll do everything in his power to make that happen."

Jaqueline leaned forward, propped her elbows on the

desk and formed a steeple with her fingers. "One way or another, we are going to get to the bottom of this. Coughlin, alert Grey that we have a possible in Vesoul."

"Already done," Coughlin said.

Armstrong nodded. "We'll leave one drone on the Vesoul for now. I don't want to reroute all of our air coverage for something that might turn out to be a false flag."

Coughlin started to protest.

Jaqueline held up a hand. "I'll see about routing another drone from southern Europe, but the skies over France are getting crowded. We can't keep up this level of surveillance long without the French noticing. I need results, soon. Do I make myself clear?"

"Perfectly," Burke said.

"Crystal," Coughlin said.

With that settled, Jaqueline decided to shake the tree and see what fell out. She said, "Are either of you familiar with the name Mateen Slevic?"

They booth shook their heads.

"He's a French national," Jaqueline told them. "He's got ties to various organized crime groups around Europe and the Middle East."

Burke said, "Is he a part of this *Le Milieu* outfit Grey was collecting intel on?"

"That's what I'm trying to find out." She turned her attention on Coughlin. "Did Grey happen to mention the name in any of his reports?"

Coughlin's eye twitched rapid-fire. He worked a smile onto his face. "Can't say that he did."

Jaqueline nodded, took a breath, let it out slowly. "I'll

keep digging on my end. You two work on tracking down Sam Gunn. Burke, I want Coughlin to know as soon as we have anything concrete. Coughlin, I want Samantha Gunn alive. Understood?"

Both men nodded and Armstrong dismissed them. When they had gone, Armstrong picked up the phone and dialed.

CHAPTER THIRTY

Noble went back to the stairs and found the knife lying at the bottom of the steps. It was a spring-assisted Benchmade with a tanto blade and better than nothing at all, but there was a saying about bringing a knife to a gun fight. In short, it wasn't the best idea. Noble gripped the weapon in a tight fist as he climbed the stairs, straining to hear any sounds of movement from overhead.

He reached the top of the steps and found the warehouse empty. Duc's messenger bag sat against the wall in the corner. Everything was there except Noble's gun and the cell phone. A quick look outside showed him Frack sitting behind the wheel of a four-door Nissan, bopping his head to music. As he watched, Frack glanced at his watch and frowned.

Noble hurried across the dusty floor, wincing at the sound his feet made on the gritty concrete. He had to move fast if he was going to catch the thug off guard. If Frack got curious and decided to investigate, he would have his gun out and be ready for trouble. That would make Noble's job twice as hard. Speed and surprise were his best weapons.

He slung the messenger bag, reversed the knife in his grip and paused. *Don't let the enemy force you to move faster than you can think.* He slipped out the side door, moving in back of the sedan. Frack had the windows up and generic Europop blasting from the speakers. The engine was idling and exhaust plumed from the tailpipe. The sky was spitting snow that melted before it could pile up.

With the knife in his left hand, Noble stepped around the corner and walked briskly toward the driver's side door. Frack saw movement in the mirror and bent forward for a better look. Noble reached for the handle as Frack fumbled for the lock. Noble was faster. He yanked open the door and jammed the butt of the knife into Frack's neck, just below the ear. It forced Frack's head to the side and stopped him from getting a look at the weapon.

"One wrong move and I pull the trigger," Noble told him.

Frack's whole body tensed. His hands hoovered over the steering wheel, fingers splayed out. His face pinched. "Okay, American, you win."

"Out of the car," Noble ordered. He gripped Frack's elbow with his free hand to stop him making any sudden moves. "Nice and easy."

Frack performed an ungainly sideways slither out of the driver's seat. Noble kept the knife hilt pressed hard into his neck. Frack put his hands out to the side, to show he was no theat.

"What happened to René?"

"He's taking a swim," Noble told him. With his free

hand, Noble frisked for a weapon and felt steel in the small of Frack's back. He reached under the man's coat and retrieved his missing Kimber Ultra Carry.

"Got any more?" Noble asked. He pocketed the knife and put the gun to the back of Frack's head.

"No."

"Don't lie to me," Noble said.

Frack hesitated.

Noble said, "Toss it in the passenger seat. Real slow."

Frack reached under his coat with his left hand, took out a Saturday night special and lobbed it into the car. Noble heard it bounce off the seat and onto the floor.

"Phone next," Noble ordered.

Frack dug in his pocket, took out a cell, and it joined the gun.

"Now your clothes," Noble said.

Frack started to protest.

Noble thumbed back the hammer and said, "Go on! I haven't got all night."

Frack shrugged out of his coat, threw it in the car, kicked off his shoes and then unbuttoned his shirt. Noble pinched Frack's ear with his free hand while he stripped down to tighty-whities.

"The drawers too," Noble said.

"Come on," Frack begged. "It's freezing."

Noble twisted his ear lobe.

Frack winced. "Alright."

He shed the underwear and tossed them in the passenger seat. Gooseflesh marched across his bare skin in ranks and he shivered from the cold. "What now, cowboy?"

"Start running," Noble told him. "If I see you again, I'll kill you."

Frack took off, naked as the day he was born, without looking back. His bare feet slapped against the slippery asphalt and silver clouds streamed from his open mouth. He reached the corner of one of the abandoned warehouses and disappeared from view.

Noble glanced around. He could see lights in the distance. It must be a mile or more to the nearest filling station. Frack probably wouldn't freeze to death if he kept running. Noble climbed into the driver's seat and put the car in gear.

He had been in Paris less than twenty-four hours and he had already been in a fistfight, a car crash, knocked unconscious, interrogated, fallen down a flight of stairs and then stomped a man to death. His suspicions of Grey had proven correct. The freelancer was working hand-in-hand with *Le Milieu* and whatever they were up to, they were willing to kill to keep it secret.

Noble swung the car around and put his foot down. He didn't even know where he was going. He picked up Frack's cellphone and wracked his brain for Armstrong's number. He should have memorized it on the flight over, but he had been too busy going over the contents of the file. Instead he dialed the switchboard at Langley and asked for the Director. Which did about as much good as dialing the White House and asking for the president.

CHAPTER THIRTY-ONE

Sam was on a park bench, huddled in her fleece, shivering against the cold. Duval sat next to her. His breath steamed up from his mouth and broke apart in the frigid air. Light snow swirled down from a silent black sky. Street lamps lit the falling flakes, turning them bright gold which melted as soon as it touched the ground. The park was a sprawling patch of green in a little village called Vesoul. University students thronged the sidewalks, bundled in oversized parkas and mittens. Most of them made their way to a Tuscan pizzeria for a slice before heading down the boulevard to one of the pubs lining the street.

Hard to believe, thought Sam. She had been a carefree college student not so long ago herself. Now she was on the run from the CIA with an international fugitive in a little French town that barely showed up on a map. Freezing on a park bench no less. She had planned this whole thing perfectly, or so she thought.

A hard tremor gripped Duval. His lips had turned an

unhealthy shade of blue. "Well," he said through chattering teeth, "we can't sit here all night."

"Why ever not?" Sam said. "Pretty view. Be a nice place to visit." After a beat she added, "In summer."

They had ditched the minivan on the other side of the wooded park, under a bald oak tree. With a little luck, the drones wouldn't spot it under the branches. But it wouldn't be long before police found the vehicle.

"Yes, well, it's winter," Duval said. "And I'm freezing."

"Me too."

"Two people on a bench in the snow are going to attract attention," Duval added. He was trying to wear down her resistance. It was working.

Sam nodded, it was a jerky movement. "I could go for a slice."

"I thought you'd never ask."

"Be sure to speak French," Sam told him. She dug into her coat and came out with a fold of Euros. "Pay cash."

"You're not coming with me?"

She shook her head.

"I'm not going alone," he said.

Sam exhaled. "Duval, the game has changed. Don't you understand? That roadblock was for us. I thought we could make it across the border, but the CIA must have put my picture out to French authorities. My face will be on every news station. I go in there and a dozen people are going to be on the phone to the police."

He sat there on the bench, clutching the money, staring longingly at the brightly lit pizza parlor. The night was winding down. It was nearly one in the morning; the shops would be closing soon and the students would wander back to their dorms for a few hours' sleep.

"Like it or not," Sam said, "You're our best bet. No one is looking for Sacha Duval, yet."

"I've got a pretty recognizable face," he said.

"Keep your hat down and your collar up," Sam told him. "And stay in sight of the windows."

His eyes went to the words *Tuscan Style Pizza* in gold script and a pained expression crossed his face. He wanted the food, but he was too scared to go alone. Sam could see the struggle taking place just below the surface.

She said, "They'll be closing soon, Sacha. It's now or never."

That sealed it.

Duval stuffed the money in his pocket and limped across the boulevard. Sam watched him go. *Please God,* she thought, *don't let anyone recognize him.*

He hauled open the door, stepped inside and stamped his feet to shake off the cold. A pretty, young French girl in dreadlocks offered a bright smile. Sam watched the exchange. Duval kept his chin tucked while he ordered, handed over a few bills and then disappeared into the back.

"Where are you going?" Sam said aloud. She sat up on the bench, oblivious to the cold. Her pulse started a slow Latin beat inside her chest, ready to do the rumba at the first hint of danger. Her eyes were wide and she stood up for a better look. Duval was nowhere in sight. Sam wanted to curse, but started praying instead.

CHAPTER THIRTY-TWO

THE SMELL OF FRESHLY BAKED DOUGH AND SIMMERING tomato sauce washed over Duval as he stepped inside. He shook off the cold. A threadbare mat showed the name of the restaurant, mostly obliterated by the foot traffic of countless college students. Square tables marched in ranks toward the restrooms. Friendly chatter made white noise that drowned out an Italian opera piping through speakers in the ceiling. A long counter took up one wall and heat from coal-fired ovens steamed up the windows.

A teenager with dreads and hazel eyes smiled at him from behind the counter. She greeted him in French, asked if he wanted a slice or a whole pie. Duval ordered a large with mushrooms, onions, green peppers, and white cheese. She scribbled his order on a pad and passed the paper into the kitchen. Duval counted out the money and, as he handed it over the counter, noticed a television in the corner with a black and white headshot of Samantha Gunn on the screen. The ticker at the bottom warned people she was armed and extremely dangerous—wanted in connection with recent terrorist activities. A lead weight dropped into Duval's belly. His bladder threatened to let go. The teenager was telling him the pie would be ready in a few minutes. Duval tried to thank her, but his tongue stuck to the roof of his mouth. The syllables came out jumbled. She gave him a curious look. He tried again and said, "I need the toilet."

She pointed him to the back of the pizza parlor.

Duval limped past the line of tables with his head down. His butt cheek smarted with every step. He pushed through the door into a cramped bathroom with a single stall and a window set high in the wall. Duval bent down, didn't see any feet and let himself into the toilet.

The words *armed and extremely dangerous* went through his head on repeat. *Terror suspect.* The CIA had really put the fix in. With the recent string of terrorist attacks scattered around Europe, people were living in a constant state of paranoia. Any time they left for work or went down the block for a drink with friends, in the back of their minds they were wondering if tonight was the night. If a nail bomb would explode and kill them while they were watching Paris Saint-Germain take on Lyon. But that's what the terrorists wanted, wasn't it? They wanted anyone who opposed them to be afraid. Rule by fear.

Duval emptied his bladder, zipped up and flushed. He stopped at the sink to wash his hands and the window caught his eye. He had put on a few pounds living in the embassy. Long hours with nothing to do and nowhere to go had taken a toll on his health. Not that he was in particularly good shape to begin with. He certainly wasn't going to be competing in any triathlons, but he might be able to fit through the window.

Sam wouldn't get far with her face plastered all over the news. Maybe he was better off on his own? He was less than a hundred miles from the border of Switzerland. From there to Montenegro would take a day. Two days if he was extra careful.

He turned on the hot water and waited for it to get warm, then splashed his face and inspected himself in the mirror. He had dark circles under his eyes and his skin was waxy pale. Living in constant fear had taken its toll. But that's what governments wanted, wasn't it? Anyone who exposed their corruption was forced to spend their life in hiding, looking over their shoulder. Rule by fear. Not so different from the terrorists.

He glanced again at the window. Sam had risked everything for him. She had given up her career with the CIA and become a fugitive. Abandoning her on a park bench in Vesoul was low, but Duval had done worse as an investigative reporter. He had scraped the very bottom of the barrel to get the story and put lives at risk when he exposed the truth. Still, he liked Sam. She was a decent person. Where would she go? What would she do?

Fear and simple self-preservation stamped out that line of reasoning. This was about survival. He needed to disappear, and Sam's face was on every channel.

"Screw it."

A sign on the wall declared *No Smoking* and asked patrons not to leave the window open. *Thank you. Management.* Duval worked the latch on the window. It had been painted over numerous times and the metal squealed in protest. Ignoring the sign, he slid the window up as far as it would go. Outside was a trash-strewn alley bathed in shadow.

He gripped the frame in both hands and heaved himself up. A grunt worked its way up his throat and his face turned beet red. Life in the embassy had taken more of a toll than he thought. His feet scrambled at the tile wall, leaving skid marks, but he managed to get his head and shoulders through.

He hung there a moment, wedged in the frame. Frigid air struck his face and the awful reek of spoiled meat brought tears to his eyes. He gasped for breath, sucked in his gut, and wriggled his body in an effort to get his hips through.

A shadow detached itself from the darkness in back of the pizza parlor. Duval saw the movement from the corner of his eye. His mouth opened to scream. His heart tried to jump out the window and take off down the alley as his body tried to scramble back inside. A hand caught his ear and twisted. His scream turned to a yelp.

Sam's face appeared in the light spilling from the open window. Her jaw was set and her mouth was a strict line. "I told you to stay in sight of the windows."

Duval's chin trembled as he spoke. "You were right. Your face is all over the news. They're looking everywhere for you."

"So you decided to ditch me?"

Duval groped for words. Hot tears of shame welled up in his eyes. "I didn't know what else to do. I panicked."

She gave his ear another twist. "Climbing out the window seemed like a good idea?"

"We have to run," he said.

"You already ordered a pizza," she said, still holding onto his ear. "If you disappear, they'll remember you."

"But—"

Sam yanked on his ear. It felt like she would rip it right off his head.

"Go back inside, get the pizza, and meet me around the corner," Sam ordered.

She let go of his ear, palmed his face, and shoved. Duval went backwards, hit the tile floor and barked in pain. His butt felt like there was a white-hot lump of coal in the right cheek. He groaned, rubbed at the wound, and used the sink to haul himself off the floor.

Sam stuck her face in the open window. "If you don't come out with a pizza in five minutes, I'm coming in shooting."

She shut the window with a rattling bang.

She's right, Duval told himself. When he didn't come out of the bathroom, the cashier would get suspicious. She'd send one of the cooks to see what had happened. He would find an empty bathroom and then they would start to talk. Duval fixed himself in the mirror, took a deep breath, and told himself to act casual. Just another guy picking up a pizza after a night of drinking.

CHAPTER THIRTY-THREE

CLAUDE COMTOIS WORKED THE NIGHTSHIFT AT HOTEL LeBlonde. He slouched in a swivel chair, a cigarette dangling between his lips and his feet stacked on the desk, watching highlights from yesterday's match. Because he slept during the day, he had missed the game, but working the overnight was better than not working at all and with France's unemployment hovering close to ten percent, Claude was thankful to have a job that paid the bills. It had been difficult at first to reset his sleep schedule. He spent the first few weeks walking around in a daze, but he had finally rewired his brain and, six months later, he was a bona fide night owl. He took a drag and stabbed the butt of his cigarette out in a plastic ashtray. The small hotel lobby was dingy and smelled of soiled laundry, stale booze, and mold.

Outside, the wind rose to a mournful howl and gusts of snow swirled against the window panes. Claude sighed, rolled his shoulders, looked at the clock. It was just after one in the morning. He had another six hours before he could go home and climb into bed. He poured a glass of red wine from a minifridge under the counter. He wasn't supposed to drink on duty, but what was the point of working the overnight if you don't bend the rules a little? Claude lit another cigarette as Vesoul Haute-Saône scored a goal against Dunkerque.

He clapped his hands together. "*Oui! Magnifique!*"

The front door opened and a gust of cold air blew into the lobby, carrying with it the smell of fresh pizza. An unlikely pair stumbled through the open door, pawing at each other. The man was older, soft around the middle, with early gray in his white-blond hair and he was clutching a pizza box in one hand. The girl was younger and Asian with a butt that made Claude sit up and take notice. They stopped in the doorway for a passionate kiss. Her hands roamed over his paunch, down to his belt. She spoke German with an odd accent that Claude couldn't quite place. German girls are kinky beasts—Claude knew from experience—and this one proved it with her dirty talk. The man looked like he had died and gone to heaven.

They staggered up to the counter, laughing, and asked for a room. She never even glanced in Claude's direction. While the man pushed a wad of cash across the counter, she nibbled his earlobe and described all the things she was going to do to him.

Must be a hooker, Claude decided as he scooped up the money. He wondered how much she cost. Maybe after the old pervert finished, Claude would take a turn. *Not likely*, he told himself. *She probably cost more than I make in a month.*

He handed them a room key and pocketed the cash. They wouldn't be here long, two hours at the most. The old pervert would want to hose off the smell of cheap hooker before going home to his wife. Then Claude would remake the bed and management would never know the difference. What was the point of working the overnight if you didn't bend the rules a little?

"Don't knock holes in the wall," Claude told them as they stumbled up the steps, still groping each other. He returned his attention to the match, but he couldn't get his mind off the girl. She was a knockout. He thought about sneaking up stairs to listen at the door, but abandoned the idea. The old man probably wouldn't last five minutes with prime meat like that on top of him.

On the television, Vesoul Haute-Saône scored another goal and Claude lifted his glass.

CHAPTER THIRTY-FOUR

SAM DROPPED THE ACT AS SOON AS THE DOOR CLOMPED shut. Duval hadn't showered in days and, with all the running and sweating, he smelled like a hog at the trough. She took a step back and turned her face away. The sour reek of his breath was even worse than his armpits. He leaned in, his mouth open for another kiss. His left hand held the pizza box while the right ventured down her spine toward her bottom. He whispered, "Why stop?"

"There's only one thing I want from you," Sam whispered.

He smiled. "What's that?"

She snatched the pizza box and crossed the room to a tattered chair by the window. Duval's face melted. His shoulders sagged like a little boy who'd just had his toys taken away.

The room was a standard affair. There was a bed with stiff sheets, thin carpets covering the floor, a television secured to a nightstand, and wallpaper that had yellowed with age. At the very least it was warm and they had food.

Sam peeled open the box lid and a look of horror crossed her face. "No pepperoni?"

"Americans and your meat." Duval reached for a slice. "You get everything you need from fruits and vegetables."

"That's why you're in such great shape?" Sam took a slice and bit into it without much enthusiasm. Pizza without pepperoni wasn't deserving of the name. Still, it was food and her stomach didn't seem to mind. After the first bite, neither did her taste buds. It was good despite the appalling lack of protein. Ten minutes later, they had devoured the whole pie.

Duval sat on the carpet with his back to the bed and a mostly eaten crust pinched between thumb and forefinger. He inspected the bit of bread, frowned and tossed it into the open box. It landed next to a stale bit of cheese. Duval rested his head against the mattress and closed his eyes. "What's our next move?"

"I'm working on that," Sam admitted.

Duval scrubbed his face with both hands. "It's useless," he moaned. "We'll never make it. America is *too* big. The CIA has *too* many resources. Might as well give ourselves up."

"Don't say that," Sam told him.

"It's true." Duval spread his hands. "Who are we kidding? Trains and planes are out of the question. They'll be watching every highway. Looking for us at every border crossing. We'll never make it out of France."

"They haven't caught us yet," Sam said.

He gave a bitter laugh. "I never should have left the embassy."

"We'll make it," Sam said. She needed time to think, and a break from his constant belly aching. She stood up, went to the bathroom door and stopped in the frame. "I got you this far. I'll get you the rest of the way. I promise."

Duval took a hit from his inhaler and said, "I'm scared, Sam."

"It's okay to be scared," she told him. "Just don't give up on me."

He managed weak smile. "I'm not giving up. Just being realistic."

Sam said, "I'm going to take a shower. Promise me you'll still be here when I get out?"

"Where would I go?"

Sam shut herself in the bathroom, turned on the shower, closed the toilet lid and sat down. Hot tears welled up in her eyes. Her face crumpled. A tight knot formed in her chest. She choked back a sob. Everything had gone belly-up. All of her carefully laid plans had crumbled. Her career with the CIA was over. Half the law enforcement agencies in Europe would be looking for her, and Duval was right: They'd be lucky to make it to the corner. Sam had done her best and it wasn't good enough.

Up until now, everything had been happening so fast that Sam had no time to think. But she had time now. She thought about what would happen when they finally caught her. She wouldn't get a trial. No jury. Just a concrete room where she would be interrogated for days. When they were done, she would be shipped off to a maximum-security prison. Fear gripped her so hard it was a physical force that shook her body. Her hands trembled and a moan worked up from her throat. She slid down off the toilet onto the grimy linoleum, rested her forehead against the cold floor and begged God to send some help. As tears trailed down her cheeks in silent rivulets, Sam prayed, *Please, God. I need help.*

CHAPTER THIRTY-FIVE

Burke dozed fitfully on one of the sofas scattered around the offices of the Operations Directorate. The action arm of the CIA works long hours. Missions in crisis mode can drag on for days and critical personnel are required to be on hand in case something breaks. Burke had located an unoccupied sofa in a quiet room that smelled strongly of lemon-scented cleaner, probably to mask a more offensive odor lingering underneath. Some joker had scrawled out a sign that read *Safe Space* and hung it on the door.

Burke wasn't really asleep. He did very little of that lately. His mind was racing through thousands of potential scenarios, all of them bad. He couldn't see any way to bring Sam out of this thing clean. It would help if he knew what she was mixed up in, but to figure that out he needed to know what Bonner had been working on, and Coughlin seemed to be doing everything in his power to run interference. If Burke didn't know better, he'd think the two were in on it together. Maybe Bonner had been running an operation off the books and Coughlin was involved? It would certainly explain a lot of things. The more Burke thought about it, the more sense it made. Why else was Coughlin so intent on Grey making the capture? That left Burke with more questions than answers. What were Coughlin and Bonner up to? And how did Sam Gunn fit in the picture?

When Burke's mind wasn't working on the Samantha Gunn problem, it was shifting through the last six months of his personal life. His stalled marriage had finally imploded and his office romance had heated up. Madeline had kicked him out and Burke was now living in a cheap efficiency apartment in Foggy Bottom. No one at the office knew he and Maddie were split, but it was only a matter of time, and there was bound to be speculation when they found out. Dana's name would come up. What a mess.

Someone laid a hand on his chest and Burke's eyes shot open. Dana leaned over him. Her button-down blouse gave a generous view of her cleavage. She smiled, checked to be sure the door was closed, then gave him a quick kiss. Her lips were soft and eager. She whispered, "Wake up, black dynamite."

Burke snorted, swung his legs off the sofa, and rubbed his eyes. "Has it been an hour already?"

Dana shook her head. "We caught a break."

Burke was fully awake now. "Sam?"

"Looks like," Dana told him. "A night clerk at a no-tell motel in Vesoul called in a possible."

Burke pushed himself out of the sunken couch. Dana followed him out the door and down the hall toward the situation room. "When did it come in?" Burke asked.

"About two minutes ago."

"Is Coughlin already in on it?"

"You kidding?" Dana said. "He's foaming at the mouth."

"What did you find out from the Ecuadorian embassy?"

"I think Duval left."

"You think?" Burke asked.

She nodded. "I talked to a junior staffer at the embassy who told me Duval was safe and sound in his apartment on the third floor."

Burke stopped and turned to face her. "And you think he was lying?"

"He never hesitated," Dana said. "I asked if Duval was still there and he said yes right away. Didn't even bother to check."

"Good girl." Burke resumed course. "Remind me to give you a raise."

They reached the door to the situation room and Burke scanned his ID badge. The electronic lock chirped and the light turned green. Burke yanked open the frosted glass door. He motioned for Dana. She entered and Burke let the door hiss shut before asking, "What's the latest?"

"We got her," Coughlin said. His sleeves were rolled up to his elbows and his eye winked. "She checked into a hotel in Vesoul, less than a mile from the autoroute exit where the police lost contact."

"Have we got a positive ID?"

"Ninety-two percent."

"I want to see it," Burke said.

Coughlin turned to face him. "It's ninety-two percent, Burke. That's textbook positive. We're moving on this."

Burke turned Jameson. "Bring it up. I want to see it."

The side of Coughlin's face went through a series of spasms.

Jameson turned to his computer and keyed in commands. The screen filled with a dozen different angles from French traffic surveillance cams around the little hamlet of Vesoul. "This is the angle in front of the hotel," he was saying. "See that couple? Watch as they get closer."

The feed was choppy. The camera strung together stills at a frame rate of one per second. The effect was like watching an old black and white from the early days of motion pictures when cowboys raced across the silver screen on jerky steeds and Charlie Chaplin took pratfalls in double time. Only this movie was colorized. Sam and her unidentified counterpart walked up the sidewalk in juddering movements. The man had a pizza box in one hand. They stopped a few meters short of the hotel entrance, had a brief conversation, walked a little more, and then right before they got to the door, started pawing at each other like a couple of teenagers.

Jameson said, "Night clerk got suspicious when there were no sounds coming from the room, then he recognized the girl from news reports and called the cops."

Coughlin stood with his fists on his hips. "Satisfied?"

There was nothing for it. Any denial at this point would only prove Burke was trying to stonewall the manhunt. He inclined his head. "That's her, alright. Back the video up."

Jameson ran the images in reverse. Sam and her friend raced backwards.

"Back, back, back," Burke said. "There! Right there!"

The image froze. Sam was talking to the man holding the pizza box and he had turned his face up.

"Nice clear shot of his face," Burke said. "Dana, who's that looks like?"

"Hard to say, boss." She put a finger to her lips.

"Looks just like Sacha Duval to me." Burke turned to Coughlin. "What would Sacha Duval be doing in France with Samantha Gunn? Any ideas?"

Coughlin looked ready to chew nails. "Cut the crap, Burke. I don't know who that man is. We have a positive on Gunn. I've already rerouted the other two drones. They'll be overhead in minutes. You did your part. Now it's time for my guys to take over."

He pulled out his cell and dialed.

Dana shot Burke a tense look. The meaning was clear; if Grey and his boys caught up to Sam, she and Duval were dead. Burke crossed his arms over his barrel chest and frowned. *What more could he do?* His job was to locate Sam. Coughlin was in charge of the ground team.

While Coughlin relayed commands to the computer jockeys, Burke said, "I'm starving. Dana, run down to the cafeteria and grab me a sandwich."

She took the command in stride. "Sure. What do you want on it?"

"I'd better write it down so you don't forget." He took a scrap of paper from Jameson's desk and a pen. He scribbled,

To DCI

Gunn found

Hotel LeBlonde in Vesoul

Sacha Duval involvement

Grey and company en route

Please advise

"Don't forget the mayo." Burke tore off the page and handed it to Dana.

"You got it." Her eyes ran back and forth over the text and she nodded before letting herself out of the situation room. Burke watched her go and then turned back to find Coughlin eyeballing him. Burke gave a tight smile. Coughlin wasn't stupid. He suspected something but he couldn't prove anything, so he shook his head and turned back to the monitors.

CHAPTER THIRTY-SIX

IT WAS AFTER NINE IN THE EVENING WHEN ARMSTRONG finally logged out of her work terminal. It would be three in the morning in France. She had just hung up with the Director of National Intelligence. Burke's message had turned the situation on its head. Sacha Duval represented a high-value target vital to national security which meant Armstrong could no longer keep this in-house. There was a time when the CIA director would have reported directly to the president. After 9/11, George W. Bush created the Director of National Intelligence position to oversee America's various intelligence agencies in an attempt to force cooperation between the rival services. Like it or not, Armstrong had to bring the DNI into the loop.

He had been at a recital for his granddaughter when he got the call and wasn't happy about being interrupted. Armstrong had spent ten minutes bringing him up to speed. She mistakenly thought he would be interested, or at the very least proactive. Instead he scheduled a 7:00 am meeting and told her not to call him after work hours. So much for burning the midnight oil. Armstrong could only roll her eyes and assure him it wouldn't happen again.

A map of France was open on her desk with a circle around the tiny town of Vesoul. If it was true that Sacha Duval was out of the embassy, he would be headed to a non-extradition country. Staring down at the map, a dozen likely targets jumped out. Duval would have arranged for asylum before taking a chance on leaving the embassy and that meant there would be a trail, so Armstrong had tasked her people with digging through Duval's phone calls and emails over the last six months.

With the meeting set for the morning and Jake incommunicado, Armstrong decided she might as well go home and get some sleep. She stood up, stretched, and gathered her purse. Her desk phone rang while she was balanced on one leg, putting on her heels. She reached for it.

"Armstrong."

A switchboard operator told Jaqueline someone had been asking to speak with the director. "The calls are coming from Paris on an unsecured line. The gentleman refuses to give his name but claims to be your nephew, ma'am. This is the sixth time he's called."

Armstrong grabbed the burner cell from her desk. There were no missed messages. She said, "What's the number?"

As the secretary relayed the digits, Armstrong punched them into the burner.

The switchboard operator asked, "Would you like me to route you through?"

Armstrong had already hung up and pushed send on the burner.

Noble picked up on the first ring. "I've been calling for hours. We haven't got long. I'm on a stolen phone. It'll probably get shut down any minute."

"What happened?"

"I had another run-in with *Le Milieu*," Noble told her. "I won't go into the details over the phone. What did Duc find out from the pilots?"

"Never mind that," Armstrong said. "We've got a location on Sam."

"Where?"

"She's at Hotel LeBlonde in a small town called Vesoul, south of Lyon. You'd better hurry. Grey has the address and he's on his way. Get there as quick as you can, but make sure no one sees you. There are eyes in the sky."

"Roger that," Noble said. Armstrong heard a car engine rev before the line went dead. The kid certainly didn't waste any time. Or words, for that matter. Armstrong wanted to know more about his run-in with *Le Milieu,* but that would have to wait. She pocketed the burner, kicked off her shoes, and dialed Duc for an update on the pilots.

CHAPTER THIRTY-SEVEN

SAM WAS SLUMPED IN THE CHAIR BY THE WINDOW with her feet propped on the corner of the bed. The empty pizza box lay on the floor drawing flies. There was a steady drip-drip-drip from the bathroom faucet and the couple next door had a screaming match in the middle of the night that lasted over an hour. Sam had wanted to knock on their door and tell them to keep it down, but didn't dare risk showing her face.

Duval lay curled up on the bed with his back to her. Every few minutes he would jerk and his hands would go up, fending off invisible attackers. He had gotten up twice to use the toilet. Blonde hair stuck out from his head at crazy angles and made him look like a mad scientist.

Neither of them were getting much in the way of actual sleep. Sam's thoughts would drift to the life she had given up and she would find herself choking back tears. Talking to God was the only way to stop the waterworks. Prayer helped calm her down. When she finally got her emotions under control, she would start thinking about her next move. Odds of making it to Montenegro unmolested had plummeted. Even if they made it, what then? Sam would spend the rest of her life as a fugitive. That would start her on another sobbing fit and the whole vicious cycle would start over.

Duval heaved himself into a sitting position, sighed and said, "I haven't slept a wink."

Sam grunted in agreement.

He plodded into the bathroom and shut the door. The toilet seat went up. Sam heard a broken stream. Could be stress, she thought, or it might be time for a prostate exam. No sense mentioning it though; it would only add to his worries.

A quick peek between the curtains showed the first rays of sunlight painting leaden clouds vibrant shades of red and orange. Sam was about to close the drapes when a police cruiser glided past the window. Fear drove the fog from her brain. She drew air in through clenched teeth and sat up. The radio car reached the end of the block and turned the corner.

A police unit on patrol? thought Sam. *Or are they watching the hotel?* She raked a hand through her hair in an effort to get her brain working.

The toilet flushed and Duval came out of the bathroom. He yawned without bothering to cover his mouth and then saw Sam. Fear seeped into his waxy face. "What is it?"

"I think they found us," Sam told him. "Put your shoes on."

Duval stuffed his feet into his trainers and started on the laces.

Sam chewed her bottom lip and went back to watching the street. She wished bitterly that she had never tipped to Bonner's plans. She could have gone on with her life in blissful ignorance. It was a horrible, selfish thought. Duval would be dead by now. *But I would be alive and free,* Sam told herself.

In the street below the window, the same police cruiser sailed silently past the hotel. Sam's stomach clenched. Her face tightened.

"Police?" Duval asked. His voice was strangely calm, like he had been waiting for this moment to arrive.

"Yeah."

He let out a trembling breath. "Maybe we should give ourselves up? I'm a French citizen. We could ask for asylum."

Sam shook her head. "The French want you as bad as we do."

"So what's the plan?"

"He seems to be circling the block. We'll wait for him to pass by again and then go straight out the front and cut through the park," Sam said. She was already on her feet, moving toward the door. "Don't look around and keep your eyes forward."

Duval nodded and fell in behind her.

She grabbed the pageboy cap off his head and stuffed it on her own. Duval started to protest and she said, "They're looking for me, remember?"

The second-floor hallway was empty. Sam lead the way to the stairs. It was an effort to keep her legs from running. Her brain urged her to sprint. She forced herself to walk quickly instead. Move too fast and you make mistakes.

Don't move faster than you can analyze the situation. That had been one of Burke's nuggets of wisdom.

The same tired-eyed clerk sat behind the desk. He glanced up when Sam reached the bottom of the steps and his face paled. He didn't move. Didn't speak. He just watched her like she might sprout an extra eye in the middle of her forehead.

She ignored him and crossed the lobby to the front door. Through the marbled glass, Sam recognized the blurred shape of a second police cruiser parked three doors down, on the opposite side of the street. The panic that was building in her chest started to bubble over.

Duval peered over her shoulder at the cruiser and said, "What now?"

The lobby door had a simple push bar and a deadbolt. Sam turned back to the night clerk. "You have the keys?"

He nodded.

"Give them to me."

When he didn't respond, Sam pulled the gun from her waistband. She kept the muzzle pointed at the floor and held out her other hand. "Give me the keys."

The night clerk shoved a hand in his pocket and came out with a large keyring. In his haste, he fumbled them and the keys hit the ground with a jingle.

"Come on!" Sam urged. "Hurry."

He stooped down, grabbed the keys and passed them over the counter. "Don't hurt me, okay?"

"I'm not going to hurt you," Sam told him.

He put his hands on top of his head and laced his fingers together like this was a robbery.

Sam slotted keys in the deadbolt until she found the

right one and turned the lock. The deadbolt shot into place with an audible click.

"Great," Duval said in a deadpan voice. "That will stop them."

Sam pocketed the keys, grabbed Duval's sleeve and dragged him toward the back of the hotel. To the desk clerk she said, "Back door?"

He pointed.

They passed through an employee breakroom with lockers and a Formica table. Beyond that was a small laundry facility. Four grime-encrusted washers stood against the wall and the smell of industrial cleaner hung in the air. One of the machines made a continuous loud clunking noise. Soiled linens were heaped on a table. One the far side of the laundry room was a stout metal door with a sign from management reminding employees to keep the door closed at all times.

Sam grabbed one of the sheets, stuffed it into an unused machine and then dug in her pocket for a lighter.

Duval grabbed at her sleeve. "I'm not going to let you burn the building down."

She shrugged him off, flicked the lighter and ran it along the edge of the sheet. "Relax. I'm not going to burn the building down." After a moment she added, "I hope."

Fire needs fuel. The aluminum washing machine and exposed brick walls of the laundry room should help contain the fire and still put off enough smoke to set off the fire detector. At least, that was Sam's plan. The cheap linen blackened and caught. Orange flame flickered along the edge of the sheet and started to spread.

Sam threw open the rear exit and stepped into a small

courtyard formed by four buildings with their backs facing each other. One of the buildings had an arched passageway for delivery trucks, but the double doors were secured with a heavy padlock.

Duval let out a breath. "We're trapped."

"We're a long way from trapped," Sam said. Her words came out a lot more confident than she felt. Her heart was ping-ponging around inside her chest and her knees were rubber. She handed the keyring to Duval. "Start trying keys. Maybe we'll get lucky."

"What are you going to do?" Duval asked.

She removed a green paracord bracelet from around her wrist and went to work unravelling it.

"What are you planning to do with that?" Duval wanted to know.

"Never mind that," Sam told him. "Get busy on that door."

CHAPTER THIRTY-EIGHT

"Turn right," Preston barked. He had his smartphone out, giving directions. Vesoul was a little college town less than two hundred kilometers from the border of Switzerland.

Grey spun the wheel and the silver Audi slewed around a corner. Tires growled on the blacktop. He barely missed the back end of a police cruiser parked at the corner. A second blue and white compact Renault was parked at the other end of the block. *Little wonder no one takes French police seriously,* thought Grey. *They drive clown cars.*

"Fifty feet on your right," Preston said.

Grey braked in the middle of the road and shifted into park. Preston put his phone away and pulled out a Sig Sauer SP2022, the weapon of choice for French law enforcement. Grey drew an identical pistol. Say what you will about their choice of automobiles, the French taste in guns was second to none. Grey cranked open the driver's door and said, "LeBeau, deal with the cops."

"*Oui.*" He climbed out, produced a detective's badge, and hustled back to the patrol car. With his native command of the language and a shield that was indistinguishable from the real thing, LeBeau easily passed as a plainclothes officer.

Grey mounted the steps to the hotel, with Preston one step behind, and reached for the handle. He yanked but door rattled in the frame. Grey lost his grip, staggered back a step and would have gone down the stairs but he ran into Preston.

"Locked," he said.

Shielding his eyes from the morning sun, Grey squinted through the marbled glass. A young Frenchman was behind the counter with a phone to his ear. He saw them. Grey took a fake police badge from his pocket and put it against the glass. The Frenchman hung up the phone and hurried over.

"Police," Grey told him in French. "Open the door,"

"It's locked." His voice was muffled by the glass.

"Unlock it!" Grey shouted.

"I can't." He coughed and waved a hand in front of his face. "She has the key and the building is on fire!"

Grey turned to Preston. "Get a tire iron."

He nodded and ran back to the car. Grey used the fob to open the trunk as LeBeau jogged up, a little winded.

"She set the building on fire," Grey told him.

LeBeau cursed.

Preston came back with the tire iron.

"Stand back," Grey ordered.

The night clerk retreated to the stairs.

Preston swung. The marbled glass spider-webbed and

sagged in the frame. A second blow rained the glass down on the cheap linoleum with a musical jingle. A cloud of smoke wafted out. The night clerk started toward the opening.

"Wait," Grey ordered and held up a hand.

Preston used the tire iron to knock shards from the frame.

When it was safe, Grey said, "Alright. Come on."

The night clerk turned sideways and slipped out, holding his hands across his chest to avoid getting sliced. "I called the fire department."

Grey scowled. Of course he did. That's what responsible citizens do. They call the fire department. Sam was a slippery one. She knew the night clerk would pick up the phone the second he smelled smoke. In a few minutes, people would be running in every direction to escape the fire, a truck would pull up with sirens blaring, and everything would be utter chaos. Grey said, "Which way did she go?"

"Out the back."

Grey turned to Lebeau. "Watch the front."

He nodded, took the night clerk by the arm, and steered him across the street.

Grey and Preston slipped inside. The smell of smoke was stronger in the lobby. They hurried past the front desk, through a door into an employee lounge with a folding table and a microwave oven. Preston touched the back of his hand to the laundry door and hissed. "Hot."

Grey raised his pistol. His heart was drumming inside his chest. Preston used his jacket to take hold of the knob. Grey nodded.

Preston yanked the door open. A cloud of greasy black smoke washed over them, stinging their eyes and burning their lungs. Bright orange flames leapt and flickered beyond the thick wall of smoke. Grey coughed and waved a hand in front of his face. Tears welled up and blurred his vision. He pulled his shirt collar up around his nose and entered with his weapon leading the way.

CHAPTER THIRTY-NINE

By the time Sam finished unbraiding the paracord bracelet, thick fingers of oily black smoke were creeping beneath the exit door. Grey would be here soon, if he wasn't already. The night clerk had probably smelled the smoke by now and called the fire department. Sam had two lengths of cord which she looped back on each other and tied with a double hitch. Her fingers were trembling, making tying the knots difficult. She had to try twice and the whole time her brain was screaming at her to hurry.

"I got it!" Duval's voice echoed in the small courtyard. He turned the key and the hasp popped open. "I got it."

"Great," Sam told him. "Open the door and come over here."

Duval swung the door wide and hesitated. He wanted to sprint. Sam could see his body edging toward the opening, like metal shavings drawn to a magnet. Panic etched itself on the lines of his face. He was fighting the urge run.

Fear triggers the fight or flight response and that doesn't leave any room for rational thought.

At the Farm—the CIA's top-secret training installation in Tidewater, Virginia—instructors teach counterintelligence operatives to overcome the fight or flight response by locking them in a room and then flooding it with tear gas. To escape, the recruits have to figure out a complicated series of puzzles. Forcing your brain to do puzzles when you can't breathe is like trying to do math with fire ants crawling all over your body. But the Escape Room was just for starters. Instructors at the Farm had plenty of other devious methods for training recruits to stay cool under pressure. People who can't keep it together wash out quick.

Sam fixed Duval with a hard look. She had to overcome his fight or flight response. In a stern voice she said, "The police will have the neighborhood blocked off. Come here. Now."

After a reluctant glance through the open door, Duval hurried back across the courtyard. Sam handed him one of the lengths of paracord.

His words came out in breathless little gasps. "What are you planning to do with this?"

She motioned to the water pipe running up the back of the building. The architecture in this part of France featured a lot of brick and exposed pipe. The buildings bristled with sewage and gas lines. And because these pipes carried waste water, they were made of sturdy lead.

Duval looked up and the color drained from his face. He shook his head. "Oh no. No way. Are you insane?"

Sam put her hands on his shoulders and forced him to

look in her eyes. "Take a breath and stay calm. We only have to make it to the first balcony."

Duval pointed at the smoke leaking from the rear exit. "You want to go back into a burning building?"

"Sacha, you need to trust me." Sam fed one of the lengths of paracord through the pipe and looped it twice. "This is child's play. Didn't you ever do this as a kid?"

Using the cord as a hand hold, Sam braced her feet against the wall and slid the cord up, then walked her feet up. Her weight on the double hitch kept the cord taut against the metal pipe. She went up a few feet and then dropped back to the ground and let the paracord slide down. "See how easy it is?"

Duval shook his head. "I can't do it, Sam. I'm not..." He motioned to her and groped for words. "Jason Bourne with boobs."

Sam arched an eyebrow.

"Sorry," he muttered.

She motioned to the pipe.

He shook his head. "I can't."

"I'll be right behind you," Sam told him. "You aren't going to fall. But we have to go, *now*. Grey is going to come through that door any second. You know what's going to happen if they put you in a black site? Death would be a mercy."

"You're trying to scare me."

"You should be scared," Sam said. "Last year I was involved in an operation that ended with a man I know, Clark Foster, shipped off to a black site. He's a hollow shell now. Spends his days sitting in a wheelchair staring out the window of a nut house. You want that?"

"Alright," Duval said. He took out his inhaler and shook it.

"You can do this," Sam assured him as he reached for the paracord. "Lean your weight back against it."

Duval took hold of the hitched length of green rope. Sweat sprang out on his forehead. He gave it a few tentative yanks to be sure it was secure. Precious seconds were slipping by. How long had they been standing here? Two minutes? Five? It was impossible to say. Inside Sam's brain a warning siren whooped. She wanted to shout at Duval to hurry it up, but that would only fluster him. Instead she fought to control her voice and said, "Nothing to it. Lean your weight back. That's right. Just like that. Now put one foot up on the wall. Now the other. See? You're doing it."

Duval was breathing hard, but he managed to get both feet up on the wall. A nervous smile flashed across his face when he didn't tumble back to the earth.

"Now push off with your feet and slide the rope up," Sam instructed.

He started to shake his head.

"You can do it," Sam told him. "You have to."

He slipped the rope up a scant two inches. A nervous burst of air escaped his lips. His whole body shook like a newborn colt trying to stand for the first time. He slid the rope up again and then slowly, carefully, moved one foot, then the other.

"You're doing it," Sam told him. "That's perfect. Now just go a little faster. You're almost to the balcony."

CHAPTER FORTY

GREY CROUCHED OUTSIDE THE LAUNDRY ROOM. SWEAT beaded on his face and chest, soaking through his sweater. He felt like he was suffocating in his winter coat. He had delved into the inferno but couldn't see two feet in front of his face and was forced to retreat. Flames leapt and danced in the thick wall of smoke and oily black clouds belched from the open door.

Preston coughed and waved a hand in front of his face, then pulled his collar up over his nose. With both of their shirts hiding their faces, Grey was reminded of playing ninja as a boy. He remembered slinking around his neighborhood at night, along with his two best friends, trying to disappear into the darkness. But this was no game and he was no ninja. If Sam managed to escape with Duval, however, Grey would disappear *permanently*.

Using hand signals, he motioned for Preston to check the smoke-filled laundry room. Preston nodded, took a deep breath in through his shirt and then ducked around the door frame. He reemerged seconds later and shook his head.

"Empty." He coughed and dashed tears from his eyes. "No place to hide either. Another door though. Leads outside."

Grey cursed. Sam had gone out the back and set the blaze to stop them from following. In the distance, Grey heard the wail of a fire engine and tramping feet from the floor overhead. The hotel guests had smelled smoke and were raising the alarm.

"She'll probably have another little trick on the other side of the door," Grey said. "Be ready."

Preston nodded.

"Moving," Grey announced.

With his shirt covering his nose, and his gun up looking for targets, he dodged around the doorframe into thick clouds of smoke. Preston was so close they kept bumping shoulders. Tears filled Grey's vision and forced him to blink. His lungs burned. He moved directly across the laundry room. Heat had partially melted the plastic shell of the washing machine. Grey motioned to the door and Preston kicked the push bar.

They both spilled outside into a tiny courtyard blocked in by surrounding buildings. The only exit was an arched passageway, designed for delivery trucks. The double doors stood open and a heavy-duty padlock lay on the cobblestones along with the key ring.

Grey let his shirt collar fall and sucked in a lungful of fresh air.

"That way!" Preston managed through a fit of coughs.

They jogged across the courtyard. Grey thrust his gun

through the narrow gap, then pushed the door wide with his toe. Faded posters for a punk rock band papered the walls, ripped and peeling in places. The low arched passage beyond emptied onto the street. They sprinted the short tunnel and peered around, but Sam and Duval were nowhere in sight.

Grey leaned a shoulder against the chipped brick wall and took out his phone. Seconds ticked by while he waited.

"This is Coughlin. What's going on?"

"Gunn is in the wind," Grey said without preamble. "Have you got eyes on the area?"

"We're looking at the target building now," Coughlin assured him. "I see smoke."

"She lit the building on fire. I need to know which way she went."

"We haven't seen anyone leave."

"She went out the back." Grey peered up into a leaden sky like he might be able to spot the drones circling. He stepped away from the wall and waved an arm overhead. "Did you see anyone go this way?"

"No." Coughlin spoke in clipped tones. "No one left that way."

Grey turned in a circle, looking for any sign of his prey. "Did you see anyone in the rear courtyard behind the hotel?"

"We don't have an angle on the courtyard, but I'm telling you, no one left. She has to be inside somewhere."

Grey motioned to Preston and they jogged back through the tunnel. All the buildings had exits that let onto the space, but they were closed and locked. Grey tugged on all the handles to be sure.

"Look!" Preston pointed to a water pipe scaling the back of the hotel. A tangle of parachute cord lay pooled around the base and shoe marks walked up the wall to the first-floor balcony.

Grey spit a curse. He hung up on Coughlin and dialed LeBeau. The scream of the fire engine drowned out the dial tone.

Preston reached for the back door. His hand closed on the latch and his eyes opened wide. He drew back with a shriek of pain. The flesh of his palm was bright pink. He bent over, cradling his injured hand. "My hand," Preston moaned. "Oh, God, my hand!"

"Come on," Grey barked. He led the way out of the courtyard, with the phone to his ear. Preston jogged after him, his blistered palm cradled protectively against his chest.

CHAPTER FORTY-ONE

SAM SUSPECTED THE DOOR ON THE SECOND-FLOOR balcony would be unlocked and she wasn't disappointed. Balcony doors are frequently left unlatched in the mistaken assumption they can't be reached from the outside. It's a mistake that covert operatives often leverage to their advantage. She was easing the door shut as Grey and Preston pounded across the courtyard to the open delivery door. A hint of smoke was rising up through the floorboards and Sam wrinkled her nose. Panic crept around the edges of her brain like the shadows pooling around an old house in the evening when the last of the light is fading from the sky but it's still too early to turn on the lights.

Duval stood at the foot of the bed, blinking stupidly at the sight of a middle-aged Frenchman stretched out naked on the sheets. The sleeping man had a paunch, skinny legs and a head of sandy hair with early streaks of gray. An empty wine bottle stood on the flimsy table next to the bed.

Sam patted him on the shoulder. "*Bonjour*, time to wake up," she said in French.

He came awake with a snort, passed a hand over his face and blinked up at her with bloodshot eyes. He must have really tied one on last night, because waking up naked with a stranger standing over him didn't seem to surprise him. He smacked his lips a few times, like he was getting a bad taste out of his mouth, and managed to croak out, "Who are you?"

Speaking slowly and in French, Sam said, "The hotel is on fire. You need to..."

She realized she didn't know the word for evacuate and looked to Duval.

"You need to leave." Duval motioned to the door. "The building is burning down."

The man's brow furrowed. He seemed slightly more confused by the presence of Duval, but his eyes went back to Sam. He grunted, swung his legs out of bed and reached for his trousers.

"Hurry," Sam told him.

"Yes," Duval said. "Do hurry."

The man motioned back and forth between Sam and himself. "Did we...?"

Sam nodded. "Yes. You were incredible. Come along now."

She took his elbow and steered him toward the door while he worked his zipper. He tried to stop for his shoes but Sam kept him moving. "Leave the shoes," she said.

Duval held the door. A thin layer of black smog gathered around the ceiling in the upstairs hall, obscuring the cheap fluorescents. The long, steady wail of a fire engine grew louder by the second. A door near the stairs opened and a woman popped her head out.

"The hotel is on fire," Sam told her. "You need to get out."

The girl darted out of her room and down the stairs in her bare feet. Sam and Duval banged on doors as they passed. "Fire! Get out! The hotel is on fire!"

Others took up the alarm and soon everybody was yelling. Doors flew open and, within seconds, Sam and Duval were hustling down the stairs along with a dozen terrified hotel guests. The smoke thickened as they reached the lobby. Tears doubled Sam's vision. She covered her mouth with an elbow. Duval took out his inhaler.

"Put that away," Sam managed to shout through the sirens and panicked shouts.

He clutched the inhaler in a tight fist, coughed, and hammered his chest instead.

Sam ushered him, along with the crowd, out through the shattered front door. She kept her elbow up to disguise her face, gripped Duval's arm and muttered instructions. "Don't look up. Keep your head down. Cough, like everyone else."

"Shouldn't be... too... hard." He wracked out between coughs.

A yellow fire engine was parked in front of the hotel. Firemen in oversized coats and helmets hustled around the truck, uncoiling hoses and directing people to safety. An ambulance fought its way along the narrow boulevard, past a cordon of police vehicles.

"Turn right," Sam said. "Turn right."

She and Duval broke off from the main group. While

the rest of the people moved toward the ambulances, they hurried along the sidewalk toward the corner. A French police officer caught sight of them trying to break free from the group, raised a whistle to his lips and gave a loud blast. "*Monsieur*, please stop."

Sam's heart squeezed painfully inside her chest. She ignored the cop, like she hadn't heard the piercing whistle, and urged Duval forward with a hand on his back. "Faster."

"Halt," the officer yelled. "You two, stop right where you are!"

Sam gave Duval a shove. "Run!"

He broke into a sprint that lasted all of ten seconds before his legs slowed to a lumbering gait. A plodding pack mule could have kept pace. A greasy patch of sweat formed on his forehead. Sam stayed one step behind. She could only go as fast as Duval was able and, right now, that felt entirely too slow.

The officer was closing the distance fast.

Sam jogged next to Duval, but her mind was racing two steps ahead. A police cruiser was parked on the corner along with another ambulance trying to fight past the traffic and a growing knot of spectators. If she could reach the corner and mix in with the crowd, she might still escape. She grabbed Duval's elbow and yanked him along. Then she spotted LeBeau near the corner with a phone pressed against one ear. A police shield hung around his neck on a chain. He spotted Sam at the same time, plunged a hand into his coat and pulled a gun.

Sam knew they were caught. With LeBeau in front and the French police officer behind, she had nowhere to go. If she pulled her gun it would start a firefight and that would only get her and Duval shot down in the street. The narrow boulevard seemed to constrict. The buildings shrank in on her. LeBeau raised his pistol and sighted on Sam's chest. She stared down the dark barrel and waited for the sound of a bullet. Cornered and out of options, Sam did the only thing she could think to do when things were bleakest: she prayed.

"God send me help," she said out loud.

An older model Nissan screeched around the corner. The driver side tires humped up onto the sidewalk as the driver threaded his way past emergency vehicles. LeBeau heard the motor and turned in time to see the car barreling down on him. He opened his mouth to scream but never got the chance. The front bumper clipped the backs of his knees and he went over the hood. It all happened so fast, and yet it was like watching in slow motion. His body impacted the windshield, cracking the glass, and his legs shot up in the air like a peace symbol. His gun went flying and he landed in a heap on the sidewalk. The crowd gasped and pressed back, blocking the ambulance trying to get through. LeBeau lay in a twisted wreck, one leg bent at a wrong angle and blood smearing the side of his face.

The driver of the Nissan laid on the brakes, the tires locked, and the driver side window buzzed down. Jake Noble stuck his head out. "Need a lift?"

CHAPTER FORTY-TWO

BURKE HAD GIVEN UP STANDING HOURS AGO AND confiscated one of the rolling office chairs. His arches were killing him. The sixty extra pounds was taking a toll. He made a mental note to lay off the potato chips. Dana would be happy to hear it. She'd been hounding him to go on a diet. Funny thing, when Madeline had hassled him about eating healthy, it was annoying. When Dana did it, Burke found it endearing. Maybe healthy relationships are all about how we label the little things?

It was 1:15 in the morning local time. That would make it 7:15 in France. The energy in the situation room was electric. A quiet bustle of activity coalesced into white noise. Coughlin had more or less taken over at this point. Burke's presence was purely functionary. Grey and his team had arrived at the hotel. Drones circled overhead. An end to the exhausting manhunt was finally in sight. Everyone was looking forward to calling it a day and heading home for some much-needed sleep. Everyone except Burke. He crossed thick forearms over his chest and watched the feed from the drones.

Sam had picked a hotel in a city block where all the buildings shared a closed-in rear courtyard. You rarely find that type of construction anywhere in the United States. The drones were in a wide holding pattern with a front view of the building exteriors. Coughlin had a phone to his ear, telling Grey they didn't have an angle on the courtyard. It would take several minutes to reroute a bird directly overhead and even then, at air speed, they would only have a shot of the courtyard for a few seconds.

On the screen, a fire engine stopped in front of the hotel as guests came pouring out. Smoke billowed up from the back of the building. Police had both ends of the street blocked with patrol cars, keeping out street traffic.

Burke watched the action unfold. A white-hot hunk of coal burned in his gut. Mentally, he screamed at Sam to get the hell out of there. *What was she thinking stopping at a hotel? She must be getting tired,* thought Burke. *Making mistakes. Come on, Sam. Get out. Run girl! Run!*

One of the screens showed a pair of individuals separate from the crowd that was exiting the hotel. A uniformed officer tried to stop them and they broke into a sprint.

"Is that Gunn?" Coughlin wanted to know.

Burke shook his head. The figure was right but a pageboy cap obscured her face. He said, "Can't tell. The angle's no good."

"That's them," Coughlin said. "Track them."

But the control team was already issuing commands to the drone operators. The pair of fugitives hurried along the sidewalk and the police officer ran after them. On the corner, a man reached into his coat and came out with a small black object that could only be a gun. Sam's steps slowed. Her hands started to go up.

Burke said, "He's going to shoot! Call them off, Coughlin!" Burke's heart clenched inside his chest. Sam was about to get shot and the only thing he could do was watch.

A four-door sedan slid around the corner and hit the man from behind, sending him over the top of the car. Everyone in the control room responded. People gasped. A few of the women let out breathless screams.

"What the hell?" Coughlin barked. "What's going on? Who is that? Did a drunk run over a cop or did someone just walk into this op?"

There was a mad scramble as techs started tracking this new development.

"All of our people are on foot," someone called out.

"It's not one of ours."

"Who is it?" Coughlin wanted to know.

"And who got run over?" Burke said. "Was that a cop? One of Grey's men?"

"I can't decide which would be worse," Coughlin said.

"For once we agree."

On screen, the pair of fugitives sprinted to the car. Burke uncrossed his arms and stood up, the pain in his feet was temporarily forgotten. He watched as the fugitives piled into the car. The Nissan reversed, swung through a backwards turn, and then shifted into drive.

Coughlin growled a curse. "Give me an angle on the driver. We need to see who's driving that car."

Burke knew it was a losing proposition. It would take the closest drone several minutes to correct course. By then the driver would change directions. Burke had no sooner thought it than the sedan slewed through another turn with the practiced skill of an espionage agent.

"Stay on the car," Coughlin ordered. "Do *not* lose that vehicle. I want a license plate number and a picture of the driver. Come on, people! Make it happen!"

While the techs scrambled to keep up, Burke eased back down into his seat.

Dana caught Burke's attention and questioned him with a look.

He shook his head, trying to communicate with his eyes. *Not now. Tell you later.*

Images of the hotel were gone, replaced by city streets and blurred treetops. All three birds were on the car, trying to correct their flight pattern to keep up with the sedan racing through the narrow streets of Vesoul. The vehicle slid through another turn, avoided a city bus, and zig-zagged through traffic. Coughlin dialed Grey and told him Sam was escaping in a four-door sedan. "Looked like a Subaru," Coughlin said. It was a Nissan, but Burke didn't bother to correct him. The car raced north and west along the park then disappeared into a tunnel.

"They might try to turn around," Coughlin told the room. "I want one drone on the entrance and the other two on the exit. Don't let them get away."

Minutes ticked by. The drones captured images of vehicles exiting the tunnel in both directions and everyone watched the screen for any sign of the sedan. The Nissan never reappeared. One corner of Burke's mouth twitched in a barely perceptible grin.

CHAPTER FORTY-THREE

Noble was behind the wheel of a black Peugeot, headed south. The sun was poking through a blanket of scattered clouds, throwing patchwork shadows on the narrow lanes of Vesoul. Sam was in the passenger seat, a pageboy cap pulled low on her head. She checked the mirrors then crowded forward over the dash and peered up into the sky.

"Relax," Noble told her. "We lost 'em. For now."

They had ditched the Nissan inside the tunnel and carjacked a young woman with a yappy poodle, who was more concerned about the puppy than the car. Noble didn't even have to threaten her. She got out, begging him not to hurt her baby. The dog had curled its lips back and issued a growl, more comical than scary, from the depths of its tiny body. Sam apologized profusely as she jogged around the front bumper and climbed in the passenger side while her friend piled in the backseat. Noble handed over the keys to the stolen Nissan, got behind the wheel of the Peugeot and shifted into gear.

Now, with the threat of drones behind them, Sam pulled the cap off, closed her eyes and breathed. Her friend splayed across the backseat, sucking on an inhaler. The acrid stench of burning plastic clung to their clothes.

"Tough night?" Noble asked.

Sam turned in her seat to face him, opened her mouth to speak, and threw her arms around him instead. He fought to control the vehicle. He had been dreaming of this moment ever since Hong Kong. Now Sam was wrapped around him and he couldn't even stop to enjoy it. A smile forced its way onto his face. He wanted to tell her how much he had missed her. Instead, he patted her shoulder with one hand and said, "Okay, don't crash us."

"It's really you," Sam spoke into his chest. "You're really here."

"It's me," Noble assured her.

She eased up on her strangle hold. "How did you know?"

Noble chewed the inside of one cheek while he thought about how to answer.

Her hands slipped away. All the happiness drained out of her face, replaced by a tightness around her eyes and mouth. She said, "You're here to bring us in?"

"Yeah." Admitting it felt slimy, like wading through ankle-deep sewage.

The guy in the backseat cranked himself into an upright position and took the inhaler away from his mouth. "What?"

Sam's face went through a confusing tangle of

emotions. Pearly tears gathered in the corners of her dark eyes. The sight drove a railroad spike right through Noble's heart.

"What's going on?" the pudgy Frenchman with the white hair asked.

Noble aimed his comment at Sam, "Armstrong sent me."

Sam screwed her eyes shut and raked a hand through her hair.

The Frenchman said, "Are you turning us over to the CIA?"

Noble's grip on the wheel tightened. "I didn't say that."

"But you're working for Armstrong," Sam said.

"I don't work for anybody," Noble said, "but Armstrong sent me."

"Then why *are* you here?" Sam wanted to know.

"I'm here to figure out what's going on, Sam. There's a dead COS and a field officer on the run. Armstrong needs to know why." Noble tilted the rearview for a better look in the backseat. "Is that who I think it is?"

Sam took a deep breath and blew out her cheeks. "Jake Noble, meet Sacha Duval. AKA Cypher Punk."

Noble craned around for a better look. Duval offered him a tight smile. Noble turned his attention back to the road and found the Peugeot had drifted lanes. He tweaked the wheel and said, "That raises more questions than it answers."

"Montenegro offered him asylum. It's a non-extradition country." Sam cocked a thumb over her shoulder. "Genius here, tried to lay in the pipeline for a defection using back channels on the dark web. He hired a smuggler to get him across the water and *Le Milieu* to escort him to Montenegro."

Noble twirled his hand in a motion that meant '*keep going*'.

"Bonner got word of the move," Sam explained. "He paid off *Le Milieu*. They were going to deliver Duval at the harbor."

While Sam spoke, the quaint houses and cracked asphalt gave way to a bleak countryside gripped by the cruel hand of winter. Noble took turns at random, looking for a place to lay low. The manhunt was on and police would have roadblocks set up along all the major highways. The drones would be expanding their search area.

Noble said, "That doesn't explain why you went off script."

"I didn't," Sam told him. "I was never part of the script. Bonner laid in the whole operation behind closed doors and hired a trio of private contractors. It was obvious he was planning something and I got curious. I wanted to know why he was cutting me out of the loop. At first I thought it was because I was the new kid, but I kept digging."

The grim hulk of a gothic cathedral reared into the leaden sky. Long yellow stalks of grass grew up around the old church. Stone gargoyles leered down from broken parapets and the sagging roof looked ready to collapse. Ancient oak doors were banded by strips of iron and secured with a rusty padlock. Several of the stained-glass windows were cracked and broken in places. Behind the old church was a forest of naked trees. Dead leaves made a brown carpet around bone white trunks. Noble parked under a barren oak.

"Why didn't you kick it up a level?" he asked. "Go to Bonner's boss? Or, hell, to the new Director herself?"

"Because I'm pretty sure Coughlin is in on it," Sam said. "Truth is, I don't know how high up it goes."

"Pete Coughlin?" Noble asked.

"Yeah. You know him?"

Noble nodded. "He ran Afghanistan after September 11. He's not much for field work. He likes to stay in the rear with the gear. So what happened?"

"By the time I figured out what Bonner was up to, the operation was already in the works. I had to move fast. I stole a van, took an MP5 and rubber bullets from a weapons cache in Paris, and raced to the harbor ahead of Bonner and his crew of freelancers."

"Why?"

"What do you mean why?" Sam asked.

"He's a wanted fugitive," Noble pointed out. "Why not let Bonner intercept him?"

"They were going to kill him."

Noble's lips pressed together in a tight line. Hollywood paints the CIA out to be a shadowy boogeyman responsible for mysterious disappearances all over the globe. Nothing could be further from the truth. The CIA collects intelligence. Occasionally that intel is used by Special Operations Groups to carry out clandestine missions, but very rarely do those missions involve assassination. Bonner must have something to hide if he wanted Duval dead instead of talking to the CIA.

Noble said, "That's a bad thing?"

Sam folded her arms under her breasts. "I can't believe you'd say that."

"He leaked classified intel and put a lot of field officers in danger," Noble said. "Good men had their covers blown and got killed because of him."

"He deserves a fair trial."

"Granted," Noble said. "But that doesn't explain why you scuttled your career to help him."

Duval stuck his head between the seats. "I'm right here, you know."

"Shut up," Noble told him.

Sam stared straight ahead and spoke through clenched teeth. "I couldn't let Bonner execute him."

"Now your head's on the chopping block."

"Fine!" Sam threw her hands up. "I totally blew it. Is that what you want to hear?"

She dashed tears from her eyes.

"Smooth," Duval remarked.

Noble turned. "Remember what I said about shutting up?"

Sam looked at the old church and said, "What are we doing here?"

"We need somewhere to lay low," Noble said. "This place has been abandoned for years."

"How do you know it's empty?"

"French people don't go to church," Noble told her.

"He's not wrong," Duval said.

"Besides," said Noble. "There's a rusty padlock on the front door."

CHAPTER FORTY-FOUR

JAQUELINE ARMSTRONG WAS BACK IN THE OFFICE BY 4 a.m. feeling like she'd hadn't slept. Her secure line buzzed all night with updates on the situation in France. By three o'clock, she had given up trying to sleep and brewed a pot of coffee before heading back to Langley. Her first stop was her private bathroom where she put on her war paint. She kept a makeup kit under the sink with everything she needed. That done, she scooped up the phone on her desk and called the cleaners, then leafed through an urgent EYES ONLY file while she waited. Ten minutes later there was a knock at the door.

A team of professionals filed in, hauling an array of equipment designed to detect listening devises. Her office was swept twice a day. Six of them went over the room, top to bottom. It was actually pretty interesting and Jaqueline had watched them work the first few times, impressed by their speed and efficiency. After the first month, the process had lost its charm. When they finished checking the office and bathroom, one of the men stepped up to Armstrong's desk. She knew the drill. She rose without a word and spread her arms.

He ran a wand over body. Top to bottom, front to back. The instrument clicked softly as it sought listening devices that might have been planted on her while she was out of the office. After the wand came *the mouse*. It resembled a computer mouse, hence the name. He ran the device over her chest, hips, down her legs and arms and then moved to the back. When he got to her left shoulder blade, the mouse gave off a rapid, high pitched bleat.

"How's the shrapnel today, Director?"

"Cold weather makes it hurt twice as much," Jaqueline said over her shoulder.

He finished and packed the mouse away as he moved toward the door. "You're clean. Office is clear."

When they had gone, Jaqueline took out the burner cell and dialed. She kicked off her shoes and lowered herself into the office chair while she waited.

Jake's voice came on the line. "I was starting to think you forgot about me."

Jaqueline told him, "Despite what some people think, even CIA directors have to sleep. How is officer Gunn?"

"A little rattled and exhausted. Otherwise okay."

"Is Sacha Duval with her?"

"What would make you say that?"

"Don't jerk me around, Noble. It's been a long night," Armstrong said. "We've got positive IDs on facial rec and the Ecuadorian embassy all but admitted he's gone."

"Why ask if the question if you already know the answer?"

Armstrong could practically hear the smile on his face. She said, "How is he?"

"A pain in the butt," Noble said. "He complains constantly. I'm surprised Sam hasn't shot him."

"Has officer Gunn said anything?"

There was a pause on the other end of the line and then Noble said, "She's under the impression Frank Bonner was on a capture-and-kill mission. Duval was the objective. Any truth to that?"

Armstrong said, "That would be very alarming information."

"Are you saying you didn't lay in the op?" Noble asked.

"No operations concerning Duval crossed my desk," Armstrong told him.

"With all due respect, ma'am, I don't like to be jerked around either. Did you send me to clean up a failed assassination?"

"Noble, up until a few hours ago, I didn't even know Duval was in play," Armstrong assured him. "Bonner never breathed a word of this. It was blind luck Duval happened to look up at the wrong time and we caught his face on camera. Burke was the one who recognized him."

"Is Burke there now?" Noble asked.

"If you mean at Langley, yes."

"Can I talk to him?"

"You can talk to him when you bring Gunn and Duval in."

There was another pause, longer this time. "Sorry. I can't do that."

Jaqueline leaned forward and propped her elbows on

the desk. "Don't do this, Noble. Do not go back on your word."

"I said I'd find Sam," Noble said. "I found her. I never said anything about turning her over to the Company."

"You have my word she'll get a chance to tell her side of the story."

"Sure, after you torture her for seventy-two hours straight," Noble said. "And then what? She goes to jail for the rest of her life? No dice."

Jaqueline massaged her temples with her free hand. "Jake, I want you to think about what you're doing. I want you to think about what this means."

"I thought about it."

"Noble, I'm begging you to do the right thing," Armstrong said. "Bring them in, and I'll reinstate you with the Company. You'll get your full pension. It will be like you never left."

The line went dead.

Jaqueline put the phone down and a smile crept over her face. Noble was in love, just like Burke had said. He would make sure Sam disappeared, probably into the Orient where she'd blend right in. No one would never see her again. It saved Armstrong the trouble of having to waterboard and imprison a traitor two months into her stint as Director. She reached for one of the thin cigars she kept on her desk.

To be young and in love. Jacqueline shook her head. She missed those days.

CHAPTER FORTY-FIVE

Burke popped a pair of aspirin in his mouth and then sipped from a can of Dr. Pepper while IMINT techs sifted through security footage from the surrounding areas. The game had changed. The arrival of the mystery man in the Nissan forced them to take a step back, reexamine all the players, and a prolonged search meant a changing of the guard. Burke had been forced to bring in fresh eyes to replace exhausted analysts who had been working all night. It meant updating a new crew on the situation, and inviting more possible leaks. It meant a logistical nightmare.

He took his time getting the new people up to speed, giving Sam a window of opportunity. Not much, but the best he could do under the circumstances. The techs were busy tracing back the movements of the Nissan in the hopes they could ID the driver. It was a painstakingly slow process. While the image professionals poured over security footage, the drones monitored the highways in an ever-expanding circle. So far, nothing.

New people brought with them new smells and of course, someone was wearing too much perfume. There was one in every crowd. This time it was a woman in a floral scent. Empty food wrappers and stale coffee added to the pungent aroma. But there was another smell, something Burke couldn't define. He put down his can of Dr. Pepper and sniffed an armpit. His nose wrinkled.

"You're pretty ripe," Dana told him. She sat next to him in a rolling office chair with her shoes off, rubbing her arches.

"You're no rose garden," Burke said.

She stuck her tongue out.

"French police found the Nissan abandoned in the tunnel," a signal tech said. He was rail-thin with dun-colored hair and a set of headphones clamped over a pair of ears big enough to pick up signals from outer space. "They switched cars."

Burke pinched the bridge of his nose. "Tell me something I hadn't figured out myself."

"The car they stole is a Black 2015 Peugeot model 308. We're combing through footage now to see if we can pick up the trail."

"Get that description to the drones," Burke said. "Any pics of the driver?"

"Not yet."

Dana shifted her weight and said, "Hmmm."

Burke turned to her. "What are you thinking?"

"I'm just a secretary, remember? I make the coffee."

"We could do with some more," Burke said.

She narrowed her eyes at him.

"Come on," Burke said. "Don't make me waterboard it out of you."

"Duval was safe at the embassy in London and our files indicate he's a physical coward," Dana said. "People like that tend to stay where they feel safe. Makes me think he didn't leave voluntarily."

Burke chewed that over. "He wasn't abducted. If a covert team had violated the embassy, we would have heard about it. They wouldn't cover something like that up. It would be front page news. Something forced his hand. Some change in circumstance made a move necessary."

"That's my point," Dana said. "Something happened and Duval was no longer safe at the embassy."

"Any idea what?"

"Two things come to mind," Dana said. "Either he found out Ecuador was going to expel him, or he learned someone was going to assassinate him."

"I found the car and I've got a picture of the driver," one of the IMINT techs announced.

Burke threaded his way between desks. The image showed the Peugeot at a stoplight. Burke recognized the driver's windblown hair and angular features right away but he said, "Get a copy of that down to facial rec. Where did they go from here?"

"We're working on that part, sir."

CHAPTER FORTY-SIX

The elevator dinged and Ezra stepped out. He had two Starbucks lattes in a cardboard drink caddy and his coat draped over one elbow. Several people greeted him as he passed. Gwen was already in her chair, light from the monitor reflected in her thick glasses and her mousy brown hair was pulled back in a ponytail.

Any discussion of leaving the Company for the private sector had vanished, replaced by this new mission. Breaking the CIA databanks was something they could sink their teeth into. It was something worth their time and talents. They had a productive first day. Not that they had made any progress, but they had been introduced to everybody in the third-floor basement and been invited out for drinks after work.

They found themselves at a tucked-away kombucha bar in Foggy Bottom frequented by Langley computer ninjas. Their work for Coughlin being hush-hush was enough to make them minor celebrities. After a few hits of kombucha, both analysts loosened up enough to test their moves on the dance floor. In a hipster bar full of computer cowboys and net rangers, they danced as well as anybody. Better by far, at least in Ezra's opinion, they had shared a dance, one tight hug, and a lingering smile with plenty of eye contact. All good progress so far as Ezra was concerned.

Progress on busting into Langley's operations database was an altogether different problem. So far, the Seven Dwarves had defeated every cipher, every code, and every backdoor hack they could think of. They had even written new code in the hopes of working around the system's redundancies, all to no avail. But Ezra's enthusiasm was undiminished. He laid awake half the night thinking about Gwen and the other half thinking of new ways to break into the database.

He crossed the floor and put a cup down next to her elbow. "Skinny caramel. Just the way you like it."

A smile played around the corners of her mouth. "Thank you."

"I've got a few new ideas." Ezra dropped his coat into an unused chair and logged into his terminal.

"Me too," Gwen said. "Last night I was thinking we could try a self-testing algorithm that would run all the various possible permutations in alternating patterns."

"That's a possibility," Ezra said.

She picked up her coffee and sipped. "You got a better idea?"

"I was thinking we could pull out the hard drives."

She stared at him.

He shrugged. "Bypass the front interface altogether and go straight to the source. It makes sense. Anyone trying to break into the system would have to know the hardware. While we're in there, we install an encrypted algorithm that would show us how the databanks are protected in real time."

She leaned back. Her brows pinched together over the bridge of her nose. "That's really clever."

"Thank you."

Before they could discuss the idea further, Coughlin stepped out of the elevator and cut across the floor to their work station. The left side of his face bunched and released in spastic patterns. His tie was pulled down and his hair was out of place. Dark circles had formed under his eyes, like he hadn't slept all night.

"Heads up," Gwen said.

Ezra swiveled in his chair.

Despite his appearance, Coughlin fixed a smile on his face. "How are my net rangers this morning?"

"Good," they chorused. The fact that Coughlin made an effort to use the lingo was appreciated.

He propped an elbow on the corner of their cubicle. "Any progress?"

"You want the good news or the bad news?" Ezra said.

"Always start with the good news."

"The good news is our system is very secure."

Gwen nodded in agreement.

"Are you saying you can't crack it?" The tick in Coughlin's eye winked several times fast.

"We still have a few tricks we haven't tried," Gwen assured him.

Ezra said, "I'd like to actually enter the database and get a look at the hardware, sir."

Coughlin blinked. "What?"

"I want to physically remove a hard drive."

"Won't that... crash the system?"

Ezra grinned and shook his head. "No. We wouldn't actually disconnect the drives. We just want to have a peek at what kind of hardware we're working with. It will give us a much better idea of any weaknesses and how to get past the security measures."

"And you're sure it won't... I don't know... fry the database?"

Ezra resisted the urge to laugh. The layperson's ignorance when it comes to computers was amazing. Sometimes he wondered how the troglodytes even managed to turn them on. "It won't fry the database."

Coughlin looked to Gwen for confirmation.

She shook her head. "Completely safe."

"How long would that take?"

"Couple of hours," Ezra told him. Always overestimate. That was Ezra's motto.

Coughlin pinched the bridge of his nose. "Do whatever it takes, just make it happen. I've got a meeting with the director in fifteen minutes. I'll check in on you later."

"Uh..." Gwen started up from her chair, rose halfway, and hung there. "We need authorization."

"How's that?" Coughlin asked.

"We need authorization," Ezra explained. "To actually enter the database."

Coughlin thought that over. For one brief second, a dark shadow passed over his face, the tick stopped, and his mouth formed a hard line. It was a look that filled Ezra with disquiet. He didn't like being on the other end of that look and feared Coughlin was about to explode in a tirade, but his face cleared just as fast and a smile appeared. It happened so fast, Ezra wasn't sure he had even seen it. Maybe it was just a trick of the light, or the product of a long night dealing with whatever was happening upstairs. Coughlin said, "I'll see that you get the necessary clearance."

CHAPTER FORTY-SEVEN

Burke entered the Director's office to find Coughlin already waiting, along with the Director of National Intelligence. An air purifier hummed softly in one corner. The space was impeccably clean with tasteful track lighting and neatly shelved volumes on the bookcases. A pair of deep leather sofas flanked a low table. Armstrong, in a pinstripe suit jacket, perched on the edge of one of the sofas. Her hair was up in a knot and a few loose strands framed her face. Half a dozen files were open on the glass table in front of her. She looked up as Burke entered. "Have a seat."

He lowered his bulk across from Armstrong. The sofa groaned under his weight. The summons had come on the heels of an eighty-eight percent facial recognition match for Jacob Noble. Burke had known it was coming, but that didn't make it any easier. His former protégé walks into an operation to hunt down his current protégé. It didn't look good. He reached for a carafe of water and poured himself a glass.

Across from the new DCI sat the Director of National Intelligence. Oliver McPherson was a Wheaton graduate and Army Staff Sergeant who worked his way up through the political system with a foot planted firmly on either side of the aisle. He supported gay marriage but opposed more stringent gun laws. How a former Staff Sergeant had managed to grab the DNI position, Burke could only guess. One thing he was sure of, anything said here would be reported directly to the president.

McPherson tipped a nod to Burke.

Burke returned it. No need for introductions. In McPherson's world, Burke was only a bit player. An operations officer was simply another cog in the wheel.

Coughlin was too keyed up to sit. He paced the floor, his facial tick torturing the side of his face. A thick file folder was clutched in one hand. Burke had never seen him so high-strung. His fingers jerked and danced like they were playing an imaginary piano.

Armstrong started the meeting by saying, "What happened in Vesoul?"

Coughlin held up the file in his hand. "A former Special Operations officer named Jacob Noble showed up out of nowhere and blew the op." He slapped the folder down on the coffee table with a sharp *thwack!* "The guy is a former Green Beret with a history of interfering in operations. Isn't that right, Burke?"

Burke fought to control his face. Not that long ago, he had used Noble to rewire a mission in Mexico City. The affair had ended in one of the most sensational shootouts in recent history. When it was over, a drug cartel was in tatters and a major U.S. politician was fending off allegations of illegal campaign funding. Only a handful of people at the CIA knew the whole story, and two of them were in this room. Burke spread his hands. "I had nothing to do with Noble's sudden appearance in France."

"Sure you didn't." Coughlin's face twitched and for a moment Burke could picture him in a straightjacket raving about bats. "Sure. It's all one big coincidence. Aren't you the guy that says you don't believe in coincidence?"

"Still don't," Burke said. "Jake Noble was Sam's introduction to the Company. He saved her life in Hong Kong. It makes sense she would call Noble when she found herself in a corner."

Coughlin said, "The guy's mother has medical bills that make Melania Trump's wardrobe look modest! He's unemployed. He lives hand to mouth. You expect us to believe he hopped aboard his private jet and rushed over to France?"

"I haven't figured that part out yet," Burke admitted.

"You mean you don't have an excuse handy."

Director Armstrong lit one of her thin cigars, leaned back in the sofa, and blew smoke up toward the ceiling. "When?"

Coughlin turned to her, his brow clouded over. "When what?"

"When would Burke have had time to read Noble in on the operation?" Armstrong asked. "He's been in on the search from the word go."

Coughlin didn't have anything to say.

"That's only one of the questions I'd like answered," Armstrong said. She rose up, went to her desk and came back with a glossy black-and-white which she laid on top of Coughlin's file, like a poker player dropping four aces. It was a surveillance photo of Sam and Duval outside the hotel. She rotated it so the DNI got a good look. "It's hard to tell with the hat, but my people assure me that's Sacha Duval."

No one spoke for several seconds. DNI McPherson, who until now had followed the debate with polite disinterest, was the first to break the silence. "Duval is in the open?"

"It would appear so," Armstrong told him as she retook her place on the sofa.

"Duval is top priority," McPherson said. "This Samantha Gunn character needs to be dealt with, but tell your people to bring Duval in alive,"

"What do you mean dealt with?" Burke asked.

"I'm not here to parse words," McPherson said. "You've got a rogue agent. That's the CIA's problem. Duval is a wanted fugitive. We need to know how this guy gets his information and what else he's holding before he leaks any more state secrets to the press. Duval is priority one."

"They both need to be brought in alive. A CIA officer is dead and Sacha Duval is somehow mixed up in the whole affair. We need answers. We aren't going to get them if Grey makes the call."

"The hell is that supposed to mean?" Coughlin said. His face did a rapid-fire twitch.

"It means Bonner was up to his eyeballs in a black bag operation and now Grey is trying to sweep the whole thing under the rug."

Director Armstrong held up a hand for silence. "Let's all get on the same page. I brought DNI McPherson here so everything is out in the open. The current administration has enough to worry about. No sense adding fuel to the fire. I have a briefing with the president in a couple of hours. He's going to want an update. He doesn't like to hear 'I don't know.' So, I want something to give him. Who knew Duval was leaving the embassy and when? Furthermore, why wasn't I made aware of it?"

All eyes turned to Coughlin. As acting head of operations, Duval would have been under Coughlin's jurisdiction. He said, "If I even suspected, I would have brought it to your attention."

"You mean you had no idea?" DNI McPherson said.

Armstrong didn't look any happier. She said, "He's on America's most wanted list. He's been under twenty-four-hour surveillance. We're monitoring all his communications. Now you're telling me he slipped out of the embassy without raising suspicions? We're the CIA for cripes' sake. How did he manage that?"

Coughlin shook his head. "I don't know. He must have had help."

Armstrong scooted to the edge of her seat and leaned forward. Her skirt hem rode up an inch. She said, "Somebody knew. I don't believe for a second that Frank Bonner just *happened* to show up at the dock when Duval was stepping off a boat. There are too many coincidences. Did Bonner indicate he was laying in any operations concerning Duval?"

Coughlin shook his head. "Absolutely not."

"You're sure?" Armstrong said.

"Bonner was a top-notch field officer with an impeccable record," Coughlin told her. "And Grey is a hired gun.

He only knows what he's told. If there's any shady business going on, I'd take a closer look at Gunn and Noble."

"That's one possible scenario," Burke muttered.

"Can you think of any others?" Coughlin asked, like he was daring the other man to come up with an answer.

"I can think of dozens," Burke said. "We won't know until we sit Gunn down and have a talk with her."

"If that's even possible," Coughlin said. "She's already killed one man. At this point, she might not be taken alive."

"Do everything you can to make sure she is," Armstrong told him. She fixed him with a hard look. "I want both Gunn *and* Duval taken into custody. Do I make myself clear?"

Coughlin's eye twitched. "Fine. Now let's discuss Jake Noble. The guy is aiding and abetting a murderer and an international fugitive. I'm asking, right out in the open, what means am I authorized to use?"

Burke's stomach clenched.

Director Armstrong leaned back and drummed the arm of the sofa with manicured fingernails. A vein pulsed in her neck. "Samantha Gunn needs to be questioned about her role in the murder of Frank Bonner, and Duval is an information gold mine. Bring them in alive if at all possible."

She stopped talking and her silence told Coughlin everything he needed to know. Without coming right out and saying it, Armstrong had given him permission to kill Noble if he got in the way.

A cruel smile turned up one side of Coughlin's twitching face. "There's nothing more to discuss. If anybody needs me, I'll be in the situation room cleaning up this mess."

Armstrong called an end to the meeting and Burke waited until DNI McPherson was gone before saying, "For God's sake, you just gave him the green light to eliminate Jake."

Armstrong puffed on her cigar. "What else could I do? Noble cut me out of the loop. He's refusing to bring Duval and Gunn in."

Burke ran a hand over his face and groaned. "That kid has a stubborn streak a mile wide and his own sense of right and wrong."

Armstrong waved away a cloud of smoke. "Duval is a high priority target. If he makes it to a non-extradition country, there's no telling what sort of bombshells he's going to drop. You want to be the one to tell the president we let him get away because we have a soft spot for a burned spy?"

"Okay." Burke puffed out his cheeks. "Okay, you're right. But I still don't like it."

"You don't have to," Armstrong told him. "I don't particularly like it, but we both knew the risks when we dropped Noble into the mix. And Noble knew what he was getting into."

Much as Burke hated to admit it, Armstrong was right. If she had gone to bat for Jake, it would have blown the lid off their little coup. Burke said, "You think Coughlin is caught up in this whole mess or is he just overzealous?"

"I think he's up to his eyeballs in a black bag operation that was supposed to stay off the records." Armstrong blew smoke. "Let's just hope Noble can untangle the Gordian knot. Meanwhile, I want you to quietly dig through Coughlin's ops and see what he's been up to."

CHAPTER FORTY-EIGHT

LeBeau had been transported to Centre Hospitalier de la Haute-Saône. Grey entered through the emergency room doors twenty minutes later. Preston was right behind him. The doors hissed open and sighed shut with a gentle push of warm air. Florescent lights reflected on green and white linoleum streaked by wheelchair tracks. Grey went to the front desk and flashed his fake badge at a heavy-set nurse with gray hair. His French wasn't as good as LeBeau's, but it was passable so long as he didn't get drawn into a long conversation. He said, "A detective was brought in a while ago. I want to know if he's alright."

"He's still in treatment," the nurse told them. "I'll inform the doctor you are here, if you'd like to wait."

He and Preston went to the big picture windows looking out at a parking lot full of cars. An ambulance pulled up to the emergency room entrance and paramedics unloaded a man on a stretcher with his neck in a brace. LeBeau hadn't looked much better. Paramedics had strapped him to a board before Grey could get close enough to ask any questions. He had been in a neck brace and his mouth was a bloody gash in his swollen face.

Preston kept his back to the front desk and took a bottle of pain killers from his pocket. His hand was blistering where he had grabbed hold of the hot door handle. It made Grey think of the Christmas movie where a pair of bumbling burglars are in a house full of booby traps. Only this wasn't funny. The skin around the burn was already turning an ugly shade of black with an angry, red eye in the center. He tried to get the cap off the pill bottle one-handed, but Grey had to help him.

Preston tipped several pain killers into his mouth and swallowed.

"Go easy on those things," Grey warned.

"My hand is killing me," Preston snarled. "I should have a doctor look at it."

"Later," Grey said.

"How long before they figure out LeBeau isn't a real cop?"

"Not long," Grey said. "Then they'll be looking for us."

"So what are we doing here?" Preston asked with a glance around the hospital waiting room. "The place is full of cameras."

"We have to make sure he doesn't talk," Grey said.

Preston stared at him. He started to open his mouth but was interrupted by a doctor in a green smock with wire-rimmed glasses. He greeted them with a reassuring smile.

"The detective is your partner?" he asked.

"That's right," Grey assured him. "Is he going to make it?"

"He lost a substantial amount of blood but he's in stable condition. He'll need surgery. He's got a broken leg and a chipped vertebra. I won't know what else is broken until we've had him under the x-ray. For right now, he's sedated, but you can look in on him if you'd like."

"That would be fine," Grey said. "Thank you."

The doctor told them the room number and then went on with his rounds.

Preston turned to him and dropped his voice to a whisper. "What are you gonna do?"

Grey felt his pocket vibrate and held up a finger for Preston to wait. He recognized Coughlin's number and put the phone to his ear. "Any word on Gunn?"

"Nothing yet," Coughlin said. "We know what vehicle they're in and I'll call you as soon as we have a location."

Grey cursed.

"My thoughts exactly. You really dropped the ball this time."

"Jake Noble showed up out of nowhere," Grey said. His voice had an edge to it and a vein throbbed in his forehead. "He snatched Sam and Duval right out of our hands."

"I saw it," Coughlin reminded him. "So did the rest of Langley. I thought our friends in *Le Milieu* had picked him up?"

"They did," Grey said. "He beat the hell out of one of their people and escaped. He put one of mine in the hospital."

"Which one?" Coughlin asked.

"LeBeau."

"How is he?"

"Not good," Grey said. "We're at the hospital now. He's going to need surgery."

"That complicates things," Coughlin said. "We can't have him talking to police."

"I'm taking care of it. Who is this Noble guy anyway?" Grey asked.

"He's former Special Operations Group."

"Oh, great. A trigger-happy idiot with a Rambo complex."

"It gets worse," Coughlin said. "Remember the snafu in Mexico City a couple months back?"

"The Mexican cartel that got wiped out?" Grey asked.

"Exactly."

Grey said, "Same guy?"

"Same guy," Coughlin confirmed. "Don't lock horns with him. He's not anyone you want to tangle with. The next time you get a chance, put a bullet in him. No messing around. We need to clean this mess up and tie off the loose ends. I just got out of a meeting with the Director. She knows about Duval and she's starting to ask questions."

Grey felt the vicious little rodent gnawing at the lining of his stomach again. He said, "What are you going to do?"

"I've got a pair of hard luck cases working to wipe any evidence from the database," Coughlin said. "I'll make sure the computer records match. You find out the name of Duval's failsafe. Do not screw up again, understand?"

"Don't worry about me," Grey said. "Just make sure the computer is taken care of."

He dropped the phone into his pocket.

Preston asked, "What's Mexico got to do with anything?"

Grey's brow wrinkled. "Huh?"

"You said something about Mexico."

Grey scratched behind an ear. "Remember the guy who duked it out with the cartel in Mexico last year?"

Preston frowned. "I remember hearing about it. We suspected it was one of our guys working off the books."

"That's our freelancer."

Preston groaned. "The guy took out an entire cartel."

"In as many words," Grey told him. "Now he's our problem. You go wait in the car. I'm going to look in on LeBeau."

Preston's mouth formed a strict line. For a moment it looked like he would try to stop Grey. They had worked with LeBeau nearly ten years. Bonds like that run deep, even in the world of counter intelligence where everyone's allegiance is suspect.

Grey grabbed Preston's sleeve and yanked, but kept his voice down. "You want to go to jail for the rest of your life?"

Preston frowned and shook his head.

"Go wait in the car," Grey ordered.

CHAPTER FORTY-NINE

"SO I LAID IN A HASTY OPERATION TO SNATCH DUVAL before Bonner could kill him," Sam was saying.

Noble sat across from her on a hard wooden pew. His bottom was numb. Wind moaned around the eaves of the old church and whistled through cracks in the stained-glass windows. Noble had his phone set to record and his elbows propped on his knees for support. Sam sat Indian style. She had spent the last half hour detailing her discovery of Bonner's plan: how she realized he was laying in an operation behind closed doors, got curious, dug a little deeper, then found out Duval was making a move and Bonner meant to assassinate him. She conveniently left out Duval's destination, but everything else was a blow-by-blow account of the last three days. Noble didn't need to interrupt her. She had been through the Farm and knew Company protocols for debriefing. She laid it all out, beginning to end.

Tears welled up in Sam's eyes as she finished her story and she dashed them away with an angry swipe of her hand.

"I didn't mean for Frank Bonner to get killed. Nobody was supposed to get hurt. My intent was to grab Duval and turn him over to the Company before Bonner could bury him."

Noble wanted to stop the video, put his arms around her and tell her everything was going to be alright. But that was a lie. Nothing would ever be the same again. It was unlikely any of them would make it out of this alive and if they did, Sam would spend the rest of her life in prison, or on the run, constantly looking over her shoulder.

It took everything Noble had to keep the video rolling while tears spilled down her cheeks. Her breath steamed out of her mouth, forming silver clouds. Noble's heart squeezed inside his chest and for a moment he wondered if it would keep beating or quit altogether. He motioned for her to continue.

"Official statement of field officer Samantha Gunn, Paris Branch." She rattled off her security clearance and number. She finished with, "Signing off."

Noble stopped the recording.

Sam sunk her face in her hands. "I really made a mess of things."

He scooted across the rickety pew, put an arm around her shoulders and she buried her head in his chest. They had set up in one of the side vestibules off the main sanctuary. The musty smell reminded Noble of an attic. Duval was in the small entryway, called a narthex, keeping a lookout. At least he was supposed to be keeping a lookout. He was probably fast asleep.

Noble said, "You did what you thought was right."

"Look where it got me," she spoke into his chest. Her body trembled with fear and cold. Noble wrapped her up in his arms. She grabbed hold of his coat with both hands like a drowning woman clinging to a life raft. Tears soaked through his shirt. Sobs hitched up from her throat.

Noble hugged her that much tighter. A knot formed in his throat. He sat on the cold, hard pew, knowing he needed to say something but not knowing what. It was now or never, the hardest part of this whole affair so far. He forced his mouth open. It took another second to get the syllables past the obstruction in his throat. "I'm glad."

Her sobs stopped short, like a razor slicing through silk. She looked up at him. Her eyes were rimmed with red. She sniffed. "You're glad?"

Noble hauled in a lungful of air. Now that he had got his words started, the pressure in his throat relaxed some and he was able to force more words out. "I missed you. Before all this..." He shrugged. "I thought I was never going to see you again. It didn't sit well with me. I thought we had a good thing going and then..."

Noble trailed off.

"Don't stop," Sam said.

"After Hong Kong, you dropped off the face of the earth. When you resurfaced, you were working for the Company. It was a bitter pill to swallow. In a way, I'm glad all this happened."

She tilted her face up to his. Their lips brushed together. Noble pulled her tight. He forgot all about the cold and the uncomfortable wooden pew. All he could think about was the warm press of her body against his. Their lips melted together. Her breath came out in trembling gasps. Sam straddled him, took his face in both hands, and kissed him deeply. The old pew creaked under their weight. Her body shook with barely restrained passion. Noble gathered her silky black hair in his hands, used it to pull her chin up, and trailed kisses down her neck. Sam let out a deep sigh.

Noble's body was on fire, but his mind went racing back to their first encounter. They had been alone in a hotel room, on the edge of passion, when Sam put the brakes on. It had left Noble confused and in a fair amount of pain, mental as well as physical. He found out afterwards she had a strict *no sex before marriage* policy. But right now she was caught in the grip of emotions. The situation was overriding her thinking. She rocked her hips against him, smothering him with kisses, while her fingers found their way under his shirt.

Noble put a hand on her chest and gently forced her back. His brain was telling him, *Shut up, now's not the time for talking.* But another part, the part that really cared for Sam, forced him to utter the words, "What about your commitment?"

"I need this," she whispered.

"You sure?" Noble said. "I wouldn't want..."

Sam put a finger over his lips. She shrugged out of her coat and pulled off her shirt. A simple lace bra cupped small breasts, high on her chest. Black hair fell down around bare shoulders. Noble gathered her in his arms and pressed his lips against her bare skin. Sam closed her eyes, leaned her head back and moaned. Her chest swelled. She tangled her fingers in his hair and directed his kisses.

After more than a year of fantasizing, it was finally going to happen. Noble felt the skies part and heard the Hallelujah choir. Whatever came next, they would deal with it together.

Sam was working on his zipper when Duval came stumbling around the corner, breathless and wide-eyed. "Somebody's coming," he gasped. "Somebody's coming down the..."

Sam gave a shriek, grabbed her shirt and covered her breasts with it.

Duval stopped midsentence and shuffled his feet. His eyes went from Sam to Noble. He muttered an apology, then pointed one chubby finger. "Someone's coming down the lane."

CHAPTER FIFTY

The fire drained from Noble's belly, like someone pulling the rubber stopper on a bathtub. The passion emptied out and left a sinking feeling in its place. Two years, thought Noble. For two years he had been longing after Sam. Now, when they were finally about to get together, Duval had come along and ruined the moment. Sam scrambled off his lap, shrugging into her shirt at the same time. Duval watched her dress with a leering grin.

Noble fixed Duval with an icy stare.

He apologized and pointed to the door. "Come have a look."

"There better be a tank division outside," Noble said as he passed.

Sam was one step behind. She had her weapon drawn and clouds steaming from her lips. Her toe caught on something hidden by the moth-eaten rug covering the stone floor and she stumbled. Neither Duval nor Noble noticed her near mishap. They were too busy with the visitors out front.

Sam stopped, pushed back the rug with her toe and found a rusty metal grate set in the floor. A drainage ditch ran diagonally underneath the church. Dead leaves carpeted the floor of the tunnel, giving off a musty odor. Where it came from and where it emptied out, Sam had no idea.

Noble went to the front of the church and peered out through gaps in the roughhewn planks that made up the heavy oaken doors. A middle-aged couple on bicycles was pedaling along the lane. The man wore a windbreaker and a cap. The woman had on a thick parka with her greying hair pulled up in a bun.

Noble's lips pressed together. He rounded on Duval. "Really? You think the old couple on bikes are agents?"

Duval spread his hands. "If they see us in here, they'll talk. Word will get around. This is France, not..." He waved a hand at Noble. "Texas."

"I'm from Florida."

Sam put her face to the gap. "They won't see us if we stay quiet."

"They'll see the car," Noble pointed out. He should have parked the vehicle deeper in the woods, but he wasn't planning on being here long. Much as he hated to admit it, Duval was right. The old couple was going to be a problem. Noble chewed the inside of one cheek.

"Maybe we should go," Duval suggested.

"Three of us pile into a car and take off from an abandoned church?" Sam shook her head. "That would really set them talking."

Noble said, "Go out there and try to sell the place to them."

Duval's brow wrinkled. "What are you talking about?"

"Go on out there, put a big smile on your face, and ask them if they want to buy the place. Try to sell it to them. You're a Paris businessman. The property has been in your family for generations. Now you're looking to unload it. Push them to buy."

"That's ridiculous," Duval said. "I can't sell them a church I don't own."

"They don't know that," Noble said. He clapped a hand on Duval's shoulder. "Listen to me. They're out for an afternoon bike ride in the countryside. They aren't looking to buy property. Given the state of their bicycles, they couldn't afford to buy land anyway. And no one wants to meet a pushy salesman while they're taking in the fresh air. If you try hard to sell the place, they'll turn their bikes around and leave."

Duval let out a nervous laugh. Fear gathered together on his face in a series of tight lines around his eyes. His tongue darted between his lips. "What if *they* own the land?"

"If that happens, you tug your earlobe like this." Noble pulled on his own ear to demonstrate. "Tell them you made a mistake. You're very sorry. We all get in the car and leave."

"That would look really suspicious," Duval said.

"It's not going to happen," Noble assured him. "But if it does, tug your earlobe, say you're sorry, and we leave. Understood?"

Duval whimpered. "I'm not cut out for this spy business. Why can't you do it?"

"Because my French isn't that good."

"No," Duval agreed. "It's terrible."

Noble gave him a hard look. "Time's wasting, Sacha.

Get out there and stop them before they get a good look at the car."

"Alright. I'll do it." Duval said, but he made no move toward the door.

Noble gave him a moment to collect his courage and, when it was clear Duval wasn't going outside without help, Noble pushed the door open and gave him a shove.

The couple saw him and slowed their bicycles. Duval waved an arm in the air. *"Bonjour! Comment allez-vous?"*

Noble watched him high-step over a patch of tall weeds across the yard. The couple greeted him and Duval launched into a sales pitch. Noble could barely make out the words from this distance, but Duval was selling hard. He motioned to the church and the surrounding hillsides. The older couple smiled politely and nodded along, but their feet pivoted away. People's feet always give away their intent. Want to know if someone's really listening to you or just waiting for you to stop talking so they can escape? Look at the direction their feet are pointing. If their toes point away, it's a sure sign they're searching for an excuse to leave.

"Not bad," Noble muttered. Inside of two minutes, Duval had managed to drive off their visitors. The couple shook their heads in unison, turned their bikes, and pedaled back down the lane. Duval had done a good job. Noble turned to tell Sam as much, but she was nowhere in sight.

He closed his eyes and cursed. She was probably already regretting her decision, embarrassed that she'd been caught in the back of a church with her shirt off. Had he totally blown his chance with Sam for a quickie? That thought left Noble numb and it had nothing to do with the chill leaking in through the cold stone walls.

"They're gone," Duval said as he slipped back inside and pulled the door shut. "It worked just like you said."

Noble glanced through the gaps. The couple was almost at the turnoff to the main road.

Duval shook off the cold. "Temperature's dropping. Going to be a cold night."

Noble grunted.

"Sorry about..." Duval motioned toward the pulpit. "I didn't know you two were a couple."

"Never mind that," Noble said. He pointed Duval to a rickety stool in the corner. "Let's talk about why you decided to make a run for Montenegro."

"I already told Sam." Duval lowered himself onto the seat and tucked his hands in his armpits. "They offered me immunity and it's a non-extradition country."

Noble nodded. "Yeah, I got that much. But that's not why you decided to leave the embassy."

"I don't know what you mean."

"Sure you do," Noble said. "You were safe and sound in the Ecuadorian embassy. The promise of immunity and an ocean breeze wasn't enough to coax you out of hiding. Something forced you out. What was it?"

Duval started to stammer out excuses.

Noble grabbed his collar and yanked him off the stool. "Let's get one thing straight: I'm not here for you. I'm here for Sam. Your life isn't worth a crushed cigarette butt to me. You're just another journalist who stuck his nose where it doesn't belong. Now we have the entire United States government trying to track us down. Eventually they'll find us. If I have to trade you for Sam, that's exactly what I'm gonna do. So if you want my help, you'd better come clean. Why did you leave the embassy?"

Duval lifted both hands in surrender. "You're right. I was forced out."

"Why?" Noble let go of him and said, "What forced you out, Sacha?"

He ran a trembling hand over his face. "Coughlin uncovered two of my sources and had them killed. I was next. The only thing he didn't know was the name of my failsafe."

"What failsafe?" Noble asked.

"A friend with a backup of all my files and instructions to go public if I die. That's why Coughlin didn't simply have me killed. He needed to question me first, so he laid in an operation to infiltrate the embassy and abduct me. It was called, uh... Operation MEDUSA."

CHAPTER FIFTY-ONE

Ezra and Gwen worked straight through lunch. Getting to actually enter the database mainframe was not only rare, it was time consuming. First there was paperwork to fill out, then they'd both been required to don bright yellow space suits, hoodies, goggles, gloves, and booties. They looked like members of a hazmat team responding to a spill.

The seven Cray-2 supercomputers (nicknamed the Seven Dwarves) were housed inside an air-controlled vault with low ceilings, bare floors to reduce static electrical discharge, and optically enhanced florescent bulbs to prevent circuit degradation. The result was a blue cave the length of a football field with seven onyx obelisks covered in blinking lights that looked like something out of 2001: A Space Odyssey.

Once inside, Ezra and Gwen went to work inspecting one of the dwarves. The tower emitted low buzzing tones as random-access memory communicated with solid state hard drives, sending information racing back to the computer terminals in the floors above. The air smelled thin and recycled. Ezra thought this must be what it felt like to work in outer space. He pictured himself as Dave, doing battle with HAL for control of the spaceship.

The delicate nature of the equipment made speed impossible. They opened the tower, took careful notes on wiring, circuitry, and hard drive components, then debated the best way to attach a small thumb drive relay. In truth, neither was eager to leave. This was a rare look inside highly classified government hardware that collected and collated trillions of minute pieces of information captured by the CIA and other intelligence agencies. They felt like kids in a candy store. When they had pushed the time as long as they could without raising suspicion, Ezra ported the thumb drive, closed up the tower, and they passed back through the static control room where they shed the space suits.

Ezra's stomach growled as they rode the elevator back to their desks, but food was the last thing on his mind. Gwen stood at his shoulder, fingers rapidly drumming her thighs. When the elevator stopped on B3, they both hurried to their cubicle.

All it took was a few key strokes. A smile crept over Ezra's face. Gwen pushed her glasses up the bridge of her nose and pinched her bottom lip in nervous excitement. She whispered, "It worked."

"Of course it worked," Ezra said, trying to sound more confident than he felt. The backdoor relay fed them real-time information on the database firewall algorithms designed to keep out hackers. They studied the information scrolling across the screen for several minutes and then said in unison, "It's changing!"

"That's why we couldn't get in," Gwen said. "The algorithm is constantly changing. Anyone who wanted to break in would have to know the pattern and timing."

"Which we now know," Ezra pointed out.

"Coughlin wanted to know if it could be done," Gwen said. "I don't think anyone in the world could break that cipher. Should we tell him it's impossible?"

"And stop now?" Ezra turned to her. "We've got an open door."

"But like you said, unless someone knew the exact algorithms and when the code changes, they could never get in."

Ezra grinned. "You and I both know we're going to break in anyway. Besides, how do we know that nobody else knows?"

"They'd need to actually enter the mainframe."

"We did it," Ezra said.

"We work here."

"Come on," Ezra urged. "We would be the only two people in the history of the Company who ever cracked the code."

An awkward smile crept over her face. "Okay."

"What was the operation name?"

Gwen searched her work station, found a yellow legal pad and said, "MEDUSA."

Ezra searched the records, located the files, then jabbed a finger at Gwen's monitor. "Should be coming up on your desktop."

"Bingo," she said.

Ezra glanced briefly at the files in question. At least a

dozen side operations were associated with the main objective and showed pages of material. They had really gone all out creating the dummy op. He quickly rooted through the directory, tagging everything he wanted removed.

"Um..." Gwen said from behind him. She pushed her glasses up the bridge of her nose and squinted at her own computer where she had one of the files open. "Did we get the right operation name?"

"You wrote it down," Ezra said over his shoulder.

"This looks like a real op."

Ezra shrugged. "They probably wanted to make it look legit."

"Wait," Gwen said.

Ezra's finger hovered over the delete key.

"Oh my god," said Gwen.

Ezra spun his chair around. "What are you on about?"

"Can't you read?" Gwen pointed. "This is a plan to infiltrate the Ecuadorian embassy in London and abduct Sacha Duval. They plan on taking him to a black site and torturing him for information before they kill him."

Ezra leaned forward. His eyes leapt back and forth as he read. The first nervous flutter turned his guts runny. Goosebumps broke out on his forearms. He shook his head. "They probably just wanted to give the file some authenticity. Maybe it's part of a war game operation? You know how Company trainers work. They're always going for hyper-realism."

"Come on. You don't really believe that?" Gwen scrolled through several of the other associated operations and their after-action reports. The Company had been watching two individuals who were suspected of passing information to Cypher Punk. A quick web search was enough to confirm that both were dead and their homicides unsolved. "They've already killed two other people with suspected ties to Cypher Punk."

Ezra licked his lips. "Coughlin never said to read the files. He just said to delete them."

"They're planning to kill Sacha Duval," Gwen said. "Cypher Punk is a hero. He exposes government corruption."

"I think treasonous is the word you're looking for," Ezra said.

"We can't let them kill him."

Ezra said, "What do you want to do?"

"Maybe we should go to someone higher up?"

"Who?" Ezra asked. "Coughlin runs Operations. He reports directly to Armstrong."

"Maybe we should be talking to the Director."

Ezra snorted a laugh. "Sure."

Gwen's lips pressed together.

"You're serious?"

She shrugged.

Ezra held up a hand. "Alright, let's say, for the sake of argument, this is some complicated conspiracy and Coughlin is bent. You want to go to Armstrong? How do you know she isn't part of it?"

"Have you got a better idea?"

Ezra dropped his voice to an urgent whisper. "You don't just walk up and knock on the Director's door."

"You don't think I know that?"

"I think we should follow orders," Ezra said. "You really want to go back to debugging code?"

Gwen deflated some. She sank back into her seat and stared hard at the worn carpet. "But what if?"

Ezra groaned. His eyes went to the screen where a black and white picture of Sacha Duval stared back at him. "I admit it sounds like a Watergate scandal, but there's no way of knowing who's in on this. We go asking too many questions and we might be the next unsolved homicides."

Gwen glanced around the sea of computer terminals on B3 to see if anyone was watching, then she reached for a thumb drive on her desk and cocked an eyebrow in question.

Ezra set his teeth together and let out air. He sounded like a tire that had sprung a leak. Trying not to move his lips, he said, "You're treading dangerous ground."

"Is that a yes?"

Through gritted teeth he said, "Yes."

She slotted the USB drive into her machine and quickly copied everything associated with Operation MEDUSA.

CHAPTER FIFTY-TWO

A HOWLING WIND WHISTLED AROUND THE EAVES OF the old church. Noble crossed his arms over his chest and put his back to the wall. His toes felt like blocks of ice inside his shoes. Humans can die of exposure in temperatures as high as fifty degrees Fahrenheit, and it had to be twenty degrees colder. At least they were out of the wind, Noble told himself. He made a rewinding motion with his hand and said, "Alright, back up. Why would Coughlin want you dead?"

"He's not the only one." Duval cupped his hands together and blew into his palms. "Frank Bonner and Grey, they were all part of it."

"A part of what?" Noble asked.

"Several years ago, the CIA's Center for Cyber Intelligence Division created a highly classified program called CyberLance."

"Sounds like something out of a William Gibson novel," Noble remarked.

"I wish," Duval said. "CyberLance is the tip of the CIA's hacking arsenal. It allows the CIA to break into virtually any system on the planet and leave behind a digital footprint that points back to a separate entity."

"What's that mean in English?" Noble asked.

"It means they can use it to spy on anyone in the world and point the finger at someone else. They could hack into the Chinese defense system, melt down a nuclear reactor, and blame it on the North Koreans. Or plant evidence on the laptop of a Fortune 500 CEO that ties him to Russian organized crime. The sky is the limit."

Noble nodded. It didn't take much imagination to see how powerful CyberLance was when used as a weapon. He said, "What's any of this got to do with you?"

"Nine months ago, someone stole the majority of the CIA's weaponized cyber arsenal, including the CyberLance program."

Noble let out a low whistle. "Any idea who made off with the files?"

"Coughlin," Duval said. "He and Bonner were going into business for themselves. With a copy of CyberLance they could sell their services to the highest bidder. Need to sabotage a business rival's manufacturing plant and make it look like it was a simple technical glitch? They can do it. Need to accuse your political rival of interfering in the election? They can make it happen."

"How do Grey and his team fit in?" Noble asked.

Duval said, "In order for the program to work, you need ground access."

"And they're the CIA's best covert entry team," Noble said. He used the door frame to scratch an itch between his shoulder blades. "That's a pretty tall claim. I assume you have proof?"

"I've got everything," Duval told him. "Names, dates, dollar figures, and the accounts where the money went. It's scheduled to release with the next Cypher Punk vault."

"How do you know all this?" Noble asked.

"I have sources inside the CIA," Duval told him. "That's how I found out Coughlin was planning to abduct me from the embassy. He knew it was only a matter of time before I released Vault 7 and blew the lid on his operation. He had to shut me up. He called it Operation MEDUSA. A Special Operations Group would infiltrate the embassy at night, take me out by force, and deliver me to a black site where Bonner could force me to give up the name of my failsafe. That's when I decided to make a run for Montenegro. I tried to keep it quiet. I used back channels, but they must have someone inside the embassy."

"They did," Sam said, walking back into the narthex. She had her jacket on and her hair pulled up in a ponytail. "The secretary you used at the embassy was on Bonner's payroll. She made a copy of every document you gave her."

Duval's brow wrinkled. The hurt was plain on his face.

Sam said, "She fled a money laundering indictment in the Netherlands. Bonner found out about it and used it as leverage."

"Way to check your sources," Noble said.

Sam elbowed him in the ribs. "Don't be mean."

"If it weren't for him, we wouldn't be in this mess." Noble gestured to Duval. "This fop leaked classified American intelligence and put a lot of good field officers in danger."

"Okay, granted," Sam said. "But that's no reason to be rude."

"No reason to be rude? He committed *treason*. He deserves to be executed."

She pulled her gun and held it out to Noble. "Go ahead, then. You want to do it? Or should I?"

Noble made an effort to soften his voice. "Okay, that was out of line, but what he did is still illegal."

"I'm not defending him." Sam tucked the gun in her waistband. "Yes, he committed a crime, but he deserves a fair trial. Not a bullet to the back of the head."

Duval stood up so fast he turned over the stool. "Listen to yourselves! I expose government corruption at the highest levels on both sides of the aisle. Instead of hunting me down, you should be thanking me."

Noble resisted the urge to punch him in the mouth. "Americans have a right know what goes on in our government. I won't argue that. Government corruption should be exposed and the people responsible punished. But the way you went about exposing the corruption was wrong. Innocent people lost their lives. You got a lot of people killed. Did you ever stop to think about that?"

Duval groped for the overturned stool, set it right, and sat down again. He was quiet for a while, staring at the ground between his feet. Finally he said, "I never meant for anybody to get hurt. I didn't know what else to do. I thought once I released the information, the world would demand justice and the people responsible would be brought to heel. Instead the world went on like it never happened. Most people don't even care."

"You nailed it with that last statement," Noble said.

"You're one to talk," Duval said.

Noble fixed him with a hard stare. "What's that mean?"

"Don't pretend," Duval said.

Noble pushed off the beam and uncrossed his arms. "What are you talking about?"

"You said yourself you aren't here for me and you don't care about the truth." Duval thrust his chin at Samantha. "You're here for her."

Noble never took his eyes off Duval, but he could feel Sam watching him and his ears burned.

Duval shrugged. "I'm just baggage. No need to burden yourselves with me. You're both spies. You can disappear. No one will ever see you again. Go on." He waved a hand at the door. "Go. I'll get by on my own."

Noble snorted. "You wouldn't make it to the end of the drive."

"Maybe I'll stay right here," Duval muttered. "Start a vineyard."

His shoulders slumped and his chin sank into his parka.

Noble held up both hands. "Alright. Relax. No one is abandoning you."

Duval looked up, like a puppy that hears a key in the lock. It was sad and endearing all at the same time. Noble thought of Shawn Hennessey and all the rest of the sad saps just smart enough to get themselves into trouble but not strong enough to protect themselves. He went to the door and peered out through the gaps before anyone saw the emotion on his face.

Emotions are the enemy, every bit as deadly as a bullet. Torres got himself killed when he let emotions get the better of him. Noble set his jaw and mentally boxed up all that sentimental bull. It wouldn't help him get the job done. Sam was in a world of trouble and the only way to help her was to help Duval.

He felt a hand on his shoulder, turned, and found Sam at his side. She silently implored him with big dark eyes.

Noble cracked a grin. "Alright, doll. Turn off the doe eyes."

To Duval he said, "I'll help, but we have to be smart about this. Making a mad dash for the border is exactly what they expect."

Sam tried and failed to hide a smile. She grabbed his collars, planted a quick kiss on his lips and pulled back beaming. "What's the plan?"

"First, we need to buy ourselves some time to think," Noble said.

Duval snorted. "Where do you buy that?"

"Hardware store."

CHAPTER FIFTY-THREE

Matthew Burke sat in a rolling chair, watching live feed from drones circling France at twenty-thousand feet. Modern surveillance was a wonderful thing, especially in places like central Europe where cameras record every major intersection in metropolitan areas. Electronic eyes capture footage twenty-four hours a day, seven days a week, and store it in government databases. It makes tracking fugitives painless and easy. Unless your target leaves the city for the countryside, where the only cameras are at gas stations and those usually back up to on-site computers.

After the tip about a carjacking in the tunnel, the team had done a marvelous job of tracking Noble's movements, until he turned down a hard-packed lane running through a picturesque countryside of quaint cottages and rolling fields. That had been four hours ago.

Coughlin paced like a caged lion, barking orders and demanding to know where Noble had gone. Why weren't they making any progress? His face twitched and his fingers clutched at the air. Damp circles formed under his arms. He kept tugging his tie until it resembled a noose hanging around his shoulders. He was on the other side of the situation room, haranguing a pretty young data expert when Dana leaned close to Burke and whispered, "He's starting to scare me."

Keeping his voice low, Burke said, "Let him rant and rave. It's not getting him anywhere."

Dana stood up and stretched.

Burke watched the lines of her body. Her breasts strained against a silk blouse and her skirt stretched tight across her hips. Several of the men near the back of the room stole glances. She was a showstopper alright but, tired as he was, Burke couldn't bring himself to appreciate the view. Given the choice between sex and a nap, at the moment, he'd choose the nap.

She came out of the stretch and asked, "Need anything?"

Burke consulted his watch. "The last forty-eight hours of my life back."

"So coffee?" Dana quipped.

"Extra cream and sugar."

"Splenda," she said before walking out the door.

Coughlin stomped past, headed for the other side of the room to harass someone else, and muttered, "Bet you're real happy, Burke."

"What have I got to be happy about?"

Coughlin stopped. His face twitched and jerked. He looked like the guy on the bus that you try to avoid. "Your buddy managed to give us the slip and helped an international fugitive escape justice."

Burke shrugged his massive shoulders. "Coughlin, I'll be happy when this is over and I can crawl into my bed."

Coughlin planted his hands on his hips and shook his head. "One of these days you're going to slip up, Burke. I hope I'm around to see it."

One of the IMINT specialists called out, "I think I've got something."

"Let's see it." Coughlin said.

A fresh wave of panic swirled in Burke's gut like cheap liquor drunk too fast. He sat up and his brows pinched.

A black and white video showed the stolen Peugeot pull into the parking spot of a store. A tall man with rebelliously long hair climbed out. He kept his face turned away from the camera, but there was no mistaking that silhouette.

"That's him," Coughlin said in a voice raw with emotion and shot full of venom. "Where is this?"

The analyst consulted his computer and said, "A retail store on the outskirts of Vesoul, 11 Rue des Saules. The store is called Pro'Bois Tout Faire Bois."

"In English," Coughlin said.

Someone else said, "It's a hardware store, sir."

"What the hell is he doing?" Coughing muttered.

Noble went inside. He was gone thirty minutes and when he came out again he was carrying a shopping bag and a coil of rope. He looked directly into the camera on his way to the car. The image specialist froze the picture. "Seventy-eight percent match," he said. "The hair makes it difficult to get good anchor points."

"That's him," Coughlin said. "How long ago was this?"

The young man consulted his computer. "Less than ten minutes."

Coughlin came to life like he'd had a shot of adrenalin straight to the heart. "I want all three birds rerouted to that location. Get me everything we can on the area. Gunn and Duval are probably held up somewhere close by. Did he pay cash or credit?"

"Cash," one of the techs reported.

Coughlin cursed. "Can anybody tell me what he bought?"

"Forty-foot length of rope and two packages of plastic BIC lighters," came the response. Image Specialists are experts at determining an object by the size, shape, and weight of the package. During the Cold War, they could look at satellite photos of crates arriving at Russian harbors and tell you if a shipment to the Kremlin hid vodka or the latest audio-video technology.

"You're sure?" Coughlin asked.

The specialist nodded. "Ordinary BIC lighters. Two packs of six. Assortment of colors. Retail price stateside, six ninety-nine."

"How do you know that?"

In answer, the specialist reached into his shirt pocket and produced an orange BIC.

Coughlin turned to Burke. "Is Noble a smoker?"

Burke shook his head. "Not unless he picked it up recently."

"What's he up to?" Coughlin wondered out loud.

"Something's not right," Burke told him.

"What do you mean?"

Burke motioned to the black and white still of Noble on the screen. "He looked right into the camera. He *wants* to be found."

"Or he slipped up," Coughlin said. "Maybe he's getting tired."

"Noble doesn't make mistakes like that." Burke said. He suspected Jake was about to pull a Houdini—intentionally allow himself to be tracked and caught only to disappear again, throwing off pursuit. Burke also knew that trying to warn Coughlin off would only make him more determined. Burke said, "He's playing you, Coughlin. He wants you to chase him."

Coughlin snorted. "Spare me the bull crap, Burke. I'm not buying."

Burke raised his hands in surrender.

Coughlin coordinated the search. The room was a flurry of activity. Within minutes a drone was tracking the Peugeot as it rolled east over a dirt road that wound through rolling hills surrounded by small vineyards. A plume of dust followed the toy-sized car on the monitor screen. Coughlin took out his cellphone and called Grey. "We've got eyes on target."

CHAPTER FIFTY-FOUR

"What do we do with it now?" Gwen wanted to know. She had the thumb drive in the palm of her hand, holding it out for Ezra's inspection like it was an archeological artifact of significant importance. A cursory read-through of the files was enough to convince Ezra that she was right: those weren't dummy operations planted for the sake of an exercise in cyber security. Dark things were hidden in those files, things Ezra wished for all the world he could un-see. Something sinister was going on and Ezra didn't want to know or be forced to do anything about it.

Gwen lowered her voice. "We can't get it out of the building."

"We could bury the files in a photo and upload the photo to one of our phones," Ezra suggested.

Gwen closed her fingers around the thumb drive and glanced around to see if anyone had heard that last remark. "Are you crazy? That's espionage. We'd go to jail for life!"

"What do you want to do?"

"I still think we should go to the Director."

"And say what?"

Gwen shrugged. "Show her the files and tell her exactly what happened."

"What if we're wrong?" Ezra said.

"What if we're *right*?" Gwen countered.

"You don't just walk in to see the Director," Ezra said.

Gwen pressed her lips together.

Ezra held up a hand in surrender. "Alright."

He reached for the secure phone on his desk. He had never had to call the Director of the CIA before. He said, "I don't even know the extension. Do you?"

"It's in the binder."

He took out the Interoffice Communications Binder and opened it to the first page. "Here it is. Right below the Director of National Intelligence. Sure you don't want to call him instead? I got the Director of National Security here too."

Gwen narrowed her eyes. "Don't be a wisenheimer."

Ezra punched the number and waited. A tight knuckle of fear formed in his chest. Could he get in trouble just for calling the Director of the CIA? He listened to the line ring and imagined himself getting told off for breaking protocol.

"DCI's office."

The voice was older and female. Ezra's thick brow bunched over his nose. Did the new Director pick up her own phone, he wondered? He cleared his throat. "Uh... Is this the Director?"

"This is her secretary. To whom am I speaking?" The tones were clipped and sharp, like a librarian with no patience for people who don't understand how the Dewey Decimal system works.

"Er, Ezra Cook. I need to speak to the Director."

"What department are you with?"

Ezra considered how to answer that. Coughlin had never said what department they were officially attached to. "I work on B3 for acting DDO Coughlin and there's... uh... something I think the Director needs to know about. Can I please talk with her?" After a moment Ezra added, "If she's not busy."

Gwen gave a thumbs-up.

"What's your clearance and priority level?"

Ezra's eyes got big. Words failed him. His tongue stuck to the roof of his mouth.

"Clearance and priority level, please."

He unstuck his tongue and said, "I don't have a clearance level to speak with the Director. I'm a computer tech. And I... well, actually, *we*..."

Gwen nodded.

"We came across something in the database the Director probably ought to have a look at. It might be something. It might be nothing. I'm not really sure. Is this a bad time? I could call back."

The elevator dinged and the sound caught Gwen's attention. Her head swiveled in that direction, then she kicked Ezra hard in the shin.

He winced and shot her a fiery look. "Whaddya go kicking me for?"

Gwen hissed. "Coughlin."

Ezra hung up the phone and forced a smile onto his face as Coughlin approached. The acting DDO looked like he was barely holding it together. The bags under his eyes were darker and his armpits were damp. His face fired in a non-stop series of spastic ticks. He thrust his chin at the phone. "Who were you calling?"

"My mother." Ezra immediately regretted the lie. It was a flimsy excuse, but the only thing he could think of under the circumstances. To sell the lie, he added, "She's sick."

Gwen put her hand in her coat pocket and kept it there.

Coughlin stared at them for several seconds then said, "Have you made any progress?"

Gwen and Ezra exchanged a look.

"Well," Ezra said, drawing out the word.

"We've made some progress," Gwen jumped in. "It's a pretty complicated system."

"You said if you could get into the mainframe you could crack the system," Coughlin said. "I got you clearance to enter the mainframe. Now did you crack the system or not?"

Ezra hesitated entirely too long. He felt like there was a fire under his seat, cooking his bottom. "Yeah, we cracked it."

"And?" Coughlin demanded.

"And we're hunting up the files right now," Gwen filled in.

"What are you waiting for?" Coughlin asked.

"Nothing," both programmers said at once.

Ezra turned to his terminal, brought up the operation reports and clicked delete. With backdoor access, he didn't need clearance to alter files or delete them entirely and no one would ever know. Just like that, it was done. No fanfare, no alarm bells. The file simply ceased to exist. Except for the copy in Gwen's pocket.

Coughlin nodded to himself, satisfied. Then he turned and started back toward the elevator.

"Um..." Ezra said. "Excuse me, sir?"

"What?" Coughlin stopped and turned back.

Ezra motioned to himself and Gwen. "What should we be doing now?"

Coughlin's forehead creased like he wasn't sure what language they were speaking.

Gwen said, "What do you want us working on, sir?"

Coughlin put his hands on his hips and considered them with cold, dispassionate eyes. *Did he know?* Ezra wondered. His face was a twitching mask of unhinged lunacy, but his eyes were hard. They hid something nasty, Ezra was sure of it.

Finally, Coughlin said, "Go back to what you were doing before and I'll be in touch."

When he was gone, Gwen punched Ezra on the arm.

"Ow!" He rubbed his bicep.

"Your mother?"

"It was the only thing I could think of," Ezra said.

"On a secure interoffice line?" She motioned to the handset. "Now he knows something is wrong."

CHAPTER FIFTY-FIVE

THE SILVER AUDI RUMBLED OVER THE HARD-PACKED lane and braked at the turn-off to the abandoned church. A hundred meters of open ground, dotted with naked trees, separated the car from the grim stone edifice. The sun had gone down, leeching the last of the warmth from the frozen hills surrounding Vesoul. Large white flakes swirled down out of the black vault of the sky and settled noiselessly on the ground before melting.

Grey was behind the wheel. Warm air poured from the vents and fogged up the windows. Preston sat in the passenger seat, wrapping his blistered hand in a fresh white bandage. The wound had begun to ooze a foul-smelling puss. Grey said, "You going to be able to shoot with that hand?"

Preston frowned. "Have I got a choice?"

"No," Grey said, "I guess not. When this is over, we'll get you to a hospital."

"When this is over, I'm disappearing," Preston told him. "I've got enough to live on. I'm going someplace warm and spending the rest of my life drinking piña coladas." He peered through the falling snow at the church. "I don't see the Peugeot."

"Probably stashed it in the woods," Grey said.

"Lot of open ground to cover."

"Yeah," Grey agreed.

"Probably knows we're coming," Preston remarked.

"Don't lose your nerve."

"This guy was a Green Beret," Preston pointed out. "We should have a dozen guys for this job."

"Yeah, that would look real good on the video feed back at Langley. Besides," Grey reached into the backseat for a pair of fully automatic MP5 Heckler & Koch submachine guns. "Noble hasn't got one of these."

He passed one to Preston, along with a pair of thirty-round magazines, and said, "We kill the Green Beret and Gunn, torture Duval, and find out the name of his failsafe. Then tell Langley nobody survived. That'll be the end of it. The new Director will be pissed, but what can she do?"

Preston jacked a magazine into the little automatic and slaped down on the charging knob. The bolt shot forward with a hard *clack*. He didn't look happy about walking into a firefight with Noble. Fear crept onto his face but he said, "Let's just get it done."

Grey cranked open the driver side door and a breath of cold air hit him. Spots of color appeared in his cheeks. The temperature had plummeted. Snowflakes lighted on his head and shoulders as he climbed out. Cold seeped through his coat and into his bones. Silver clouds rose like ghosts from his open mouth. Preston glanced at him over the roof of the car and Grey nodded. They started across the long stretch of open ground.

CHAPTER FIFTY-SIX

SAM'S FINGERS WERE PINS AND NEEDLES. SHE STOOD with one shoulder against the stone jamb, watching snow drift down through cracks in the weathered timbers of the door. She could see a large, skeletal oak ten yards away, but the road was lost from view. The night was preternaturally still and sound travelled in the quiet. Noble was in the nave, working on his science project. When he finished, he had several meters of rope doused in lighter fluid, wrapped around brightly colored BICs.

Sam kept her attention focused on the yard, but her lips remembered his kisses and she could still feel his eager hands on her skin. The memory kept her warm in the gathering cold and set her heart galloping. A pleasant fire formed in her belly at the thought of Jake holding her tight. Sam chewed her bottom lip. She wanted him with a longing that was close to a physical ache, making it hard to focus on anything else. The thought was almost enough to make her forget about the world of trouble she was in. If she lived—

and that was a big if—she would spend the rest of her life in hiding. Was one night with Jake too much to ask?

She silently cursed Duval. If not for his whistleblowing, none of this ever would have happened. Sam wished she had turned a blind eye Bonner's operation, and then immediately regretted the thought. Duval was a little man with a coward's heart who had tried to do the right thing. He had broken a string of international laws along the way, but his intentions were noble.

Jake appeared at her side without warning. One minute she was alone, the next he was standing there next to her, peering through gaps in the boards. Sam started and put a hand to her chest. "How do you do that?"

"Do what?"

She opened her mouth, about to say he had snuck up on her, and thought better of it. Instead she said, "All set?"

He nodded and held up the length of rope. It looked like a long string of Christmas lights with BICs instead of colored bulbs and gave off the stench of lighter fluid. Noble strung the concoction across the narthex, in front of the door, and under the stained-glass windows.

"I never thanked you," he said.

Sam's brow pinched. "For what?"

"Mexico," he said. "You saved my life."

"I don't think Hunt would have really killed you," she said, but the words sounded false, even to her ears. She glanced at him from the corner of her eye. He was at the door, peering into the dark. A narrow shaft of starlight illuminated his profile. Sam said, "He still has a limp from the shrapnel. Blames you, by the way."

Noble chuckled. "I don't know what you see in that guy."

"Is that jealousy I hear?"

"No," he said. After a few seconds he added, "Yeah. Maybe. A little."

"If it makes you feel any better, I'm through with him."

"Finally figured him out, huh?"

"Let's just say I got a peek behind the curtain."

After Mexico, Sam had seen the real Gregory Hunt. Anger and jealousy were eating him up. When Foster took a tumble, Hunt's rising star had fallen back to earth fast. He was cleared of any intentional wrong doing, but his all-star status with the Company was shot. He spent his days riding a desk. His nights were spent chasing skirts and boozing. He resented Noble and resented Sam because of Noble. Things between Sam and Hunt had finally ended in a crazy screaming match.

One setback had been enough to derail Hunt's entire life. Sam doubted if he would ever find his footing again. Noble, on the other hand, had lost his career with the CIA, lost his home, was saddled with his mother's medical debt, and he just kept on dealing. He put out life's fires one at a time with the same quiet efficiency he did everything else.

A wave of bitter regret gripped Sam. She realized she had bet on the wrong horse. Hunt was a boy, obsessed with status and prestige. Noble was a man. He wasn't the most eloquent man in a room, probably never would be. Sam never expected him to quote Baudelaire, but you could count on him when the chips were down. And right now, every chip Sam had was on the table.

Jake's mouth twisted into a frown. "Just as well. You deserve better."

A tight knot of nervous tension formed in her chest. She tucked a loose stand of hair behind one ear. "Maybe you want to pick up where we left off?"

"Can't right now," Noble said.

She blinked and cleared an obstruction in her throat. "Are you seeing someone?"

"Yeah," he whispered.

Sam felt the earth beneath her feet crack and fall away. In some secret corner of her heart, she had thought Noble was a sure thing, someone she could keep on the back burner in case the stable guys with the good careers didn't work out. Now he was gone, slipped through her fingers. She had waited too long.

"Oh. I see," she said. "Well, she's a really lucky girl."

Noble turned to her in the dark. His brow wrinkled in confusion then he shook his head. "No, I meant I see someone out there." He motioned to a gap in the planks. "They're here."

"What?" She stuck her face to the boards and peered out into the gloom, using her peripheral vision to scan for movement. The human eye has two different kinds of receptors; cones in the center of the pupil detect color, and rods on the outside of the pupil detect shape and movement. Rods make it possible to detect a black cat at night from the corner of your eye, but cones make it disappear when you look directly at it. Sam said, "I don't see any..."

A dark figure detached itself from the deeper black and moved in a crouch with a machine pistol clutched in both hands. A moment later she spied a second figure moving across the field. They were keeping plenty of space in between them.

"Wait," Sam said. "I see them. Going to be hard to hit anything in the dark."

Her knees felt like runny eggs. Despite popular Hollywood portrayals, the CIA doesn't train their people for open conflict. The Farm teaches recruits basic weapon skills and hand-to-hand combat for emergencies, but the focus of spy training centers on espionage skills. When they need guys with combat training, they recruit soldiers from Special Forces, guys like Noble. Sam slipped her gun from her waistband, cradled the weapon in both hands and concentrated on controlling her breathing.

"Noble?" she said.

"Yeah?"

"Don't kill them if you don't have to."

He hesitated a moment, then nodded. "It's so dark out here I probably can't hit anything anyway." He took a step back from the wall, pushed his Kimber straight out in front of him, and aimed through a split in the boards. "Ready?"

Sam sighted on the indistinct shape of a man moving in the darkness. The two figures were less than twenty meters away now. Their feet made soft shuffling noises in the dead grass. Sam slipped her finger into the trigger guard and said, "Ready."

"Now."

CHAPTER FIFTY-SEVEN

Grey stopped twenty meters from the darkened church and took a knee. Instinct screamed a warning to his brain. The night was eerily quiet and the cathedral squatted in the dark like a grim stone monolith, glowering at him with blank eyes. Stone walls and thick stained glass made it a perfect defensive position. Noble would have the front door guarded. It was the only weakness. The boards were warped and the metal bands were caked with rust. The rivets looked like bloated boils. Either Noble or Sam, maybe both, waited on the other side. Grey waved until he got Preston's attention.

Crouching with the H&K stuck out in front of him, Preston acknowledged Grey with a quick shrug.

Grey cradled his submachine gun in the crook of his left arm, pointed to Preston, and then signaled for him to circle around the building. Preston gave the thumb and forefinger for *Okay*. He turned and started around the side of the church, giving the front door a wide berth. There was bound to be a rear exit, and Grey wanted to be sure Noble didn't slip out the back while they were coming in the front.

They should have a dozen guys to cover the church from every angle but that wasn't an option. Things were happening too fast and by the time they rounded up a crew, Noble would disappear again. Like it or not, Grey had to make do with just himself and Preston.

Keep your eye on the prize, Grey told himself. Stop Duval and his confederates from opening the next Cypher Punk vault or go to jail for life. Grey had over three million dollars sitting in an account in the Cayman Islands and a house on the beach. He wasn't about to watch it all go up in smoke. He should have cut ties with Coughlin and Bonner after the first million, but there was always more money to be made. At least a dozen times, Grey had told himself he would do one more job. But one job lead to the next. Now he was stuck cleaning up Coughlin's mess. *Find out the name of Duval's failsafe and then you can quit,* thought Grey. *Buy a new identity and head to South America.*

He rose to a crouch and started for the corner of the building. He hadn't gone two steps when the bullwhip crack of a gunshot shattered the silence. Grey saw the flash and heard a lead slug burn past his shoulder. His heart leapt up inside his chest and started to dance.

Twenty meters on his right, Preston threw himself to the ground and mashed the trigger. The night came alive with the sound of small arms fire. Bullets hissed and snapped. Preston triggered his weapon with wild abandon, shooting at the front of the dilapidated cathedral. Tongues of fire leap from his muzzle. Empty brass spun through the air. Bullets whined off stone and hammered holes in the stained glass.

Grey sighted on the front door and squeezed. The little automatic spit a stream of bullets. Warped timbers splintered under the impact. He held the trigger down until the bolt fell on an empty chamber with a muted *clack*, dropped the spent magazine, and dug a fresh one from his pocket.

Every farmhouse for two miles must have heard the shots and be dialing the police right now, thought Grey. He rocked the new magazine into his H&K, chambered a round, and sighted on the front of the church.

———

Inside the narthex, Noble had fired two quick rounds and then put his back to the wall. Grey and Preston responded with a full auto barrage. Heavy led slugs drilled through the rotting door and ricocheted off the walls. A round snapped against the stone over Noble's shoulder and set his ears ringing. He turned his face away and grimaced. What he wouldn't give for a pair of earplugs right now. *An AR15 and a bulletproof vest would be even better.*

Sam was on the opposite side of the door with her back to the wall. She narrowed her eyes against the onslaught. Her brow pinched and her lips pressed into a thin line. Strands of silky black hair fell across her face. Noble waited for a lull in the action and then gave her the signal to move. She nodded, took a breath and then sprinted toward the opening to the nave.

Noble covered her movement with three shots. He wasn't aiming, just firing blind. His instructors at Fort Bragg would have recoiled at the idea of undirected fire—never shoot at a target you can't see—but desperate times call for desperate measures. It was a waste of ammo, but got a response. Another long peal of automatic fire punished the front of the church, chipping away at the stonework and turning the door into kindling.

Noble tucked the gun in his armpit. It was like ramming a hot curling iron under his arm. Ignoring the searing pain, he crouched down and dug a BIC from his pocket. It took him three tries to get a flame. He touched the fire to the frayed end of the rope and ghostly blue waves raced along the cord, engulfed the first of the lighters and started to melt the plastic. The orange body bubbled and warped, blackening around the edges. Noble sprinted from the narthex before the first sharp *pop*.

Grey and Preston answered with a deadly burst. From outside, it was hard to tell the difference between an exploding lighter and a gunshot. As the fire engulfed the rope, melting another lighter every few inches, it added to the din. The end of the rope was stuffed inside a half-full gas can that would create a nice big bang. A stray bullet blew a chunk out of a stained-glass window and hissed over Noble's head.

He pulled his shoulders up around his ears and yelled to be heard over the constant barrage. "Time to go!"

Sam dropped down through the open drainage ditch, ducked her head and disappeared into the dark, scrambling on hands and knees along the tunnel. Noble hopped in after her and pulled the heavy steel grate into place. Damp leaves mushed under his hands and feet.

———

Grey sprinted to a scrawny tree and put his shoulder against it. As far as cover went, it was lousy, but it made him feel safer. Either his mind was playing tricks on him, or that last shot had been from a .22 caliber with a reduced load. It sounded too soft and high pitched. But it got a reaction. Preston hammered the front of the church with another long barrage. Every shot was a bullet that might accidentally kill the French journalist.

"Hold your fire!" Grey yelled.

Preston kept squeezing off rounds, sending lances of pain through Grey's ears and into his brain. By the time he made himself heard, a flicker of orange fire was crawling up one corner of the door. Grey cursed. They had managed to set the place on fire. Another sharp crack made him flinch. This time he was sure of it. *That was no gunshot.* Sounded more like a firecracker. Noble had rigged a distraction to keep them busy.

Grey called out, "Preston! I'll circle round back. You go in the front."

A sharp pop brought their shoulders up around their ears.

When Preston didn't move, Grey shouted, "Now!"

Preston popped up off the lawn and sprinted toward the double doors. Grey hustled toward the side yard with his gun leading the way. He was expecting Duval to emerge from the back of the church, trying to sneak away under the cover of darkness. Two more sharp pops like fireworks went off, followed by a rending explosion that shook the ground under Grey's feet. An orange fireball blew out the windows and sent chunks of stained glass sailing through the air.

Noble followed Sam along the low drainage tunnel. She was just a shadow in the deeper darkness up ahead. Damp soaked through the knees of Noble's denims. His hands squished in cold mud and soggy leaves. In his hurry, he got distracted, cracked his head a good one against the curved roof and cursed.

"You okay?" Sam hollered back. Her voice echoed in the enclosed space.

"I'm good," he assured her. "Keep moving."

They hadn't gone far when the gas can ignited. The deafening *whomp* sucked all the air from Noble's lungs and he had to stop. Hearing was gone, replaced by a high-pitched dial tone. Briefly, he wondered what kind of long-term damage this was doing to his ears. He would probably be deaf when he got older, but that was a small price to pay. He got his hands and feet moving again and ran into Sam's bottom. He reached forward and gave her a push.

The crawlspace emptied into a shallow drainage ditch running through the woods in back of the cathedral. Noble scrambled over a bed of sharp rocks, scraping his knees in the process. Sam helped him to his feet. He stood with his hands on his thighs, breathing heavy. Sam pushed a tangle of damp hair away from her forehead, smearing dirt on her brow in the process. "We have to keep moving."

Noble nodded, too out of breath for words. They went crashing through the woods, naked branches clawed at

Noble's cheeks. Exposed roots snagged his toes. His heart rode in his throat and his lungs burned. It was an effort to keep pace with a woman ten years younger. Sam ran flat out, her long legs eating up ground, dodging between trees like she could see in the dark.

CHAPTER FIFTY-EIGHT

BURKE WAS ON HIS FEET WITH HIS FISTS CLENCHED AND his fingernails biting into his palms. The large center screen showed two figures creeping across the ground toward a rambling structure. It was hard to be sure from the angle, but the analysts assured him it was an old cathedral. Drones circled overhead. Both units had switched to Starlight video, turning Grey and Preston into white phantoms picking their way across a field of black. The situation room watched the approach with baited breath. Dana was at Burke's side, one hand over her mouth.

"Coughlin, I'm telling you for the last time," Burke was saying. "Call your men off. Tell Grey to stand down. They need to wait until we can get a Quick Reaction Team over there."

Coughlin snorted and shook his head. "And let Gunn slip away again? No chance."

Burke rounded on him. "Noble is a former Green Beret, for cryin' out loud. He's going to take these two apart."

Coughlin, his eye twitching, shot him a nasty look. "Grey and Preston both have military backgrounds."

"But you don't." Burke jabbed a finger at Coughlin's chest. "You're about to get them both killed. Or Duval."

"This is happening, Burke. Now get your finger out of my face before I have you thrown out of this situation room. You did your part. You found them. Now I'm going to do mine, so back off."

Burke shook his head and turned back to the action on screen.

The ghostly white apparitions came within a dozen yards of the structure. A brilliant flash caused the picture to bleed out momentarily while the cameras adjusted to the change in illumination. Burke had seen enough firefights through a Starlight scope to know a gunshot, even without sound. A brief but intense exchange of rounds followed. It was like watching an avant-garde science fiction movie. White ghosts sent arcs of laser light zipping at the front of the church. There was a brief lull and then another brilliant display. Then one of the attackers rushed the front door while the other went around the side. Before either man could reach the building, a major heat signature washed out the picture.

Burke's mind struggled to make sense of what he was seeing. Had he just watched Jake Noble and Sam Gunn blown to bits? When the image adjusted, the cathedral was a white-washed conflagration. Bright spots of fire illuminated the field of black. For one brief second, Burke thought he glimpsed a flash of muted white in the trees behind the church, but it was impossible to say if it was a person, an animal, or just flaming wreckage.

Coughlin took a breath and let it out slowly. His fists were planted on his hips. "What the hell just happened?"

One of the analysts turned in his seat. "Looked like an explosion, sir."

"Did they hit a gas main or something?" Coughlin wanted to know.

Burke said, "We won't know until we go through the wreckage."

Coughlin said, "Get fire and rescue units en route in case there are any survivors. Keep two drones overhead. I want to know if anyone comes out."

A chorus of *Yes, sirs* greeted his request.

Coughlin said, "I'll inform the Director."

"Do that," Burke said, watching him go.

Dana laid a hand on Burke's shoulder and whispered, "I'm sorry."

Hot tears of pain and sorrow gathered behind Burke's eyes. It felt like someone had dropped a load of cinder blocks on his chest. He cleared his throat. "Excuse me a moment. I need the restroom."

CHAPTER FIFTY-NINE

Coughlin started across the floor of the Operations Directorate, shot a quick look around the sea of cubicles to be sure no one was looking, then ducked into an unused conference room. The long, windowless cube had nicotine stains on the walls and a table the size of a battleship crammed up the space, but it was swept twice a day for listening devices, so Coughlin wasn't worried about anyone picking up his conversation.

He perched on a corner of the table, dialed, and put the phone to his ear. The muscles around his left eye convulsed. Stress and lack of sleep made the myoclonic twitch worse. The uncontrollable jerk had earned him grade school monikers like Winky Pete and Mr. Twitchy. College hadn't been much better. Coughlin didn't score his first date until the ripe old age of twenty-two, and she had been a wallflower with Coke-bottle glasses and a lisp. In his career with the CIA, the involuntary contraction had kept him out of field work, but that wasn't always a bad thing. It's hard to get shot when you're running an operation from the other side of the globe. However, it meant he was constantly one move behind the action, making decisions after the fact, trying to collect information on a fluid situation and adapting as new facts came in.

Grey picked up with a brusque hello.

"What happened?"

"I'm not sure," Grey said. Coughlin could hear the crackle of flames in the background. "They started shooting and next thing I know the whole place goes up in a ball of fire."

"What about Duval?" Coughlin said.

"Not much chance he lived through that," said Grey. "The place is a wreck."

"You'd better pray he's still alive." Coughlin stood up and paced the narrow space. "He's the only one who knows the name of his failsafe. If that next Cypher Punk vault gets released, we're going to find out the hard way what dirt he's got on us. If it's even half what we suspect, we are looking at life in prison."

"What do you want me to do?" Grey said.

"Get in there and sift through the ashes," Coughlin told him. "If they're dead, I want to see the bodies. And be quick about it. Police and fire are on their way."

"Fine," Grey said, "I'm on it. What about the computer?"

"My two hard-luck cases managed to hack the database and delete all of the MEDUSA files. I think they might be suspicious, but they can be dealt with."

"And who's going to do that?"

"I will," Coughlin told him.

Grey snorted.

"Just because I don't work in the field doesn't mean I'm afraid to get my hands dirty," Coughlin told him. "I've got my end under control."

"A fat lot of good that's going to do us if Duval is dead," Grey said.

"And whose fault is that?" Coughlin massaged the skin around his eye in a useless attempt to relax the muscle. "I practically dropped him in your lap."

"Don't pin this on me," Grey said.

"Why not?" Coughlin said. "It's your fault."

"First Sam Gunn shows up out of nowhere and kills Frank, then this Noble guy comes along. How is that my fault?"

"I'll make it your fault," Coughlin said. "I'll march into the Director's office right now and pin this whole thing on your head. I know all about your account in the Caymans. I'll freeze your assets. You won't make it out of France alive."

"You bastard," Grey said.

"If you don't want to spend the rest of your very short life looking over your shoulder," Coughlin said, "get in there and find those bodies. If they're dead, get on the first plane to D.C."

"What do you have in mind?" Grey asked.

"Maybe we can use CyberLance to incriminate Frank Bonner and Sam Gunn. They're both dead. We can make it look like they were in on it together and had a falling out. CyberLance is the perfect tool to make that happen."

He hung up and ran a hand over his face. This whole thing had gone balls up. With Duval dead, Coughlin could only wait and hope the fallout from the Cypher Punk release wasn't as bad as Duval claimed it would be. If it named names, then Coughlin would have nowhere to hide. He tugged at his collar. It felt like a noose tightening around his neck. He could go home, pack a bag and disappear, but that would be an admission of guilt. He thought about CyberLance and the pair of computer nerds in the basement. Frank had been their resident tech guru. Not that he had any great skill with computers, but he had known enough to put CyberLance to use. Maybe it was time for one last hack. Coughlin formulated a hasty plan. He would need some leverage, which meant one of the techies had to die. It appeared he would be getting his hands dirty after all.

CHAPTER SIXTY

Burke and Dana shared a high-top at the Smoke & Barrel, a trendy D.C. watering hole known for expensive bourbon. The clientele is a mix of corporate lawyers in bespoke suits and college kids in Georgetown sweatshirts affecting a knowledge of good liquor. An old Charlie Parker tune was on the sound system and a basket of curly-cut fries sat untouched on the table between them. It was just after four in the afternoon and the crowd was still thin. By six the place would be packed and the volume would peel paint from the walls, but for now it was quiet enough. Burke nursed a drink while a fat man in an apron ran a broom over the floor. The bristles made a soft whisking sound against the hardwood.

Dana reached across the table and laid a slim white hand over Burke's meaty black paw. "I'm really sorry, Matt."

He nodded, took her fingers and gave them a squeeze. "Noble was a good soldier. They both were."

Her brow pinched. She said, "I've never seen Coughlin like that before. He was possessed. He took the whole thing way too personally. I don't believe for a second it had anything to do with Frank Bonner being killed. I think he wanted to make certain Gunn didn't live long enough to talk to anybody."

"I'm sure of it. Only I don't know why," Burke said. "Now we'll never know. Everyone involved is dead."

"Or working for Coughlin," Dana pointed out.

Burke nodded. "You can bet your garter, Grey is never going to roll on his boss."

They sat in silence for a while, each lost in thought. It had been a long couple of days. Burke picked up his whiskey and swirled the amber liquid around in the glass. He was not normally one for hard liquor. A strawberry daiquiri was his drink of choice, but today called for something stronger. He sipped and pulled a face.

"Speaking of my garter." Dana lowered her voice to a throaty whisper. "How'd you like to walk me home and help me out of it?"

Burke's lips pressed into a thin line and turned down at the corners. "It's been a long day," he told her. "How 'bout a rain check?"

Her cheeks flushed. "Is something wrong?"

"No, I'm just tired."

She slipped off her stool and held out a hand. "At least walk me home?"

"Sure."

He dropped a few bills on the table, took Dana's hand and led her up a flight of stairs to street level. A blustering wind tugged at the hem of his overcoat. To Burke, it felt late, like the stars should be winking in a cold black sky, but an orange sun still hung in the clouds and their shadows stretched out behind them on the sidewalk. They strolled along, Dana clinging to his arm, and Burke cloaked in his grief. It was hard to imagine Jake Noble dead. Burke's mind refused to accept the idea. Partly because Jake wasn't the type to leave anything to chance, not if he could help it. And because, if true, Jake's death was Burke's fault. He loved the kid like a son. He would never tell that to Jake, but they both knew it. The thought that he might have sent Jake to his death left a hole right in the center of Burke's chest.

They walked in silence until they reached Dana's stoop. She wrapped her arms around his neck and pecked him on the lips. When he didn't reciprocate, she pulled back. A frown creased her forehead. "Did I do something wrong?"

"It's nothing," Burke lied. The truth was, he had been talking with Madeline the last few days. He had gone through the house last week to pick up some clothes and found her under the sink, trying to fix a busted pipe. Burke asked if she needed any help and afterwards she made coffee. They sat around the kitchen table, reminiscing about their first apartment in Savannah. It had been a two room flat in a rundown slum that needed constant repair.

Sitting in the kitchen, with mugs of warm coffee in their hands and ice frosting the windows, they had chatted about old times, laughed a lot, and Burke realized how much he missed his wife.

Dana was young and vibrant, with long blonde hair, a narrow waist, and a killer set of thighs. She was everything a guy could ask for in bed, but deep in his heart, Burke still loved Madeline.

Too bad it took him so long to figure it out.

Dana said, "Is it the job?"

Burke shook his head, put his hands around her waist and pulled her into a kiss. He should have thrilled at her touch, but the magic was gone. The forbidden fruit had lost its flavor. Instead of sweet nectar, her lips were a bitter reminder of what he had lost. It left a taste like ashes in his mouth.

Dana pulled back and said, "Something's wrong."

"I stopped through the house the other day," Burke admitted. "Maddie was there."

She loosed her hold on his neck and took a step back. "I thought you two were finished?"

"We were," Burke said, then corrected himself. "We are."

She waited.

Burke said, "It's complicated."

"It's complicated?" Dana's brows climbed her forehead. She dug in her purse for her keys. "Why not just admit you're getting back with your ex?"

"It's not like that." Burke reached for her arm.

She shrugged him off and slotted her key in the door. Pink splotches formed on her cheeks and tears streaked her mascara. She choked back a sob. "You're a bastard!"

"Dana, come on, don't be like that."

"Go to hell," she said and slammed the door in his face.

Burke stood on the front step, a bitter wind tugging at his lapels, wondering how he had managed to destroy, not one, but two relationships. There was only himself to blame. He had waited too long to figure out he still loved his wife. Now Dana was through with him and Maddie would never forgive him for the affair. Burke stepped down off the porch and shivered at the cold.

CHAPTER SIXTY-ONE

Gwen Witwicky left Langley just after six. She was behind the wheel of an electric green VW Beetle, crossing the Francis Scott Key bridge toward Georgetown. The tires hummed on a layer of slush. An icy drizzle had left a layer of cold and wet on the roadway. Overhead, the sky was as an iron-gray dome shot with darkly ominous hues that reflected Gwen's mood exactly. The excitement she felt at getting reassigned had evaporated in a confusing tangle of impending doom.

The Company didn't exactly have a squeaky-clean history. What clandestine intelligence agency does? But Coughlin's story about deleting operation files as an exercise in cyber security had all the consistency of soggy cardboard. The more Gwen turned it over in her mind, the more holes she poked in the narrative.

No paperwork. No computer logs. No written confirmation of reassignment. No official word from the Wizard or anyone higher up the chain. Just a verbal directive from

Coughlin. Worse, no way to prove Coughlin had given the order.

Had she and Ezra been duped? They had broken into the CIA database, one of the most secure networks in the world, and erased classified information. It was a federal offence and there was no way to prove they had acted under orders. The thought left a noxious feeling in Gwen's gut and a sheen of sweat formed on her forehead. She dialed back the heater.

You have a copy of the files, Gwen reminded herself. Or, at the very least, a copy of the files existed. She couldn't leave the building with a flash drive and she didn't dare leave it on her desk. So she had hidden it. She was in the women's restroom, sitting on the toilet with the thumb drive in her pocket, when she got the idea. Using a hairpin to jimmy the lock on the toilet paper dispenser, Gwen had secreted the USB drive at the back of the metal housing. She could only hope the cleaning crew didn't replace the toilet paper roll between now and tomorrow morning.

And then?

Her phone was held by a plastic clip suction-cupped to her windshield. Gwen tried to unlock the mobile with her thumbprint, but a strong crosswind on the bridge kept buffeting the car and fouling up the connection. She let out an annoyed sigh, snatched the phone out of the holder, and finally managed to unlock it. With one eye on the road, she scrolled through her contacts until she found Ezra. She was halfway across the bridge, with a clear lane of traffic ahead, when she pressed call.

There was a small bump and the crunch of plastic bumpers kissing. Gwen's eyes flashed to the rearview mirror where she glimpsed a dark sedan. By that time her car was already out of control. The front end of the Beetle weaved back and forth over the slippery blacktop. She dropped the phone. It landed in the floorboard and she could hear Ezra's voice. "Gwen? Gwen? You there?"

Gwen gripped the steering wheel in both hands. Her foot stamped down on the brake. The tires locked and the car went into a slide. Rubber howled over wet asphalt.

Behind her, the dark sedan sped up. The engine revved and the bumpers met again. Hit a car on the back bumper, right behind the driver's side, and it will force the vehicle into a sideways skid. That's exactly what happened to Gwen. She realized what the driver of the dark sedan was doing as her little Beetle started to drift.

"Gwen!" Ezra's voice came from the floorboards. "Gwen, what's going on?"

She remembered her training moments too late. She should have been driving with one foot on the gas and the other on the brake so she could transition faster. She should have steered into the skid instead of trying to force the vehicle back true. Now she had lost control of the car and was along for the ride. A terrified scream filled her ears and Gwen realized it was coming from her.

The Beetle humped up on two wheels like a dog taking a leak. Gwen's world tilted precariously and seemed to hang there. The dark sedan never stopped, never slowed. The engine revved and forced the Beetle over onto its roof. Gwen slammed into the driver side door. Glass shattered. Door panels crumpled. The airbag burst from the steering wheel, flinging Gwen's arms aside and rocking her head back with the force of a heavyweight boxer delivering a knockout punch. She clung to consciousness through sheer willpower. The horrific shriek of metal on asphalt filled her ears. The earth tipped upside down and Gwen was thrown into the safety belt with bone rattling force. All the loose change and lost French fries that had fallen into the floorboards over the years now came flying up to the roof. The car continued to slide, filling Gwen's ears with that awful shrieking sound. It seemed to go on forever. Then, finally, stopped.

Gwen hung upside down. She could still hear Ezra calling her name. Her hands dangled on the crumpled roof of the car and darkness closed in on her.

CHAPTER SIXTY-TWO

THE TOWN OF NEUCHÂTEL DATES BACK TO MEDIEVAL Europe. The old-world village of half-timber houses is in northern Switzerland, nestled on the banks of a crystal-clear lake of the same name. Residents speak a smattering of French, German, Italian, and Swiss. Europe's rich culinary diversity joins together in Neuchâtel to form an epicurean's dream.

Noble wedged their stolen vehicle into a parallel spot on a quiet street lined with cars, opened the driver's side door, got out and arched his back. His breath steamed up in front of him. A crisp, white layer of snow blanketed the cobblestone boulevards and the warm scent of baked goods spilled from the open door of a bakery across the street.

"Smells good," Sam said. She blew into cupped hands and rubbed her palms together.

Noble twisted his shoulders to one side, then the other. Vertebra made loud popping sounds.

Sam sneered. "Getting old."

"It's not the years," Noble told her. "It's the mileage."

Sam cocked her head to one side. "Is that from *Die Hard?*"

"Close," said Noble. "Indiana Jones."

"Does all your wisdom come eighties action movies?"

"Most of it. Yeah."

Duval climbed out of the backseat and took in their surroundings. "Why are we stopping here?"

"Because one of us has been driving all night and needs a break," Noble told him. "We also need food and a clean set of wheels."

"You two change cars like most people change underwear," Duval said. "We could be in Italy before sundown. Why not keep going?"

"Relax," Noble said. "They'll spend hours sifting through the rubble. By the time they realize we didn't burn up in the fire, we can be cruising down the Baltic coast. We bought ourselves a little breathing room."

"All the more reason to go now," Duval said and then fell silent at the sound of feet crunching in the snow.

An old couple, walking arm in arm and bundled in parkas, offered a cheery "*Guten tag.*"

Sam smiled at them as they passed. "*Guten tag.*"

"*Salute,*" Noble said in French.

Duval tucked his chin and turned his face away.

Sam waited until the couple was out of ear shot, then said, "Way to look suspicious."

"I'm scared." Duval lowered his voice. "You would be too if your face was all over the news."

"My face *is* all over the news," Sam said.

"Let's stretch our legs," Noble told them.

He grabbed Duc's messenger bag from the backseat and tossed the keys to the stolen car in a trash bin on his way past. They strolled along the twisting lanes, just a couple of tourists, until they spied a restaurant busy with a breakfast crowd.

Walking inside was like stepping back in time. The dining room had a low ceiling with exposed beams and a cheery fire crackled in the hearth. There was no annoying sound system blasting pop music and the customers didn't have to yell to be heard. The atmosphere was subdued but festive. The three fugitives gathered around a table near the fire and ordered breakfast. Noble waited until the waiter came back with their food and Duval had something in his belly before saying, "We need to decide our next move."

Duval put his fork down, swallowed, and wiped his mouth with a napkin. "How do you mean?"

"You have to make a choice," Noble said. "You can go to Montenegro, but you can't hide forever."

"What are you talking about?"

"You were safe in the embassy," Noble told him. "Coughlin couldn't touch you as long as you stayed put. A guy like Coughlin doesn't care about non-extradition countries. He knew the next Cypher Punk release was going to expose him and he needed to get you out in the open."

The color drained from Duval's face. He glanced over his shoulder like there might be an assassin at the next table. "You think he set it all up? Made me believe they were going to kidnap me in order to get me out of the embassy?"

Noble nodded. "That would be my guess. When you left the embassy, you played right into his hands. If he didn't catch you when you crossed the channel, he could send

Grey and his team of thugs to pick you up in Montenegro. He needs you out in the open so he can find out the name of your failsafe."

Duval buried his face in his hands. "How could I be so stupid?"

Sam reached across and patted his back.

"Remember who you're dealing with." Noble cradled his coffee cup in both hands, enjoying the warmth. "Coughlin has been running counter-intelligence ops for decades. It's one of the oldest tricks in the book—force your enemy to go left by convincing him you want him to go right."

Duval asked, "What can I do?"

"Fight back," Noble told him.

"What are you suggesting?"

"We turn around," Noble said. "Drive back to Paris. Lure Grey and his team into the open. We use their own plan against them. Get them to incriminate themselves."

Duval made a skeptical face. "You're joking."

Noble laid out his plan for them.

Sam thought it over. "It could work. It would need cracker jack timing."

"No way." Duval shook his head. "We barely escaped France with our lives. Now you want me to go back?"

"It's the last thing Coughlin would expect," Sam told him.

A pathetic little laugh escaped Duval's lips, like he was hearing a joke that wasn't particularly funny. "Easy for you to say. You both know how to fight. You've been trained. I'm a reporter."

"Like I said, you've got a choice to make." Noble crossed

his arms and propped his elbows on the table. "You either spend the rest of your life on the run, or you take down Coughlin. Those are your only two options."

Duval let out a breath. His breakfast sat unfinished. He looked like a cornered animal. "I can't," he said. "Don't you understand? I'm not like you."

"You don't have to be a Green Beret," Noble said. "Sam and I will do all the heavy lifting. All you have to do is follow my lead. My plan will put Coughlin and his accomplices behind bars. You'll never have to worry about any of them ever again."

Duval stared at the tabletop and his face clouded over.

"Do it for Sam if not for yourself," Noble said. "She risked her life to save you. Help her clear her name."

His eyes went to Sam. She caught his gaze and her lips pressed together in a tight smile. Duval looked away and shook his head. "I'm sorry. You both helped me and I'm grateful for that, but I'm not sticking my neck out. I'll take my chances and run. If you won't help me get to Montenegro, then I'll go alone. But I'm not going up against Coughlin and his gang of hired killers."

Noble picked up his fork and speared his crepes. He spoke around a mouthful of food. "At least take a minute and think it over."

CHAPTER SIXTY-THREE

EZRA STOOD IN THE DIM FLUORESCENT LIGHT OF A hospital room, staring down at the bruised and battered form of Gwen, feeling like the contents of his stomach would come rushing up. He was scared and angry and he felt very small. He groped behind him for a chair and lowered himself into it. The harsh smell of industrial disinfectant invaded his nostrils and his shoes squeaked on linoleum.

An oxygen tube was stuck up Gwen's nose. Clean white gauze covered her head. She looked tiny and broken. Angry welts covered her lips and the skin around her eyes. Her nose was swollen and rimmed with dried blood. Her heart rate monitor spiked and dipped like clockwork. That was a good sign.

Tears welled up in Ezra's eyes. *What had they gotten themselves into?*

One of her hands was laying on the coverlet. Ezra

reached out and covered it with his own. He gave a little squeeze. "I'm so sorry, Gwen."

"How is she?"

Ezra started at the voice and twisted in his chair. Coughlin stood in the doorway. His hands were stuffed in the pockets of his long beige overcoat and his hair was slicked back. A concerned frown turned his mouth down at the corners and his left eye jerked. Ezra had never noticed the sinister quality behind Coughlin's eyes before. He had always been distracted by the twitch. After all, who wants to think bad of a guy with a nervous tick? But Ezra saw it now. He saw the cold, calculating stare behind those dark eyes and it made him shiver.

Ezra licked his lips and fought to keep his hands from shaking. "Doctor says she's in a coma. Might not wake up."

Coughlin came over and stood beside the bed, hands still in his pockets. He looked down at Gwen and the truth hit Ezra like a sledge hammer. Coughlin had put Gwen in this hospital bed and he'd done it himself. He hadn't hired anybody. He had seen to it personally.

"I came as soon as I heard," Coughlin was saying. "Terrible thing when one of our own ends up hurt. Did they say what happened?"

"Traffic accident," Ezra heard himself say. "Her car flipped over."

The whole scene felt dislocated and surreal. Ezra was sitting here talking to the very man who had tried to kill Gwen and might try to kill him next. He kept expecting Coughlin to pull out a silenced pistol and shoot him between the eyes. Part of his brain was telling him to get up and run for the door, call the nearest cop. But he couldn't leave. Coughlin may have come to finish the job. Besides, even if there was a cop in the hall, what would Ezra say? He had no proof. All he had was a thumb drive, and Gwen had hidden that in the women's restroom back at Langley.

"Times like these always remind me how fleeting life is," Coughlin said. "You never know what's going to happen. One day you're out for a morning jog when a truck jumps the curb and the next thing you know, it's lights out. Could happen to anybody. Any time. Makes you want to hang on to every second, am I right?"

Ezra sat motionless in the chair. He felt like a deer staring into the eyes of a hungry bear. His bladder threatened to let go and sweat rolled down the undersides of his arms. He managed to nod.

Coughlin smiled. It was lifeless motion that pulled his lips up into an ugly grimace. "I just came by to see how she was doing. I'll let you two be alone. I'm sure you have *a lot* to think about."

He came around the bed and laid a hand on Ezra's shoulder. It was everything Ezra could do to sit there and not jump up out of his seat. He wanted to scream and howl. He wanted to hit and kick and gnash his teeth. But fear kept him pinned to the cheap plastic chair. He hated himself for being a coward and hated Coughlin more.

"Stay safe," Coughlin said. "I wouldn't want anything like this to happen to you too. After all, I've got more work for you."

Ezra managed another nod. It was a slow up-and-down movement, a silent admission of his own inferiority and inability to do anything but obey. Coughlin gave his shoulder a squeeze and walked out the door. Alone with Gwen once more, tears welled up in Ezra's eyes. He put his head down on the bed, gripped her cold hand, and wept.

CHAPTER SIXTY-FOUR

Large slabs of ice floated on the surface of Lake Neuchâtel, edges grinding together with deep groaning voices that echoed across the wintery landscape. Tree limbs sagged under heavy loads of snow. The air was perfectly still and a pale-yellow sun was climbing in the east. Sam and Noble strolled along the edge of the lake, their hands stuffed in their pockets and their collars turned up against the chill. Their feet crunched in the snow and their shoulders occasionally brushed together. Neither seemed to mind. Sam decided to test it by giving a gentle nudge. Noble swayed, came back, and gave as good as he got. One side of his mouth turned up in a grin. They shared a laugh. Sam threaded her arm through his and hooked her hand back in her pocket.

Not far away, Duval sat on a bench, gazing out over the lake. It had taken another hour of coaxing, but he had finally relented, promising to consider their plan if only they would let him finish his breakfast. Now they were giving him enough room to think without letting him out of their sight. He was huddled in his overcoat with a thoughtful frown on his face. Further along the sidewalk, a knot of spectators gathered to watch a group of old men in Speedos, flabby bodies covered in goosebumps, as they prepared to plunge into the icy waters.

Noble stopped and leaned on a concrete balustrade, letting his eyes roam the blue jigsaw puzzle of the lake. Behind them a group of children screeched in laughter as they launched snowballs back and forth.

Sam propped her elbows on the barricade. "I'm glad you're here."

"Me too," said Noble.

"This will put you in bad with the Company."

He chuckled. "I wasn't exactly high on their friends list."

"What about your mother?" Sam asked.

She felt the muscles tense beneath his windbreaker. "I'll figure that part out as I go."

"I'm sorry," Sam said.

"For what?"

"For getting you mixed up in this," she said. "Sorry for everything. I made a mess and I dragged you right down into the middle of it."

He shrugged. "I would have done the same."

Sam glanced along the snow-covered sidewalk at Duval still huddled on the bench. "Think he'll come around?"

Noble followed her gaze. "I'm not holding my breath. He's motivated by fear. Scared people make bad decisions."

"What motivates you?"

Noble's brow furrowed and his dark eyes scanned the

surface of the lake, lost in thought. His chewed the inside of one cheek while he pondered the question. It was likely something he'd never considered before, at least not in so many words, not consciously anyway. Sam knew she had struck a chord. And she knew the answer to the question even if Jake didn't. He was motivated by some powerful internal compass that only he could read—a moral code printed on the walls of his heart—and he followed the promptings without regard for countries, politics, or institutions.

He turned to her and their eyes met. Sam felt herself being pulled down into deep pools. He opened his mouth to speak, but his eyes jumped to a spot over her left shoulder. "Looks like he made up his mind."

Sam felt like a balloon with all the air let out of it. She turned and saw Duval shuffling along the sidewalk. Rotten timing as usual.

He stopped in front of them, stuck his inhaler in his mouth, and took a drag. He gave it a good shake, tried again, then stuffed the empty inhaler back in his pocket. "Alright," he said. "I'm in. What do you need me to do?"

CHAPTER SIXTY-FIVE

Women use the restroom roughly every seven seconds, or so it seemed to Ezra, who was back in his cubicle on the first floor pretending to work. In reality, he was watching the door to the women's room and keeping a mental head count. He needed to sneak inside and get the thumb drive before someone found it, or accidentally tossed it in the garbage, but for every one woman who came out, two more went in, usually in pairs.

Butterflies zipped around inside his stomach at the thought of walking into a women's restroom. The doors were situated in a hall which opened directly onto the sea of cubicles where anyone could see who was coming and going. The risk was huge, but one he had to take. He needed that thumb drive and the files it contained. It was the only evidence. Without those files, it was Ezra's word against Coughlin's.

Dark circles ringed his eyes and his clothes were wrinkled. He hadn't slept. Instead he spent the whole night watching the street below his apartment. A dark sedan had followed him home from the hospital and when he got to his building, Ezra found his front door open. He had hovered in the hall for what felt like an hour, listening for any sounds from inside. After a few deep breaths, he worked up the courage to enter. Someone had turned his place inside out. The sofa cushions were slashed, drawers were emptied, and several of his collectible action figures lay broken on the floor.

After checking to be sure the apartment was empty, Ezra had wedged his ruined sofa in front of the door and spent the hours until dawn standing at the window with a gun in his hand.

The restless night had taken its toll and now Ezra could barely keep his eyes open. His coat was rumpled, his tie was missing, and he hadn't shaved. His lips moved silently as he did arithmetic in his head.

Forty-nine cubicles on this wing and six offices. Twenty-seven female employees. It seemed like a statistical impossibility that the restroom would be empty at any given time. It was 5:15 a.m. Fourteen of the women had been to the toilet already. Five had been twice. And Carol Peters had been three times.

There were four women in the restroom at the moment. Ezra twirled a pen and clicked it repeatedly. *Click-click-click*. His tongue was a dried-out slug suction-cupped to the roof of his mouth. He rocked in his chair and willed the women to finish up and get out. The door swung open. One woman emerged as another two got up and threaded their way between cubicles.

Ezra wanted to scream in frustration. How much coffee

did they drink? The two women going in met two coming out. That left three. Ezra planted his feet and readied himself to move.

While he waited, the elevator doors rolled open and a cleaning man pushed a cart to the nearest cubicle. He was a small man in coveralls with a neatly trimmed goatee and thick spectacles. He emptied the trash from the cubicles into a specialized receptacle on his trolley. It had a flanged trap that allowed rubbish to be pushed in but not taken out. When the receptacle was full, it was taken down to the basement and incinerated. The design prevented anyone using trash to pass classified intelligence.

One of the women came out of the restroom, trailing toilet paper from her heel. She was tall with a lot of blonde hair and too much makeup. She gave Ezra a baleful look on her way past. It was a look that said all men are the same, but some are lower than others. Ezra knew which side of that equation he landed on.

He triggered the pen. *Click-click-click.*

Two women remained in the bathroom. The maintenance man moved along the outside row of cubicles, emptying trashcans and running a small shop vac whenever he found a mess that needed cleaning. He made his way toward the hall, stopped his trolley outside the men's room door, and unfolded a yellow plastic sandwich board that read *Closed for Maintenance.*

Sweat broke out on Ezra's brow. Would the janitor clean inside the women's room? Or was there a woman for that? Ezra had never bothered to find out. He thought back over the last several months and couldn't remember ever seeing female cleaning staff.

He worked the pen. *Click-click-click.*

One of the women came out of the restroom door, talking over her shoulder. The other must be at the sinks, almost ready to leave as well.

Ezra stood. Fear flooded his limbs. He had to force one foot in front of the other. He still held the pen and he dropped it on an empty desk as he passed. A bead of sweat trailed down his cheek. The breath caught in his chest. He was halfway across the office. The cleaning man propped open the men's room door and went to work with his shop-vac. The steady drone of the vacuum drowned out the friendly chatter of an early morning at the office.

Ezra was almost at the door when the last woman emerged. Now was his chance. He glanced around, made sure no one was watching, then darted inside.

Right away he noticed the smell was better than the men's room. It smelled like lemon scented air freshener instead of armpit. You wouldn't want to wear it as cologne, but it didn't make you gag either. Was the cleaning crew responsible for that? Or did women themselves take care of it, he wondered?

He closed the door behind him, quickly crossed to the second stall on the left-hand side and locked himself in. The small metal box that housed the toilet paper was locked, but Ezra set to work with a pair of paperclips. Dark circles formed under his arms. His fingers trembled. He expected the door to bang open and hear a loud voice demanding to know what he was doing in the women's room. The lock finally turned. Ezra jerked open the housing and reached behind the half-finished roll of toilet paper. His fingers closed on the thumb drive. Relief flooded through him and a grin spread over his face.

Ezra pocketed the thumb drive, let himself out of the stall, and crossed the bathroom floor. Almost home free! A surge of victory swelled up in his chest. He reached for the door handle, yanked, and was staring into the eyes of a middle-aged woman. Her eyebrows crept up her forehead and her lips parted in an unspoken question.

Ezra cleared his throat, slid past her into the hall, and gave the only excuse that came to mind. "I self-identify as a woman."

CHAPTER SIXTY-SIX

Burke arrived late to work the next morning and found a message from the Director. She wanted to see him as soon as he got in. His first thought was the situation in France. They had either gone through the wreckage and found three bodies, or none at all. Either way, Burke's stomach twisted up in knots. Good thing he'd skipped breakfast. Five minutes later, he was sitting in Armstrong's office, waiting for her to finish up in the bathroom.

A manila file folder laid on the massive desk along with a framed picture of a gawky teenager in braces and pigtails, bearing a striking resemblance to Armstrong.

Burke listened to the sink running and his mind raced through all the possibilities. Would she have asked for a face-to-face if they were alive? Maybe. Probably not, Burke told himself. Either Sam, or Noble, or both were dead. Armstrong had called him into the office to break the news personally. A tight fist cramped down on his guts. They were his recruits, his responsibility. Burke thought of them as his children. He took a deep breath and prepared himself for the worst.

The sink turned off. The bathroom door opened and Armstrong circled around behind her desk. She had her hair up in a bun and held in place with a plastic clip. Her jacket and skirt were pinstriped and immaculately pressed.

"Sorry to keep you waiting," she said.

"No problem."

Armstrong sat down, picked up the file folder and her brow creased.

Oh, dear Lord in heaven, they're both dead, thought Burke.

Armstrong passed the folder to him.

He flipped it open and a lead weight came down on his chest like an anvil. He was staring at a black and white surveillance photo of him and Dana together on her porch. For a moment, Burke was sure he was having a heart attack.

He finally found his words. "You had me tailed?"

"I made it perfectly clear my first day on the job, I was here to put the Company back on the straight and narrow," Armstrong said. "I expected more of you. Wizard vouched for you, said you were one of the best. Now I have to question his judgement as well. What were you thinking? How long did you think you could get away with it?"

"I guess I've got some explaining to do," Burke said.

"I wish you would," she said. "You're a married man sleeping with your secretary, and you know the policy on inter-office romance. What if one of our enemies had found out about this? They'd be using the information to blackmail you right now. For that matter, how do I know that hasn't happened already?"

Burke closed the file. The photos threw a spotlight on his infidelity. Seeing them somehow made it worse and Armstrong's disappointment hurt more than the shame of being caught.

Growing up in Savannah, Matt's grandmother had dragged him to church every Sunday. He vividly remembered sweating through his button-down shirt and the feel of the hard wooden pews while a Baptist preacher spit fire and brimstone. *"Your sins, brothers and sisters, will find you out! Yes, sir! Make no mistake. You think it's a secret but the Loooord knows, brothers and sisters. He sees! And your sins will find you out! On the day of the LOOORD, Jeeeesus will shine a light on your sins! Can I get an Amen?"*

The idea of his sins *finding him out* had terrified young Burke. In those days, he had dreaded Nanna Momma finding out he stole a stick of gum from the Woolworth's counter. Or that he had cheated off Charlotte Bridger's math test. As he got older, that fear got lost along the way. The idea of sin and salvation seemed to dull with time and experience. People did bad things all the time and no one ever found out. Working for the CIA, Burke knew this better than most. But his sins had found him out at last, just like the old preacher said they would.

Burke cleared his throat and said, "I messed up."

Armstrong leaned back in her chair and crossed her arms. "That's all you got for me? 'I messed up?'"

Burke placed the file on her desk. "What else is there to say? I made a mistake. If I could go back in time, I'd handle it differently, but I can't."

Armstrong let out a frustrated sigh.

"If someone has to be punished," Burke said, "it should

be me. Dana is young. She's got her whole life ahead of her. Don't take this out on her. It's my fault. I instigated it."

"Funny. She said the same thing."

"She's good at her job," Burke said. "She's got a bright career ahead of her. Don't destroy it because of one indiscretion."

"Noted," said Armstrong. "Do you have anything else to offer?"

He shook his head.

Armstrong picked up the folder and tapped the edge of the desk with it. "You've got a long history with the CIA, Burke, but I can't let this slide."

He gripped the arms of his chair. His legs felt disconnected from his body. The walls of the office seemed to expand and Burke felt like a tiny man sitting in a chair much too big for him. He realized it was like being a nine-year-old boy, his feet dangling off the edge of a hard wooden pew, sweating through his Sunday best. His sins had found him out.

Armstrong's face was hard, but her eyes had compassion. "I always have need of good operators with field experience, so I'm going to give you a choice."

Burke felt himself nod and heard words coming out of his mouth. "I'm listening."

"You can contest this and it'll get dragged out into the light. There will be an investigation and your reputation will be ruined," Armstrong said, "Or you can turn in your resignation and walk away with your dignity intact. Set up a private intelligence agency and I'll send work your way whenever I need something kept off the record."

Burke snapped back to the present. "You want me to be a mercenary?"

"I believe the official term is private contractor." She held his gaze without flinching. "Either way, it'll allow you to take early retirement and collect a few paychecks on the side."

Burke almost laughed. He had made Jake the same offer two years earlier and Jake had been in no position to refuse. Now the tables had turned. With his marriage falling apart and a divorce on the horizon, early pension wouldn't cover the cost of living. Burke had no choice. He nodded. "I'll have my resignation on your desk by the end of the day."

Armstrong fed the folder through a shredder under her desk. The motor whirred to life and turned the photos into confetti. "For what it's worth, I'm sorry it came to this."

"I made my choices," Burke said, as if that settled the matter. He still felt disconnected from his body. Part of him kept expecting to wake up in a cold sweat and realize it was all a dream. He stood up and went to the door.

"Oh, Burke," Armstrong said. "One more thing."

He stopped with his hand on the knob.

"They went through the church and didn't find any bodies," she told him. "What do you make of that?"

"For what it's worth," he said, using her own words, "Jake Noble was one of the best field officers I ever trained. We lost something special when we lost Jake."

She leaned back in her seat, considered the statement and nodded. "I'll bear it in mind."

CHAPTER SIXTY-SEVEN

Grey paced the grimy safehouse in Paris, his hands stuffed in his pockets and a frown lining his face. The aging wood floor creaked underfoot and the stink from the bathroom filled the apartment. It had taken them most of the night to sift through the ashes and realize there were no bodies. Duval was in the wind, probably halfway to Kotor by now. His laptop and passwords were gone with him, along with any hope of finding out the name of his failsafe. The rodent was loose in Grey's belly again, gnawing at his guts. Grey hadn't slept all night and he could use a good stiff drink, but that would only make the pain in his stomach worse.

Preston was perched on a windowsill, changing the dressing on his hand. The ugly burn had turned raw and gave off a putrid stench like rotting flesh. Without looking up, he said, "What are we going to do?"

"I don't know," Grey admitted.

"You were the one who convinced me to throw in with

Coughlin and Bonner, remember?" Preston said. "You said it would be so easy. We'd make a pile of cash and no one would ever find out. That's what you said. Now what the hell are we going to do?"

"Give me time to think," Grey said.

They had people in Montenegro, but no one had reported seeing anyone matching Duval's description. Ditto Gunn or Noble. All three had disappeared.

"I'm running," Preston said. He finished wrapping his hand and stood up. "I'm going today. Right now, in fact."

"Where would you go?" Grey spread his hands. "The CIA will eventually find us."

"Duval managed to disappear," Preston pointed out.

Grey flashed him an annoyed look. "For now. But he can't stay invisible forever."

Preston said, "I'm not waiting around for him to expose us. I'm cleaning out my accounts and making a run for it."

He started for the door.

"Sit down," Grey ordered.

When Preston didn't stop, Grey jerked the pistol from his waistband. "I said *sit down.*"

Preston stopped, his hand on the knob. "You going to shoot me, Grey?"

"If I have to."

Preston stood there several seconds, staring down the dark aperture of the Sig Sauer. After a minute, he took his hand off the knob, crossed the room and dropped into a swivel chair. "The Cypher Punk release is tomorrow at noon. That gives us less than twenty-four hours to find Duval, learn the name of his failsafe, and eliminate him before proof of our little private enterprise is all over the web."

"If we scatter, it'll only confirm our guilt," Grey told him. "Duval hasn't released anything yet. We've still got time to figure this out, but we have to stay calm and use our heads."

Preston snorted. "What's your plan then?"

Grey perched himself on the edge of the desk and crossed his arms, gun still in hand. "Maybe it's time to flip the script?"

Preston leaned forward and narrowed his eyes. "I'm listening."

"Coughlin threatened to hang this whole thing around our necks. What if we beat him to the punch? He's been running side operations and we've been doing all his dirty work." Grey stood up and went back to pacing. "The way I figure it, we can pin the whole thing on him and claim we had no idea the orders weren't coming direct from the top."

Preston considered the idea and nodded. "That could work. We'd need a way to hide our funds."

"That can be done with a few phone calls," Grey pointed out. "We bounce the money through several Swiss banks to muddy the trail, then call up the new Director and say we've got a few concerns about Coughlin. She'll suspect, but she won't know for sure. At worse it makes us look incompetent, but they can't prove we weren't acting under orders. We'll be blacklisted, but we've still got our freedom. After a few years, when no one is watching us anymore, we start drawing money from our accounts."

"I like it," Preston said.

Before they could put their plan into action, Grey's

phone buzzed. He scooped it up, frowned at the unknown number and answered. "Who is this?"

"You tried to kill me last night and missed."

Grey mouthed a silent curse.

Preston was on his feet, his eyes wide. He waved to get Grey's attention and mouthed, "Who is it?"

Grey held up a finger for him to wait. He said, "Noble?"

"That's right. I've got a business proposition for you."

"I'm listening," said Grey.

"You want Duval, and I want a half million dollars, cash."

"That's a lot of money." Grey snatched a pen and a scrap of paper from the desk. He scrawled *Noble wants 500k for Duval.*

"Don't play games with me," Noble warned. "Jerk me around and I'll hang up. You'll never hear from me again. I'll go public with the info on Duval's laptop. Where will that leave you? Have you got the cash?"

"I can get it," Grey said. "What about Sam? How's she feel about this?"

"She's dead," Noble said. "She wasn't on board with my plan to ransom Duval, so I killed her."

Grey asked, "How do I know I can trust you?"

"Because if you don't pay up, I'm turning Duval over to the FBI and collecting the bounty on his head. It's not half a million, but it's better than nothing. I'm giving you first crack at the hottest commodity on the market. Five hundred thousand dollars is a small price to pay for your freedom. Have we got a deal?"

"When and where?" Grey asked.

"Croix-Rouge subway station," Noble said. "Be there by midnight with my money or I walk away."

Grey started to say it would take a while to collect the funds, but the line was already dead. He turned to Preston. "He's right here in Paris and he wants to meet. Tonight."

"Are we going to pay him?" Preston wanted to know.

"We're going to kill him," Grey said. He dialed Mateen and put the phone to his ear. When the French mercenary came on the line Grey said, "Gather your troops."

CHAPTER SIXTY-EIGHT

ARMSTRONG SAT AT HER DESK, HER LAPTOP OPEN, watching black and white surveillance footage of Sam Gunn shooting Frank Bonner. The feed was a parting gift from Matthew Burke, his way of saying no hard feelings. Armstrong watched the loop over and over again, inspecting every detail, looking for some piece of evidence that would unravel the puzzle. She was hoping for anything that might tell her why Samantha Gunn had killed Frank Bonner and escaped with Duval. So far she had nothing. She couldn't even decide who shot first. It looked like everyone started firing at the same time. She was still engrossed in the video when there came a knock at the door.

She blinked, like a woman coming out of a deep trance, and minimized the video. The clock on the wall was pointing to 2:27 p.m. "Enter!"

Duc stuck his head in and Armstrong waved him to a seat.

"What did you find out?" she asked.

"Noble was right." Duc parked his massive frame in a chair and laced his fingers together in his lap. "The co-pilot was the weak link. I spent most of the day rattling his cage."

"Who did he blab to?"

"The co-pilot told a hangar attendant and the hangar attendant told Coughlin."

It shouldn't have come as a surprise. Coughlin had gone after Sam a little too aggressively from the very start. It didn't feel right to Armstrong, but she didn't have enough time in the Director's seat to trust her instincts yet when it came to spies. To make matters worse, she had just been forced to fire the one man whose instincts seemed spot on. With Burke typing up his resignation and the Wizard laid up in the hospital, Armstrong felt like a captain without a crew.

She said, "No loose ends?"

Duc shook his head. "The co-pilot and hangar attendant are at a secure site. They won't be blabbing to anyone for a while. Want me to have a sit-down with Coughlin?"

"Not just yet," Armstrong said. "We know Coughlin blew Noble's cover, but we still don't know what any of it has to do with Sacha Duval or why Gunn killed Frank Bonner."

"Let me strap Coughlin to a chair and ask him," Duc said.

Armstrong shook her head. "Coughlin is acting DDO. We can't sit him down without proof."

"What now?" Duc wanted to know.

Armstrong lit a thin cigar, then leaned back and blew smoke at the ceiling. Noble and Gunn had gone to ground and Armstrong couldn't expose the co-pilot without admitting she had dropped a burned spy into the middle of the operation. She needed to unmask Coughlin without exposing herself at the same time. With Burke gone and Noble incommunicado, Armstrong's options were limited. She took another drag and considered her next move.

"Oh," said Duc. "I almost forgot. There's a pencil-neck weenie on your receptionist's sofa. Been waiting all day to talk with you."

Armstrong's brow pinched. "What? Who?"

Duc shrugged. "Think he works in the basement. His name's Eddie, or Elmore. I'm not sure."

"What does he want?"

"He wouldn't say."

Armstrong mashed the intercom button. "Mrs. Farnham, is there someone waiting to speak with me?"

"An analyst by the name of Ezra Cook has been here three times asking to see you, ma'am. I keep telling him you're busy, but he seems quite insistent."

"Did he say what it was about?"

"No, ma'am. He said it was '*eyes only.*' He used those exact words."

"Is he there now?" Armstrong asked.

"He was here just a moment ago," Farnham said. "Would you like me to get him back?"

"Yes, thank you." Armstrong turned off the intercom, pointed her cigar at the closed door and told Duc, "Sometimes I think she goes out of her way to make my life harder."

CHAPTER SIXTY-NINE

The Croix-Rouge subway station was built in the twenties and in service less than a decade. It was shut down at the start of World War II and never reopened. Over the years, the station has played host to the French resistance, street gangs, drug dealers, and the city's homeless population. In the early two-thousands, police broke up a rave here, rounding up more than two hundred people. After that, the government sealed off the tunnel to prevent any more underground parties. Now it was a forgotten platform deep beneath the streets of Paris.

Finding Croix-Rouge had been as simple as a Google search at a local internet café. Waiting until the Mabillon metro station on Boulevard Saint-Germain was empty and then slipping away from the platform had been the hard part. They waited nearly an hour for a break in the crowd, then leapt down and hurried along the tracks. Sam kept expecting a train to come along and flatten them, but they reached the access tunnel and Noble defeated the rusty padlock with little difficulty.

Because the station was still wired into the electrical grid, it had current. A handful of flickering bulbs in wire cages threw off enough light to see. Unused rolling stock stood at the platform, doors open, waiting for passengers that would never come. The air smelled dank and stale, like a basement in bad need of sunlight and a thorough cleaning, but at the very least they were out of the wind. Broken bottles crunched underfoot and garbage littered the tracks. Graffiti covered every inch of the sloping walls and, underneath all the gang signs and profanity, were posters dating back to the late twenties. Beyond the empty train cars, tracks stretched away into darkness. One fanciful corner of Sam's brain kept expecting to see Morlocks come creeping out of the shadows.

Duval was sitting on one of the hard wood benches of an abandoned car with his back to the wall, shaking from the cold. They had gone over the plan a dozen times but Duval had the most to lose and he wanted assurances. Noble had handled him well; patiently talking him through each part of the operation and countering any objections.

On the bench next to Duval was a ruggedized laptop and microdots along with recently purchased medical supplies, glowsticks, more BIC lighters, and climbing gear.

Sam marched in place and blew into cupped hands while Noble negotiated with Grey for the exchange. She smirked when Noble claimed he had killed her. When he hung up, Sam said, "Do you think they'll even try to get the money?"

"Not a chance," Noble said.

"The first thing he's going to do is call Le Milieu," said Duval. "And Mateen will bring half a dozen hired guns."

"At least," Noble said.

"That's your plan?" Duval waved a hand at the gear piled on the seat. "The two of you against a pack of thugs. You're armed with handguns and BIC lighters."

"We've also got glowsticks." Noble picked up one of the plastic tubes and brought it to life with a twist.

"We can't possibly lose," Duval remarked. He pointed to Noble's weapon. "Have you even got a full clip?"

"Mag," Noble said.

Duval's face scrunched up. "What?"

"They're called magazines, not clips," Noble told him and produced the two extra mags.

"That's something, I suppose," Duval said.

Noble picked up a length of red and orange climbing rope. "Wish we had time to test this equipment. You're sure they'll use the barge?"

Sam said, "It's where Bonner planned to take him."

Noble nodded and turned to Duval. "Time to get you ready for the party."

Duval stood up, took a breath and said, "Get it over with."

"You're ready?" Noble asked.

Duval's shoulders crept up around his ears and his eyes narrowed. All the muscles in his body tensed. "I'm ready."

"You sure?" Noble said.

"Just do—"

Noble's fist shot out and connected with Duval's nose. There was a flat smack. Duval's head snapped back.

"Ow!" He bent over double and cupped both hands to his face. "Did you have to hit me so hard?"

"We have to make it look realistic." Noble took him by the arm and steered him back onto the bench. Blood ran down his parka and dripped on the floor. Duval huffed and spluttered, sending red droplets flying from his lips.

"You didn't have to hit me so hard," he complained through a mouthful of blood. "My nose is ruined."

"Want me to set it?"

"No!" Duval held up one blood-smeared hand. "No, thank you. You've done enough."

Noble shrugged. "That's me. Always helpful."

Sam shot him a look.

He tried and failed to hide a grin.

Sam sat down next to Duval and flipped open a folding knife.

He leaned away from the blade, his eyes wide. "What are you going to do with that?"

"Try to relax," Sam told him. "Just a shallow prick. Scalp wounds are terrific bleeders."

"Aw, come on!" Duval said. "Do we have to?"

"It has to look like you've got a head wound," Noble said. He snaked an arm around Duval's neck, putting him in a headlock. Duval strangled out a protest and his hands clutched at Noble's arm. It was like a watching a rodent try to escape the grip of a python.

Noble held him while Sam pushed the knife point into Duval's scalp just above the hairline. A rivulet of dark blood dribbled from the tiny cut. Sam cringed. She felt awful about causing the cowardly reporter any more pain. He was in for a world of that, but Noble was right, they had to make it believable.

"Ow! Ow! Ow!" Duval said, "Are you doing brain surgery?"

Noble let go and Duval shrugged him off.

Sam set the knife aside and opened a small medical kit. She tore open an alcohol swab and wiped the wound clean. Duval's face lit up in pain. His mouth stretched and a string of curses poured out.

"Language," Sam reprimanded. She ripped open a pad along with gauze and wrapped the wound, allowing some of the blood to run down over his forehead for effect. His nose was starting to swell and dark rings had formed under his eyes. When Sam was done, he looked like a proper accident victim.

He probed gently at his head, inspected his fingers, frowned.

"Now for the hard part," Noble told him.

"I never should have agreed to this," Duval said.

"It's the only place they won't check." Noble picked up one of the microdots. "Drop your drawers and lift your undercarriage."

Duval's ears turned pink.

Sam stood up. "I'll be outside."

CHAPTER SEVENTY

Sam made her way along the line of rolling stock to the last car. The air in the abandoned station was old and stuffy, in bad need of circulation. A moldering tarp lay in one corner along with the remains of a hobo's cook-stove. Through grime-streaked windows she could see tracks marching off into oblivion. The distant roar of a subway train rumbled past. Her whole world had shrunk down to this shadowy cave deep beneath Paris. In the next few hours, she would go up against Grey and a group of hired thugs, armed with a handgun and BIC lighters. Not exactly an arsenal. Duval was right; their chances were slim at best.

Sam wiped dust from a bench before sitting down. She propped her elbows on her knees and tried not to think about all the things that could go wrong. A premonition struck and she felt certain one of them was going to die, maybe all three. She couldn't say why. It came to her like a peal of thunder that rattles the whole house. Her heart trembled inside her chest and sweat broke out on her forehead. The shadows seemed to darken and gather into menacing shapes. She screwed her eyes shut and prayed. *Don't let it be Jake. If one of us has to die, God, let it be me.*

Noble's voice intruded on her thoughts. "Cold?"

Sam looked up and forced a smile onto her face. *Should she tell him? No,* she decided. It would either spook him, or he would laugh it off and tell her she was being a hysterical woman. And maybe she was. Maybe she had spooked herself. She said, "Praying."

"We need all of the help we can get." Noble stuffed his hands in his pockets and settled onto the bench next to her.

Sam scooted over to make room. "Thought you didn't believe?"

When he didn't answer, she said, "Do I detect a chink in the armor?"

"Right now," Noble began slowly. "I'm open to some divine intervention. It'll take a miracle to pull this off."

"What brought on the sudden change of heart?"

Noble shrugged, thought it over, and said, "Odds were stacked against us in that rock quarry in Hong Kong and we came out alive. I don't know if you have a direct line to God or a horseshoe shoved up your butt, but you're the luckiest person I know. If praying will bring on some of that luck, by all means, pray."

Sam felt like her heart would burst right out of her chest and go tap-dancing across the empty platform. She swallowed to contain her excitement. "Maybe if we make it out of this alive, you'll reconsider this whole faith business?"

"I'll make you a deal," said Noble. "Get in touch with whatever higher power is taking requests, and if we make it out of this alive, I'll attend a church service with you, but you have to go to dinner with me."

"Are you asking me on a date?"

A slow grin turned up one side of his mouth. It was hard to be sure in the dim light of the station, but Sam thought she saw a hint of color in his cheeks. He nodded. "I know a café in Brussels. They only accept cash and there aren't any cameras. What do you say?"

"Deal." A smile lit up her face and burned off some of the cold. She leaned in to kiss him. His hand cupped her cheek, urging her closer. Their lips melded together. Sam didn't know how long it went on; it seemed like forever, but it ended too soon.

Noble broke off the kiss and whispered, "Plenty of time for that later. We got work to do."

CHAPTER SEVENTY-ONE

A pair of Range Rovers and a fire-engine red Alfa Romeo parked against the curb on Saint-Germain, across from the Mabillon metro entrance. Upscale boutiques and bakeries lined the boulevard. Light from their windows spilled across the cold, wet pavement in cheery bright pockets. A group of business execs in wingtips and overcoats emerged from the subway entrance, laughing at some joke.

Mateen sat in the passenger seat of the Alfa Romeo, looking out the window at the entrance to the underground through a narcotic-induced haze courtesy of prescription strength pain relievers. His jaw was a mass of hurt. Percocet took the edge off and made the pain manageable, but he felt like he was moving through fog.

Warm air poured from the vents, misting up the wind-shield. The driver of the Alfa Romeo, a native Frenchman named Claude, took one look at the metro entrance and cursed. "We can't tote a bunch of hardware down the steps. We'll have the police here in no time."

Grey leaned forward. "What are you so scared of?" He had a black duffel bag stuffed with old newspaper on his lap. Preston sat next to him. It was like having a pair of nervous old women in the car. They fidgeted and rocked and drummed their fingers. Mateen wanted to tell them to relax, but they were too keyed up.

Grey said, "There are eight of you and one of him."

"That's what he wants you to believe," Mateen said. He was regretting his decision to work for the American spooks. So far a broken jaw was the only thing he had to show for it. Now he was caught in the middle of a war between counter-intelligence agents and all the money in the world can't fix dead. Broken jaw aside, Grey was becoming increasingly difficult to work with. He was making demands, accusing Mateen and his men of incompetence, and questioning their methods. If that duffel bag actually had a half-million dollars in it, Mateen would shoot Grey and take the money for himself.

Live and learn, Mateen told himself. *Finish this bit of business and be done with it.* He returned his attention to the subway entrance. Noble had done an excellent job of picking the exchange point. It was in a high-traffic area, making it impossible for Mateen's crew to go in heavily armed.

Mateen picked up a small handheld radio from the center console and pressed the talk button. "Hand guns only. We don't want to start a panic."

He opened the passenger side door and cold air rushed into the car. The sudden change in temperature made his jaw ache. At a silent command from Mateen, the Range Rover doors opened and six mercenaries in overcoats piled out.

———

Noble and Duval had taken up residence in a train car at the far end of the platform. Croix-Rouge lay in near total darkness. The few remaining bulbs had been smashed out and the shards scattered over the ground in front of the entrance. The station was now lit by the ghostly green radiance of the glowsticks. It gave the underground vault the haunted feel of a Hollywood horror movie. Noble had spent the last two hours parked on a hard seat, his feet up, staring out the window at the deserted platform. The hours slouched past like some slothful beast. Minutes stretched into vast, uncharted oceans. Noble checked his wristwatch. The hands were pointing at five to midnight. He thought of Sam and his mother and a lifetime later he glanced at his watch, but the hands hadn't moved.

Noble had once spent two days lying in a rock crevice on the side of a mountain in Afghanistan. Long stretches of time with nothing to do is par for the course in Special Forces. It made sitting in a bombed-out subway station easy, but the cold was seeping into his bones, making his joints hurt and his fingers stiff. *Too young to be getting old,* he told himself. He rolled his shoulders to keep them loose and flexed his fingers.

Duval paced, breathing hard like he had just run a marathon. Broken shards of glass crunched under his shoes. Every few minutes he would stop for a glance out the window, rub his hands together, pace some more and then stop for another look.

"Relax," Noble told him. "It'll happen when it happens."

"How can you be so calm?"

"Worrying about it won't help." Noble checked the action on his weapon, spied a round in the breech and let the slide slap forward. In truth, he was probably more nervous than Duval, Noble just knew how to hide it better. He had joined the United States Army at the age of eighteen, fought in conflicts all around the globe, and after more than fifteen years come to realize you never really get over the fear. You just learn to deal with it. Some guys cracked jokes, others prayed, and some chain-smoked. No matter the method, it came down to silencing the demons in your skull, those voices that kept insisting this time your luck would finally run out.

And then what? Noble chewed the inside of one cheek. What happened after? That was the question Noble struggled with. Not the dying part. That was easy. After he died? Then what? "Hello darkness, my old friend"? Or *Hallelujah Choir*? Sam certainly believed in a creator. So did Noble's mother. Jake told people he didn't believe, but the truth was he feared there might actually be a god and that was unfortunate, because Jake was mad. Mad at losing his father. Mad at the cancer that had nearly killed his mother. Mad at the villainous scumbags who raped and murdered and ripped the world apart. He was mad as hell and he wanted answers. All he got were more questions.

Duval did another lap of the car, wrung his hands, and

peered through the dirt-streaked glass. "I can't take this anymore."

"Heads up," they heard Sam's voice coming from Noble's pocket. They had a pair of burner phones on speaker. It was the best they could do without hands-free radios. Those were a little harder to buy last minute than climbing gear. Her words came through muffled but clear. She said, "I've got movement in the access tunnel."

Noble directed his voice at his pocket. "I read you, Sam. Stay out of sight and fall back to your position."

Duval looked stricken. The last of the color drained from his face, leaving him a waxy shade of pale. He swallowed with an audible click. "*Mon Dieu,*" he stammered. "*Mon Dieu,* I don't think I can do this."

"Too late to change your mind." Noble stood up and shook out his legs, then hunkered down in front of the window. His heart was slamming against his chest. Seconds ticked past before he glimpsed the beam of a flashlight spilling from the access tunnel that opened onto the Croix-Rouge station.

Duval joined him at the window. "*Mon Dieu, Mon Dieu.* They're here."

Noble said, "Try to relax, will ya? You're making *me* nervous."

"I can't do this," Duval hissed. He put his back to the wall of the train and covered his face with both hands. "There has to be another way. Call it off."

Noble caught his sleeve. "Don't lose your nerve."

Duval yanked his arm free. "Easy for you to say. I'm taking all the risk!"

"In a few minutes those mercenaries are going to try to kill me," Noble told him. "You've got the easy part."

Sam's voice came from Noble's pocket. "Duval, listen to me; you can do this. Everything is going to be fine. I promise."

More flashlight beams spilled from the passage as the mercenaries got closer. Duval squeezed his eyes shut. His face crumpled into an ugly mix of terror and sadness. A long mewling sound escaped his throat. "I hate this plan."

"I'm not crazy about it either," Noble admitted. "But it's too late to turn back."

The first of the mercenaries filed through the accessway onto the platform. Boots crunched in broken glass and flashlight beams played around the abandoned station, along the line of cars.

CHAPTER SEVENTY-TWO

GLOWSTICKS WERE SCATTERED NEAR THE MOUTH OF the access tunnel, shining on the ground like radioactive turds on cracked concrete. Noble used the light to count heads. He tallied up eight bad guys along with Grey, toting a duffel bag, and Preston with his hand wrapped in thick gauze. Mateen, with his broken jaw, emerged from the tunnel last and the group fanned out across the platform, putting some distance between themselves in case this was a double-cross. It told Noble these guys were professionals and this wasn't their first rodeo. They weren't going to scatter when the bullets started flying. They had come here to kill Noble and they weren't leaving until the job was done.

"That's far enough," Noble shouted.

The hired guns oriented on his voice. Flashlights reflected off the grime-encrusted windows of the subway car. Noble shrank from the light and yelled, "Show me the money."

"First show me Duval," Grey shouted back.

Noble grabbed Sacha by the arm and hauled him in front of the glass long enough for them to see the bloody bandage wrapped around his head, then shoved him out of view. "I want to see the money or the deal's off."

Grey held up the duffel bag. "It's all here. Send Duval out to me. I'll put the bag down and we walk away."

"How do I know you won't double-cross me?" Noble said.

Grey tossed the bag halfway across the platform. It landed with a soft flop instead of the heavy thud half a million dollars would make. Grey lifted both hands and took a step back. "Happy? It's all yours. We just want Duval."

So far so good, Noble told himself. Grey thought he was the player instead of the other way around. Noble turned to Duval. "Showtime. Stick to the plan and remember what I said—keep 'em talking. That's key."

When Duval didn't move, Noble grabbed his collar, steered him out the door, and gave him a shove. "He's coming out!"

———

Mateen dug a bottle of pills out of his pocket, shook a pair into his open palm and tossed them back while Grey was negotiating for the reporter. It wasn't long before a bruised and battered Sacha Duval came stumbling out of the train car. A white bandage was wrapped around his skull and his blond hair stuck up in places. He held up both hands and started to stammer. Preston darted forward, grabbed Duval's collar, and dragged him away from the train.

So far so good, Mateen thought to himself.

Grey and Preston herded the struggling reporter across the platform. They had him by the elbows and his feet barely touched the ground. Spittle flew from his lips as he begged for his life. *Pathetic*, Mateen thought. He handed Grey the keys to the Alfa Romeo and said, "Don't scratch the paint."

"Make sure you kill him this time," Grey murmured. Then he and Preston shoved Duval toward the dark access tunnel. Duval started to scream but Preston stuck a gun in his ribs. "Make a scene and I'll pump a round into your guts."

Duval stopped shouting. He walked on stiff legs like Frankenstein's monster, supported on either side by the corrupt CIA agents. Mateen waited until they had disappeared into the dark, then turned to his men and drew a thumb across his throat.

CHAPTER SEVENTY-THREE

NOBLE SHIFTED HIS FEET, CLEARING AWAY THE GRIT under his shoes. He wanted a stable shooting platform—for the first shot anyways. His attackers had the advantage in both numbers and firepower, but Noble had the gift of sight. Between the glowsticks and flashlights, Noble could see them, but they couldn't see him. Amateurs like flashlights because it makes them feel tactical and because humans have an instinctual fear of the dark. But flashlights make perfect targets. Just aim at the light and pull the trigger.

As Duval was ushered away from the platform, Noble spoke softly into his phone. "Get ready, Sam."

"Roger that," she whispered back.

The exchange and the money had all been a lead-up to this. Play time was over. With Duval out of the way, both sides could drop the act and get down to business. No more subterfuge. No more games. It was kill or be killed. Noble took in some air and let it out slow.

At a silent command from Mateen, the tunnel came

alive with the steady crack of small arms fire. Bullets hissed and snapped, obliterating the windows in a shower of glass. Muzzle flashes winked, blurring Noble's vision. He sighted on nearest gunman and squeezed the trigger. Two loud bull whips sounded inside the subway car and the Kimber kicked. Brass shell casings spun from the breech, clattering over the floor.

The slugs caught the hired gun high on the chest and knocked him backwards, but Noble didn't see it. He had bent down below the window frame and duck-walked to the open door. Lead impacted the walls with bone-jarring force. The old train car had been constructed of heavy timber and overlaid with aluminum. The wood and metal design caught most of the hollow-point rounds, but not all. Bullets chewed through the sides of the train, buzzed around Noble's head, and imbedded themselves in the benches with loud *thwacks*. Noble's nerves hummed like high tension wires. He could feel his pulse pounding in his ears. Smoke trailed from the barrel of his weapon and the smell of cordite hung in the air. He leaned around the open door frame, aimed at a flashlight beam and fired.

The shot was rushed and missed, but served its purpose. The hired guns saw the muzzle flash and focused on the middle of the car, pumping rounds through the door. Noble turned and sprinted to the end of the train. The emergency door stood open and Noble leapt down onto the tracks while Mateen's crew obliterated the subway car with a hail of gunfire.

"Sam," Noble yelled. "I'm headed your way!"

"I'm ready," she said.

Noble stuffed the pistol in his waistband, pulled three

glowsticks from his pocket and gave them a quick twist before tossing them over his shoulder.

————

Mateen ducked his head and pulled his shoulders up around his ears. The pain killers were dulling his senses and slowing his reactions. He knew he needed to get behind cover, but everything seemed to be happening so fast. One of his men was down, screaming in pain, another was tending to the wounded man. The rest were firing blind. The cavernous subway station echoed with the sharp thunder claps; it felt like white-hot needles stabbing Mateen's eardrums. He jogged to a pillar, put his shoulder against it, and leaned out far enough to see the train. His crew had turned the open doorframe into matchsticks.

"Hold your fire," Mateen yelled through clenched teeth and winced at the shot of pain. He wanted another pill, but that would have to wait. If he ever laid hands on the girl, he was going to make her suffer before she died. He put his free hand to the side of his throbbing jaw and yelled again. "Hold your fire!"

The guns fell silent, the last shell casings rolled to a stop and an oppressive quiet crowded the station. The wounded man had died or passed out; either way, he was no longer making noise and in the absence of sound Mateen caught the quick stab of heels in gravel echoing softly from the tunnel behind the abandoned train. "He went down the tracks," Mateen said. "Get him."

———

Sam had her back to the wall, using a crumbling stone arch for cover. This section of the tunnel was built with alcoves that made perfect ambush points. Sweat gathered on her forehead despite the cold and her heart thudded inside her chest. She gripped a BIC in one hand and the other held a spring with a flint attached. Noble had showed her how to take the disposable lighters apart, attach the flint striker to the spring and use it as a tiny flashbang grenade.

Le Milieu gunmen hammered the side of the train with a continuous barrage of small arms fire. Windows blew out with a small sound barely audible over the whip crack of barking pistols. The cacophony of noise filled the deserted tunnel like a symphony of jackhammers in an amphitheater. Sam narrowed her eyes and her lips peeled back in a painful grimace. She wanted to cover her ears and scream.

When Jake jumped from the back of the train, Sam flicked the lighter, ran the flame over the flint and watched it turn red hot. *Slow and steady*, she told herself. *Just like they taught at the Farm.*

Noble shouted into his phone and Sam let him know she was ready. He tossed a handful of the glowsticks over his shoulder. Seconds later the green luminescence filled the tunnel in back of the train with a ghostly light. The guns stopped, then the French mercenaries shouted commands and came around the back of the car with their weapons leading the way. The first man dropped down onto the tracks and advanced. Sam could just make out his silhouette limed by the light of the glowsticks. At the same time, Noble went sprinting past her position.

Sam recalled the first time she had ever shot a man. She was on a ridgeline above a rock quarry in Kowloon, terrified out of her mind, but determined to save her friend. A lot had changed since then. Instead of a scared college girl with no weapons training, she was now a trained field officer for the CIA.

The striker was glowing white-hot when Noble dashed by. Sam leaned out, hurled the flint at the ground in front of the hired guns and turned her face away. It impacted with a thunderous pop and a brilliant flash.

The lead gunman gave a surprised shout and threw a hand up in front of his face. The explosion had no force behind it, just a burst of light and sound, but in a dark space it could render a man blind for several seconds.

Sam pulled her Springfield XD-S, sighted on his chest and eased the trigger back, trying not to anticipate the recoil. The weapon jumped and the man went down on his back with surprise still etched on the lines of his face.

The rest of the gunmen sprayed the tunnel, blasting chunks from the walls and sending rounds skipping off the tracks. The sound was deafening. Sam ducked behind the arch and waited for the hailstorm to end.

Meanwhile, Noble had stopped, taken a position in an archway further up the tunnel and returned fire. The glow-sticks revealed his targets and a third mercenary caught a bullet in the belly. He jackknifed over, clutching his bloody stomach and moaning in pain.

Sam used the distraction to turn and sprint along the tracks. Her ankle, still tender, sent stabbing pains racing up her leg with every step, but she willed herself to keep moving, pumping her arms for speed. Bullets snapped past her ears and whined off the walls. A stitch formed in her chest. She darted past Noble's position, to an open tunnel on the left and threw herself behind cover.

While Noble fired off the rest of his mag, Sam heated another flint with her lighter. Her hands shook so badly it took three tries to get a flame. Noble's Kimber locked back on an empty chamber. He dropped the spent mag, reloaded and racked the slide. The gunmen were advancing up the tunnel, firing as they came, using the arches for cover. Noble yelled, "Sam?"

"Almost," she yelled back. The flame slowly turned the flint red then white and she shouted, "Now!"

Noble leaned out, squeezed off two rounds, then sprinted for the side tunnel. As he ran past, Sam reared back and flung the glowing flint at the advancing gunmen. Another brilliant flash lit the tunnel.

Blinded, the hired guns all started firing at the same time. One of the men in front caught a bullet in the back and was thrown face down on the track, screaming in pain.

Sam and Noble retreated along the side passage to an adjoining tunnel barred by a heavy gate. They had scouted it out before making the exchange, picked the rust-covered padlock, and left the door open. Near as they could tell, it was the only other exit from Croix-Rouge for several miles. Any other escape would require the hired guns to travel long loops of dark and deserted track. Noble went through first and snatched the padlock off the ground where they had left it. Sam was on his heels. She leapt through the opening and swung the gate shut with a loud clang. Noble threaded the hasp, snapped the lock, and gave it a tug to be sure it held.

CHAPTER SEVENTY-FOUR

GREY STOOD ON THE PROW OF A RIVER BARGE DOCKED west of Pont Neuf. A thin layer of fog blanketed the Seine and formed halos around the lights of the distant bridge. Oil drums were lashed to the open deck of the barge and old tires protected the gunwales. Waves lapped at the rusty hull while a blistering cold tugged at the hem of Grey's dark wool overcoat. He reached into his pocket for his cell, stripped off a glove with his teeth, dialed, and put the phone to his ear.

The Alfa Romeo was parked on the street. Preston and Duval waited inside the car with the heater running. Fifty meters further up, a commercial vessel had pulled in to dock. Crew members ambled up the stone steps, weary after a long day while deck hands lashed the ship to the wharf. A fog horn gave a mournful cry in the distance.

Coughlin picked up after a dozen rings. "You'd better have good news."

"We got him," Grey said. "The package is secure."

Coughlin breathed a sigh of relief. "Have you found out the name of his failsafe?"

"Not yet," Grey said.

"What are you waiting for?"

"We just got to the river," Grey told him. "I'm waiting on another ship to unload."

"Why?"

"It's one o'clock in the morning in the dead of winter," Grey said. "Two guys wrestling a third man below decks in the middle of the night might look suspicious."

"I forgot about the time difference," Coughlin said. "Let me know as soon as you have a name."

The line went dead before Grey could say another word. He stood on the prow, his coat flapping around his knees, watching the last of the sailors stumble up the steps. When they had gone and the quayside was finally empty, Grey signaled to Preston, then made his way along the gunwale to the pilothouse.

The powerful diesel came to life with a series wheezing coughs that turned into a throaty rumble, whipping the water behind the barge into white foam. While Preston herded Duval out of the car and up the gangplank, Grey hurried to release the mooring lines. The journalist allowed himself to be dragged along the deck to an open hatch, begging for his life, promising to tell them anything as long as they didn't hurt him. Grey threw off the last of the lines and then hustled back to the bridge. The sound of the engines throttled up and the old rust heap pulled slowly away from the stone jetty.

CHAPTER SEVENTY-FIVE

BURKE SAT BEHIND THE WHEEL OF HIS CAR STARING AT his two-story brownstone. The sky overhead was iron gray. Small flurries of snow accumulated along the wipers and quickly turned to wet. After handing in his resignation, Burke had driven around aimlessly for several hours, cruising the streets of the capital, not sure where he was going. Somehow, he ended up here. He had needed someone to talk to, but Maddie wasn't home. Burke's mind was racing and going nowhere, like a hamster in a wheel.

For an organization which prided itself on keeping secrets, news of Burke's sudden retirement had spread fast. People stopped him on his way out of the building to shake his hand and congratulate him on his years of service. Burke had smiled and offered up excuses for his sudden departure. The rumor mill was working overtime and there was a lot of speculation but no one really knew for certain. No one but Burke, that is. He had been fired, even if he was the only one who knew it. He had lost his job, early retirement would take a chunk out of his pension, his marriage was in shambles, and he would lose the house. Maddie would surely get it in the divorce.

How had he screwed things up so badly?

He passed a hand over his face. The engine idled and a column of white exhaust rose from the tailpipe. Rain sensors occasionally triggered the wipers. They streaked across the windshield, throwing off the buildup of slush. Burke could do as the Director had suggested and start a private intelligence firm. There were plenty of ex-CIA employees who freelanced, but fifty-eight was too old to start all over again, and contract work meant taking jobs that were less than ethical.

Burke snorted and looked at himself in the rearview. "Since when did you start worrying about ethics?"

Where was all that moral outrage when he had stepped out on his wife with another woman? Matt shook his head. Here he was, sitting in the driveway of his former home, worried about morals. Funny how we pick and choose our ethics.

While he pondered the implications of his own morality, a blue Escalade pulled into the drive. Burke angled his rearview.

Maddie was in the passenger seat with her hair pulled back and a few loose strands framing her face. A glossy red stain covered her lips. A handsome black man with a shaved head was at the wheel. From the way he sat, it was easy to see he was tall. Six-four, maybe six-five.

There was a gun in Burke's glove box and he pictured himself getting out, walking back to the Escalade, and emptying the weapon into Mr. Tall and Handsome.

While he watched, Maddie and her new beau shared a brief exchange. Her date wore a look of concern at the strange car in the drive. Maddie shook her head and dangly gold earrings swayed. Mr. Tall and Handsome leaned across the seats. Maddie offered her cheek.

Burke's tenuous grip on composure weakened. It felt like a cinderblock pressing down on his chest. *What did you expect? That she would wait around for you?* He had thrown away their marriage and she had every right to see someone new.

The passenger door opened and Maddie climbed out. A clingy black dress with a plunging neckline hugged her curves and three-inch heels sculpted her calves. She wrapped herself in a faux fur and ducked her chin as she hurried up to the side of Burke's car.

He buzzed the window down.

Maddie had a nervous smile on her face. "I wasn't expecting..."

Her smile ran away, replaced by concern. They had been married a long time and she could still read him. She saw the look on his face and said, "What happened?"

He started to talk but didn't know where to begin. Instead he hiked up his shoulders and said, "Sorry. I didn't know you were on a date. I should go."

"He's just a friend from work," Maddie said. "It was the first time and it was only dinner."

"All the same," said Burke, fighting to control the emotion behind the words. "I'll leave you alone."

"Don't shut me out, Matt. I've known you too long. Something's wrong."

"It's nothing," Burke tried to say.

Maddie turned back and gave her date a goodbye wave. He put the Escalade in reverse, backed out of the driveway, and disappeared down the road. Maddie opened the passenger door and climbed in next to Burke. "What's going on, Matt?"

A frown creased his forehead. He cleared a catch in his throat and started to talk. He told her everything.

CHAPTER SEVENTY-SIX

FEAR COURSED THROUGH DUVAL'S VEINS. WITH EVERY beat of his terrified heart, his arteries felt like they would explode. And Grey hadn't even started in on the torture yet. They had stripped him naked, strapped him to a chair in the hold, and checked for listening devices under the bandage wrapped around his head—just like Noble had said they would—but they hadn't bothered to check under his scrotum.

A single bulb in a wire cage lit rusty bulkheads and stagnant puddles gathered on the metal floor. Waves lapped at the hull and water dripped from a leaky pipe in the ceiling, making a steady *plunk-plunk-plunk*. Duval shivered against the numbing cold. His nose was running. He could feel it inching down his upper lip toward his open mouth but there was nothing he could do about it.

Preston had gone topside, to take over at the wheel, leaving Duval alone with Grey. "You made a real mess of things," Grey said. "You know that? Langley is starting to ask questions and I don't have answers."

"Please," Sacha said. The word came out in sections, broken up by pathetic hitching noises: *puh-huh-leas*. Noble had told him to act scared, do a lot of begging, and that part was proving easy. He was scared out of his mind. It was the other part that was next to impossible. Duval licked his lips and said, "Please, don't kill me. Let me go and I'll never tell anyone about CyberLance, I promise. Just let me go."

He was begging for his life, but he was also stringing Grey along, trying to tease information from him. Noble had coached Duval on the art of counter-interrogation. It required the person being interrogated to extract an admission of guilt from the one doing the interrogation.

"While they're questioning you, you're questioning them," Noble had said. *"Don't make the mistake of answering their questions directly. Answer questions with questions. Get them to spell out their crimes on tape. It's the only way to prove Coughlin stole CyberLance and is selling the service to the highest bidder."*

"But don't let on that you're trying to get a confession from them," Sam had added. *"You have to make it look natural."*

"It will help if you can act scared," Noble had said.

Duval had never been so scared in his life. His fingers and toes were numb and his bladder felt like it would let go any second.

Grey crossed his arms over his chest. "Let you go?" He shook his head. "We need to have a chat. This is about information. You have it and I want it."

"What information do you want?" Duval asked. "I

thought you already knew about CyberLance? If you didn't help Coughlin use it, then who did?"

"Where's your laptop, Sacha?"

"It was destroyed," Duval told him. "What do you want my laptop for?"

Grey shot out a hand.

Duval had just enough time to clamp his eyes shut and draw his shoulders up. The open-hand blow caught him on the cheek and rocked his head to the side. The sharp clap sounded incredibly loud in his ears. Duval hadn't realized he screamed until the sound faded.

"Where's the laptop, Sacha? You had it with you on the boat. Where is it now?"

"I told you. It was destroyed," Duval said. "All the proof I had that Coughlin was using CyberLance is gone. Tell Coughlin it was broken. That's who you work for right? Pete Coughlin?"

"Shut up." Grey hit Duval with another stinging slap.

Duval sobbed. "Please, I'm telling you the truth."

"What about your failsafe?" Grey asked. "Who else has access to the Cypher Punk vaults? Who releases the information if you die?"

Duval shook his head. "No one, I swear."

"You expect me to believe that?"

"I'm telling the truth."

"I want names," Grey said in a soft, almost friendly tone.

"There's no one," Duval insisted.

Grey said, "You have a third informant and it's someone inside the CIA. I want to know who."

Duval felt the cold hand of fear grip his guts. "How did you know that?"

"You received a data dump of classified info. That's how you knew about operation MEDUSA," Grey said. He grabbed a fistful of Duval's hair and wrenched his head back.

Duval's chin shot up toward the ceiling. He choked back a shriek.

"Think we're stupid?" Grey shouted in his face. Spittle landed on Duval's cheek and he winced. Grey said, "We've been feeding out false information trying to trace it back to you through your moles."

"Who?" Duval said. "Who's been feeding false information? Coughlin?"

Grey let go of his hair. "What's it matter to you? We know you've got someone inside the CIA and we know that person is your failsafe. You're going to give me a name or you're going to die slowly."

Grey took an unmarked bottle from a self and gave it a shake. Liquid sloshed around inside.

Duval's chin trembled. Tears welled up in his eyes and doubled his vision.

"That's right," Grey told him. "You're going to die, Sacha. But you get to decide how much it hurts."

He thumbed the cap off the bottle and the smell of bleach assaulted Duval's nostrils. His heart hammered wildly inside his chest. His body shook like a dog with worms. *Where in the hell were Noble and Sam? Why didn't they stop this?* Grey was going to kill him and there was nothing Duval could do to stop him.

"Tell me the name of your failsafe and I'll make it quick," said Grey. "Hold out on me, and we'll find out how much bleach you can drink before it eats a hole in your stomach."

"I don't know his name!" Duval was shouting now, desperate for this psychopath to believe him. "I don't know his name. He never told me. You have to believe me!"

CHAPTER SEVENTY-SEVEN

NOBLE TWISTED THE STEERING WHEEL. HE WAS IN THE
driver's seat of a stolen plumber's van, speeding west along
the Quai des Tuileries, following the line of the river as it
looped through the heart of Paris. The fading script on the
side of the van promised "Fast, Professional Service." The
owner wouldn't realize the truck was missing until he
arrived at work in the morning. Noble jogged around a
slower-moving Passat and back into his lane. Plumbing tools
crashed around in the rear of the van. The driver of the
Passat mashed his horn. Noble ignored him and watched
the side streets, looking for a glimpse of the river barge.

"We're going to lose him," Sam said. She was in the
passenger seat with the ruggedized laptop open on her
thighs. Duval's terrified voice came from the speakers, a
faint but audible signal broken by static. The climbing gear
lay on the floor between the seats. Sam listened to the
exchange and shook her head. "Jake, he can't hold out much
longer. Turn here."

"Give him more time," Noble said.

They heard liquid splashing and frantic gurgling noises. Noble frowned. A tight knot formed in his chest. The splashing sound stopped and Duval wretched. It sounded like he was tossing up his guts. Noble tried not to imagine the scene and focused on the information instead.

"Who's your failsafe?" Grey demanded.

"I don't know his name," Duval spluttered. "Listen, I've got money. How much is Coughlin paying you to cover his tracks? I'll double it. Name your price. Anything!"

A flat hard smack distorted the speaker.

"Try again," Grey barked.

"I'm telling you, I don't know his name," Duval said.

There came the sound of liquid sloshing inside a bottle. "Want some more?"

"No, please. No more."

"Tell me his name!"

"You have to believe me," Duval said. "I don't know."

Noble said, "Come on, Sacha, keep him talking."

Sam shook her head. "Jake, we've gotten as much as we're going to get. We have to pull him out."

They were coming up on Pont Alexandre III and Sam said, "Turn here."

From the speaker, they heard Duval take another face full of bleach. Grey demanded a name over more retching noises.

"He calls himself Groot," Duval spluttered at last. "That's all I know."

Noble cursed and cut the wheel. The van slewed through the turn, tires slipping on a scrim of ice. Sam braced one hand against the dash and held the computer with the other. The stolen van swerved around the tail end of a delivery truck, narrowly avoided an oncoming taxi, and veered back into the right lane.

Armed with his contact's cryptonym, Grey no longer had any more use for Duval. He would kill him and dump the body in the water. That gave Noble and Sam minutes, maybe less, to get on the barge and extract Duval before Grey put a bullet in him.

Noble stamped the gas. The old plumbing van raced onto Pont Alexandre III, past the towering winged horses that flanked either end of the bridge, and zigzagged through traffic. They could see the glass and steel dome of the Grand Palais in the distance.

Grey made a phone call and they heard him say, "It's me. Does the name Groot mean anything to you?"

Noble reached the middle of the bridge, mounted the empty sidewalk and stamped the brakes. The wheels locked and the van slid. The front bumper swerved back and forth. Tools tumbled forward, crashing and clanging, before the van slowed to a stop.

"He claims that's all he knows," Grey was saying.

On Noble's left, passing under Pont des Invalides, he spied the dark outline of the barge plowing through the fog-shrouded waters of the Seine. Running lamps made halos in the mist.

Noble threw open his door and Sam tossed him a climbing rope. He caught it one-handed and hurried to the railing, trying to gauge where the barge would pass under the bridge with nothing more than instinct born of countless hours at sea. Sometimes it pays to live on a boat.

Sam crossed around in front of the truck, coiling a rope

around her forearm. Wind caught a few loose strands of her black hair and pink spots bloomed in her cheeks. "We're only going to get one shot at this," she said.

"Don't remind me." Noble looked at the barge, then over the railing at the churning waters below, moved several meters to his left, and set to work feeding rope through his harness.

Sam chose a spot far enough apart that she would still land on the deck, but not so close that she risked colliding with Noble on the way down. Her chest rose and fell. Air exploded from her lips in short bursts. Her hands shook as she worked the rope.

"It's so close," Sam said, looking at the distance between the bridge and the deck of the ship. The barge had almost reached Pont Alexandre III. It would be passing under any minute. "We could almost jump."

"Don't try it," Noble warned.

"No," said Sam, "Just giving myself encouragement."

"Try to relax," Noble told her. "Focus on your breathing."

She nodded, took a breath and let it out slow. A cold wind whipped the waters of the Seine into white froth. Sam's eyes went to the barge. She could hear the sound of the big diesel motor and see the pilothouse. She said, "They're going to see us."

"Not much we can do about that," Noble told her. He secured his line to the railing with a carabiner, gathered the length in one hand and waited.

Sam chewed her bottom lip.

A few motorists slowed to watch, thinking this was some extreme sport stunt.

As the barge disappeared under the bridge, Noble hurled his length of rope over the railing. The line unspooled in the darkness and the excess plopped on the prow of the barge as it emerged from under the span. He grabbed the railing and climbed over. Sam threw her rope and scrambled out next to him. The barge was chugging beneath them, their view of the deck getting bigger.

"Hey Jake," Sam said and glanced over at him. She had her legs braced against the bridge, her right hand gripping the line and her left hand braking the excess. They were poised over the abyss, their landing zone getting bigger by the moment, precious seconds slipping away. "If anything happens..."

"Don't get all mushy on me," Noble said and fixed a smile on his face. It came off looking like a nervous grin. "We still have work to do."

Sam nodded.

Noble pushed off from the edge and let himself sink, using his left hand to brake the rope and slow his descent. The line purred as it played out through his harness. Friction heated his palms and his crotch felt like it was on fire. He caught a glimpse of the pilot in the wheelhouse. For one brief second, he locked eyes with Preston, then his feet touched the deck. He let his knees buckle to absorb the impact. It was like leaping off a first-floor roof onto concrete that was moving. Noble stumbled, but managed to recover.

Sam wasn't so lucky. She staggered and went down on her side with a sharp hiss.

Line continued to play out through Noble's harness as the barge motored away from the bridge. He stooped, gripped Sam's elbow and urged her up. "You okay?"

She put weight on her left ankle and grimaced. "I can fight."

Noble grabbed her line and jerked it free of the harness, before casting off the rest of his own. For the moment, they were sheltered by a stack of oil drums and a huge winch stand. The deck of the barge rumbled beneath their feet. Water churned and babbled around the prow. Standing on his toes, Noble could make out the pilothouse. He dropped back down and said, "You take starboard. I'll take port. We'll meet at the hatch. Got it?"

Sam's mouth was a thin line. The pain was obvious on her face. Her ankle was hurting bad. It would swell up like a balloon tomorrow, but she was determined to stay in the fight. She nodded.

"They'll be shooting to kill," Noble told her. "You do the same."

"Let's end this," Sam said.

CHAPTER SEVENTY-EIGHT

PRESTON, INSIDE THE PILOTHOUSE, SAW THE TWO figures rappel down and disappear behind the stacks of oil drums. He recognized Sam straight away and the other had to be Jake Noble. Those two didn't know when to quit. Preston snarled a curse and toggled the intercom switch. "Grey! We have company. Grey, do you hear me?"

The small speaker gave a hiss of static and then Grey's voice came over the system. "Police?"

"No," Preston barked. "Sam and Noble. They just fast-roped onto the ship."

"How did they do that?" Grey wanted to know.

"They dropped down from the bridge." Preston told him. "What do you want me to do?"

"Stay at the wheel," Grey said. "Do what you can from there. I'm coming up."

Preston glimpsed the top of Noble's head as he moved along the port side gunwale. He cast a look around the pilot-house, spotted a fire extinguisher hanging by the door, and grabbed it off the peg. He felt a stab of pain. His face pinched. His hand was a mass of melted skin and puss-filled blisters. It hurt even when he wasn't using it. It was doubtful he could hit a target across a dinner table, never mind a target on the deck of rolling ship.

He turned the fire extinguisher around and used the blunt end to smash the windshield. Glass rained out of the frame. Cold air and salty mist filled the pilothouse, blowing papers around like dry leaves. Preston dropped the extinguisher. It landed with a hollow *bong* and rolled across the floor. A dark splotch of blood had soaked through his bandage. Using his right hand wasn't going to work. Preston gripped his pistol in his left and thrust it out the shattered window.

———

Grey switched off the intercom. A growl worked its way up from his chest. This whole operation had gone completely off the rails. Coughlin's scheme to draw Duval out into the open had backfired and thrown a big bright spotlight on them. Even if they found the failsafe and killed him before he could release the info, the damage was done.

Grey turned a menacing glare on Duval. Dried blood caked one side of the reporter's face and his eyes were puffy red slits. He looked small and pathetic in the chair, like a terrified wildebeest surrounded by lions.

"Your friends are here," Grey told him. "But don't get your hopes up. They won't be here long."

Grey reached under his jacket for his gun, stepped through the hatch and moved along a short passageway, up a flight of steps to the galley. He heard the sharp crack of a pistol over the steady rumble of the engines.

————

Noble edged along the port gunwale, his Kimber in one hand, the other hand gripping the icy railing for support. A stack of old drums provided some cover. The slowly rolling deck caused them to shift with creaking voices. The barge plowed through the water at a steady ten knots, kicking up chilly white spray from the bow. Cold drops hit the back of Noble's neck and sent a shiver tip-toeing up his spine. His arms and legs felt electrified.

Over the sound of the waves, Noble heard breaking glass, craned his head up for a look and saw Preston thrust a handgun out the shattered window. Noble pulled his head in like a turtle crawling back inside its shell. Bullets punched through the metal drums with piercing shrieks. Two holes appeared less than an inch from Noble's face and pissed out streams of brackish water. Noble crouched and put his shoulder to the cold metal bellies. They were filled with saltwater for ballast. *Good thing they weren't full of gasoline*, thought Noble. The whole barge would be a fiery inferno by now.

He took a breath, leaned out, and squeezed off two rounds. Fire leapt from the muzzle. Thunder clapped. The rolling ship caused his shots to go wide and Preston replied in kind. More lead hornets stung the rusty drums.

————

Sam had her back to the oil drums, her weapon clutched in both hands, easing along the starboard gunwale. Her heart beat a rapid tattoo on the inside of her chest. An icy spray caught her in the face and she spit out saltwater. The harsh jingle of breaking glass made her stop. Gunshots ripped through the air. The sound felt like a rubber band snapped against her eardrums. There was an answering volley from the port side.

Sam edged along the row of barrels until she could see the hatch. She peeked in time to see the wheel spin. The rusty scrape of the hinges was barely audible over the furious exchange of gunfire. The hatch swung open and Grey filled the frame, a gun in his hand. His face was a mask of cold fury and his eyes locked on Sam

She brought her weapon up, settled the front sight on his chest and yelled, "Drop it, Grey!"

His hand came up with the gun.

Sam felt her finger tighten on the trigger. The weapon kicked. An empty shell casing leap from the breech, went spinning over the railing and into the dark waters. The bullet struck Grey high on the right shoulder. His face pinched in pain. He stumbled backwards and squeezed the trigger. His shot skipped off the wall of drums and forced Sam to retreat. When she looked again, Grey was hauling the hatchway closed. She raised her weapon, but it was too late. The metal door clanged shut and the wheel turned, driving the locks in place.

From the port side, Noble continued to trade shots with Preston in the pilothouse. Their bullets hissed and cracked, filling the air with the promise of a quick and painful death. Sam ducked her head and sprinted across the deck. She reached the hatch and gave it a pointless tug. The wheel refused to budge.

A searing lance of blinding pain twisted Grey's face. The bullet had gone in just below his collar bone. At first it was just numbness, like the aftereffect of being punched hard, then a crippling shockwave raced from the ragged hole in his shoulder to his brain and made his legs want to buckle. Blood welled up from the wound and soaked through his overcoat. He could feel it running down the underside of his arm. A wave of nausea hit and he had to clutch at the bulkhead for support. He had never been shot before. He knew it was painful, but he never imagined it would be *this* painful.

The pain turned to hatred, and focused in on Sam like a shark that smells blood in the water. She was to blame. She had started the dominoes falling. If not for her, Duval and his failsafe would be dead and no one would be any wiser. Grey would have gotten rich working for Coughlin and retired with more money than he knew what to do with. Now that future was gone and all because of Samantha Gunn. Grey hurried across the empty galley to a second hatch that opened onto the stern.

CHAPTER SEVENTY-NINE

A HAILSTORM OF LEAD RICOCHETED OFF THE TOPS OF the oil drums. One round buzzed past Noble's ear and hit the water with a tiny burst of foam. He put his back to the barrels, bent his knees, and sank down a few inches to keep from getting his head shot off. His eyes narrowed against the constant barrage and his mouth formed a strict line. Preston held the high ground and could keep Noble pinned until he ran out of ammo.

Noble considered retracing his steps, trying to circle around, but that would only bottleneck him and Sam together, making them easy targets. He needed to deal with Preston. He stuck his gun up over the barrels and fired blind. The Kimber locked back on an empty chamber and Noble dug in his pocket for his last mag. His shots inspired a loud reply. Angry lead hornets buzzed around the barrels and stung the lids. Noble winced at the sharp metal *thwacks*.

Think of something fast, he told himself.

Sam appeared at the corner of the pilothouse with her back to the wall. Preston wouldn't be able to see her from his angle. If he wanted to shoot her, he would have to lean out the broken window. Sam kept her weapon close to her chest and shouted to be heard. "You okay?"

"Never better." He winced as another bullet sizzled overhead.

"I clipped Grey," she hollered. "But he's still alive and he locked the hatch."

"There's another way below decks," Noble shouted and pointed along the narrow ledge which circled the pilothouse. It had no railing, only a frayed rope for a handhold. It was a risky maneuver, but they had to get inside or be cut to pieces out here.

Sam stepped out, glanced along the ledge and then turned back to Noble. "You going to be alright?"

"I'll be fine," Noble said, thinking of Duval. Every second they wasted out here brought him another second closer to execution. Noble said, "Get to Sacha before Grey kills him."

Sam nodded and started to turn.

Noble saw movement at the rear of the pilothouse and fear flooded his belly. Grey stepped around the corner, one hand pressed against his shoulder and the other aiming a pistol. Noble couldn't fire without hitting Sam. He opened his mouth to shout a warning and never got the chance. Grey fired four quick shots. A series of rapid bull-whips split the air. Sam jerked and strangled out a cry. Her eyes opened wide in fear and surprise. Her body tensed. Then she was falling.

She dropped over the side, hit the dark waters with a splash, and disappeared below the surface.

"No!" Noble screamed. The fear turned to hate, boiling over and setting his brain on fire. He thrust his gun out and triggered a volley, but Grey was already gone. He had ducked back around the corner before Sam even hit the water. The bullets ricocheted off the wall in a series of violent sparks.

Crushing grief threatened to cripple Noble, turning him into a howling lunatic crouching on the deck of the ship. But he couldn't let that happen, not yet. Sam was dead and the men responsible had to pay. A rip formed in Noble's soul and a terrible blackness oozed out. Preston and Grey had to die. Nothing else mattered.

He didn't stop to think about what he did next. He was on autopilot: a heat-seeking missile aimed at a target. Noble grasped the top of the barrels and hauled himself up. His face formed a grim mask. He wasn't worried about getting shot. If he died, so be it. He clambered atop the oil drums, heedless of the danger.

The move was so sudden and unexpected that it took Preston by surprise. His eyebrows went up and his mouth dropped open. By the time he recovered, Noble was standing up and taking aim. Preston raised his weapon to fire.

Noble centered his front sight and pulled the trigger until the slide locked back. Bullets stitched Preston's chest and shoulders, driving him backward. He hit the rear wall of the pilothouse and slid down, leaving a trail of dark blood.

Noble dropped the empty Kimber. It bounced off the

lid of a drum and fell down between the barrels with a clatter. A blast of cold air whipped through his hair as the barge rolled slowly on the river. Noble stripped off his coat and wrapped it around his hands, then ran and launched himself at the open window.

He sailed across three meters of open space, stretched out his arms, and managed to grasp hold of the window ledge. Fragments of broken glass shredded the coat and sliced into his palms. His body impacted the wall of the pilothouse with a muffled bang. His feet scrabbled at the slick metal until his toes found a rivet, then he pulled himself up over the frame and through the shattered window. Mean little shards buried themselves in his arms and legs. The pain fueled his hate.

Preston lay on the floor of the pilothouse, covered in his own blood. Fear flashed in his face as Noble climbed over the control panel. His words came out small and strained. "Help me. I need a hospital."

"You need an undertaker," Noble told him as he shook off the jacket.

Preston whimpered and spittle flew from his lips. He held up one blood-stained hand and croaked out, "Wait. It was all Coughlin. I just follow orders."

Ignoring the wounded man's pleas, Noble glanced around and found Preston's weapon. He picked it up, pressed the muzzle against Preston's forehead and pulled the trigger. The gun thundered and the back of Preston's head sprayed across the floor in a violent shout of pulpy red mass.

CHAPTER EIGHTY

Jaqueline Armstrong sat behind her desk with her heart pounding gently in her chest, while she listened to the torture of Sacha Duval. It was just after seven o'clock D.C. time.

A computer cowboy named Ezra Cook sat on the sofa, sweating through his shirt. His hair was disheveled and he had dark circles under his eyes. He had arrived at Armstrong's office an hour ago looking like he hadn't slept. He apologized profusely for interrupting and then demanded she see the information on a flash drive.

Armstrong had listened to his story and then cross-checked the files against Langley's database only to find them missing, verifying Cook's claims. Before she could act on this new information, she got a call from her knight errant. Noble had given her an ISP and told her to start a trace. He had relayed the feed from the ruggedized laptop to a cellphone and from there to the CIA's SIGINT office. The tech gurus in signal intelligence recorded the incoming call and uploaded the feed, with a slight delay, to Armstrong's office.

Duc leaned a shoulder against the bookshelf, his muscular forearms folded over his barrel chest, and listened in silence, a slight frown on his face and his beard sticking straight out.

The head of SIGINT, a lifer named Bob Moberly, sat across from Ezra. He had run a quick scrub to make sure it was genuine and then cleaned up the audio. It was hard to listen to. Armstrong had witnessed recordings of enhanced interrogations before. Torture, while sometimes necessary, was never pleasant. But it sounded like Grey was enjoying himself. When Duval finally cracked and divulged the name of his source, Ezra sat up a little straighter.

"That name mean something to you?" Armstrong asked.

He shook his head and shrank back down in the sofa.

"You sure?" Armstrong asked.

Ezra shrugged. "It's a character from a movie."

Armstrong nodded. "I go to the movies. You sure it doesn't ring any other bells?"

Ezra shook his head again.

On the recording, Grey was making a phone call, but the voices started to break up. Static interrupted the feed and then it shorted out altogether. Armstrong looked to Bob Moberly.

"The boat moved out of range," he explained.

"That's all we've got?" Armstrong asked.

Moberly said, "That's it, I'm afraid."

She frowned. "Have we had any word from Noble or Gunn?"

Duc shook his head. "We have a drone inbound to see if they can pick up the boat and a local contact en route."

"That recording came through less than fifteen minutes ago," Moberly said. "Near as we can tell, the situation is still unfolding."

Armstrong jabbed the intercom button and her secretary came on the line. "I need to see Coughlin in my office right away."

"I believe he's preparing to leave for the day."

"Call down stairs," Armstrong said. "Don't let him leave the building."

While they waited, Armstrong backed the recording up to the part where Grey made the telephone call. She checked the log and compared that to the local time in D.C.

When Coughlin arrived, he looked no better than Ezra. His eyes took in all the players and his face went into a series of spasms. He tried to smile, but it came off a snarl. "You wanted to see me?"

Armstrong played the recording for him.

Coughlin stood there, his hands at his side and his face a twitching mask of silence.

"May I see your phone?" Armstrong said.

Realization dawned on Coughlin's face. When he didn't move right away, Armstrong turned to Duc.

The big Navy SEAL uncrossed his arms and took a step in Coughlin's direction. The threat alone was enough. Coughlin reached into his coat pocket and came out with his cell. Duc passed the phone to Armstrong.

She glanced at his call log and said, "Well, what do you know. Matches the time of Grey's call."

Coughlin's nostrils flared. "That doesn't prove anything."

"How do you explain this?" Armstrong asked and turned her monitor so he could see the MEDUSA files.

Coughlin's eye twitched. He stood there several seconds and then said, "All that proves is that I laid in an operation to force Duval out of the embassy. So what? He leaked classified information for cryin' out loud. You should be thanking me. If it wasn't for Gunn, Duval would be at a black site right now, spilling his guts."

"If it wasn't for Gunn, Duval would be dead, and we'd be chasing rumors," Armstrong countered.

"He's guilty under the Espionage Act," Coughlin said. "Gunn helped him escape!"

"Yes, he is guilty," Armstrong agreed. "And he'll stand trial. So will you."

A sneer turned up Coughlin's mouth. "For what? Tricking Duval into leaving the embassy isn't a crime. Hell, we should have done that years ago."

"You laid in an operation without approval and erased classified information from a restricted database," Armstrong said. "That's a federal crime."

"We bury black ops all the time," Coughlin said.

"I have people going through your personal files right now," Armstrong informed him. "Are they going to find a copy of the missing CyberLance program?"

Coughlin didn't know what to say, so he stood there, a statue staring silently at his accusers. He opened his mouth once but shut it.

Armstrong said, "What about Gwendolyn Witwicky?

Did you run her off the road or did you hire someone to do it for you?"

Coughlin was going to jail and he knew it. He closed his eyes and shook his head. "Collateral damage."

Up until that point, Ezra had sat on the sofa with his fists clenched. Now, he leapt up and swung a wild haymaker. Coughlin was caught by surprise. His head snapped back and he went down in a heap. Ezra followed him to the floor, pummeling Coughlin with tightly balled fists.

Duc stepped forward, grabbed Ezra by the collar and lifted him off with no more effort than a man lifting a spare tire from a trunk.

Coughlin cranked himself up on one elbow. His lips were cut and bleeding. He ran a hand under his busted nose, leaving a bright red streak on the cuff of his jacket. His eyes bored into Armstrong like poison darts, but he had nothing more to say. His scheme had unraveled and it was only a matter of time before the investigators fitted all the pieces together.

"Duc," Armstrong said. "Escort Mr. Coughlin to a holding site until we can arrange for his debriefing."

"With pleasure."

When they had left, Armstrong turned to Cook. "I'll see that Ms. Witwicky gets the best treatment available."

He ducked his head. "Thank you, ma'am."

"Before you go," Armstrong said. "Are you absolutely certain the name Groot doesn't mean anything to you?"

Ezra swallowed hard and said, "No ma'am."

Armstrong leaned back in her seat. She was thinking of the banner hanging on the wall on B3. She had noticed it her first day on the job as she was touring the building, giving pep talks to the troops. She had thought it funny at the time, even if it was against protocol, and chose to ignore it. Now she looked hard at Cook and nodded. "Go home and get some sleep, Mr. Cook."

CHAPTER EIGHTY-ONE

DUVAL'S NERVE ENDINGS WERE ON HIGH ALERT. Sitting there and listening to the gunfight overhead made him feel small and helpless. He was sweating despite the cold. Large beads of perspiration ran down his naked skin and puddled on the floor at his feet. He blinked several times in an effort to clear his vision. Everything was blurry, like he had been swimming too long in a heavily chlorinated pool. A fuzzy halo surrounded the lightbulb. Duval wondered what kind of long term damage the bleach had done. Was he disfigured for life? His face felt like a puffy mass of bruises and chemical burns and his stomach was raw.

As soon as Grey left him alone, Duval had gone to work on the handcuffs. After securing the microdot, Noble had glued a handcuff key along with a razor blade to the small of Duval's back using medical adhesive and silly putty. When he finished, it had looked like an old scar. Duval didn't think such a simple trick would work, but with a dash of blood on it, the scar looked real enough. Now, Duval peeled back the edge with trembling fingers. It was a slow, tedious process, made harder by the fact that his hands were shaking so badly. His fingers jumped around like nervous insects looking for a place to land.

While he worked, the thunder clap of pistols had faded away and the sound of the engines cut out. Duval kept expecting Sam to come through the door any second, but the seconds stretched into minutes and minutes dragged by with agonizing slowness. *Who had won the fight?* If it was Sam and Noble, how come they didn't come rescue him? If it was Grey, why wasn't he here? A thousand bleak scenarios crowded Duval's mind.

Focus on the handcuffs, Duval told himself.

He slowly pulled away the thin layer of putty and dried blood. The medical glue ripped out the small hairs on his back. Duval winced, more from expectation than any real pain, like saying ouch when someone snaps you with a rubber band. It doesn't really hurt, but you're conditioned to think it will. Thanks to Grey, Duval's understanding of pain had been forever altered and the small sting of pulled hairs no longer counted for much.

Duval gripped the wad of putty in his right hand and gently probed with his thumb, searching for the handcuff key and fearful of the razor blade. Doing all this behind his back, using only his sense of touch, took time. When he finally managed to separate the key, he dropped the rest of the wad and set about trying to slot the key in the cuff.

Do not *drop it,* thought Duval.

The head of the key kept slipping off the metal plate with a tiny shriek. Duval was moaning quietly to himself and rocking back and forth. The strain of waiting to see who came through the door first had utterly exhausted him. He growled in frustration and tried again. He felt the key find its home and a surge of victory swelled his chest. A nervous smile flickered across his face. He gave the key a twist and the bracelet popped open.

Duval hooted in triumph.

In his mind, he was already sprinting, stark naked, across the deck of the ship, diving into the water and swimming to freedom. He stood up so fast he turned the chair over. It hit the ground with a flat smack. Duval winced at the sound, but he was too shot full of adrenaline to worry about the noise.

He quickly removed the other cuff, let it clatter on the floor, and looked about for something to use as a weapon. His eyes settled on a big, heavy wrench. He hefted it. It had a nice weight. Duval gave an experimental swing. He felt silly standing there naked with his pudgy belly and his pasty skin, swinging a wrench, but he also felt primal, like a cave man with a club. He thought of Grey dousing him with bleach, thought about the humiliation of being stripped and handcuffed to a chair, thought about the years imprisoned in the embassy, living like a fugitive, and Duval got angry. His swollen red face worked into a hard frown. He took another swing and this time the wrench whistled through the air with deadly intent.

CHAPTER EIGHTY-TWO

Noble checked the action on Preston's weapon. Blood from his lacerated palms smeared the pistol grip and the slide. The jacket had offered some protection, but not much. A few of the cuts would need stitches, but that would have to wait. Noble's body felt like a high tension wire with too much juice running through the lines.

Preston's Sig had one round in the chamber and one in the magazine. Noble patted the dead man's pockets, leaving bloody hand prints. All he found was a cellphone, car keys, a wallet, and a bottle of pain killers. Preston had been down to his last mag, but two bullets was one more than enough to deal with Grey.

The control panel was a simple affair. Noble throttled the engines back and flipped the switch to *off*. The motors died with a cough and the sudden silence was deafening. The barge slowed and then drifted, bobbing on the current in the middle of the river while waves lapped gently against the hull.

A Jim Morrison lyric popped into Noble's head. He whispered, "No one here gets out alive."

Clutching the weapon in bloody palms, Noble went to the ladder that led to the galley, crouched and scanned both directions. When no one shot at him, he sat down, swung his legs over the side and dropped to the deck. He landed with a bang. The impact sent lances of pain through aging knees. All the hard miles he had put on his body were finally catching up with him, but none of that seemed to matter anymore.

An open hatch let onto the stern and cold air blew in. Noble checked his corners, cleared the bow of the ship, then hauled the hatch shut and locked it. If Grey was inside, then he was somewhere below decks and Noble would find him sooner or later. If he was outside, he could stay out there and freeze while Noble cleared the hold.

Another ladder led down to the belly of the ship. Pipes and machinery created a maze of twisting passages. It was twenty degrees warmer down here and reeked of burning oil. Sweat gathered on Noble's forehead. He wiped his hands on his trousers and adjusted his grip on the weapon.

There was a small scuffing noise and the rattle of chains from the far side of the hold. Noble trained his weapon on the sound, held his breath, and waited. The only illumination came from red emergency bulbs in wire cages. Noble stepped over a pipe that stretched across the path and circled the compartment. He caught movement from the corner of his eye and threw himself behind a bank of pressure dials just in time.

Bullets whined off the metal and bounced around inside the hold, rebounding off the hull. It was like being stuck inside a deadly pinball machine. The enclosed space magnified the sound of the shots and left Noble's ears ringing.

He leaned out for a peek, caught sight of Grey darting across the passage, and gave chase. Noble ducked under a low pipe, rounded a corner, and took an elbow to the face. His nose broke with a wet crunch and his head snapped back. Pain sent him reeling. Warm blood spilled over his chin and the coppery taste filled his mouth. Grey had lured him into an ambush, waited for him to round the corner, and then nailed him.

Before Noble could recover, Grey grabbed a fistful of hair and slammed Noble's head against the bulkhead. The gun slipped from limp fingers and lights danced in his vision. He felt the boat tip and the deck came up to meet him. He landed on his left side with blood welling up around a nasty gash in his forehead.

There was a cold heartless laugh from overhead. The sound came to Noble's ears like something out of a distant nightmare. He gave his head a shake, blinked to clear his vision, and the image of Grey swam into view. Noble brought his hand up to shoot and his fingers closed on empty air before he realized he was no longer holding the gun.

"It's over, Noble. You lost." Grey gave him a kick to the ribs that curled Noble up. "I killed your girlfriend and now I'm going to kill you. When I'm done, I'm going to kill the reporter too."

Grey reared back, a football player lining up for a field goal. Noble balled up and took the blow on his forearms.

The bones creaked, threatening to break. It was like getting hit by a sledge hammer.

"I'm going to take my time and enjoy this." Grey delivered another devastating kick.

Noble barked in pain, rolled onto his other side to avoid having his arms broken and he spotted the fallen pistol. His eyes opened wide. He lunged for it.

"Oh, no you don't!" Grey stepped past him and shot a toe at the handgun, sending the weapon skittering across the floor to disappear behind a set of pipes. He followed up with three more kicks to Noble's ribs.

Noble drew in a tortured breath. Pain and fatigue were taking their toll. A tight knot formed in his throat at the realization that he would die here in the engine compartment. He thought of Sam: saw her eyes as she fell and heard the splash when her body hit the water. It was like someone hit the mute button on the pain and a deadly rage filled him.

Noble lunged up, grabbed Grey around the waist and wrestled him to the ground. Grey went down hard. His skull bounced off the metal floor with a solid *thud*. Noble straddled him and slammed a fist into Grey's mouth. His knuckles mashed Grey's lips and knocked a tooth out. Noble continued to pound until he felt the small bone in his left pinkie finger snap. A shot of exquisite pain raced up his arm and into his brain. He switched to elbows, bashing the boney point of his forearm into Grey's cheekbones with devastating impacts punctuated by flat, hard smacks that echoed around the engine room.

Grey cried out in pain, threw one arm over his face in an effort to protect himself, reached in his waistband and drew his pistol. The slide was locked back on an empty chamber, but Grey swung it like a paperweight. The steel frame connected with the side of Noble's head and fireworks popped inside his skull.

Grey hit him twice more and Noble pitched over on his side. It felt like his head would split open. He clung desperately to consciousness, knowing if he blacked out, it would be the end. He would never wake up. It wasn't the thought of dying that scared him, but the thought of failing Sam.

Grey staggered to his feet and reached behind the pipes for Noble's fallen pistol. Noble tried to stand. He needed to stop Grey from getting the loaded gun, but a wave of dizziness hit and he went back down, clutching a steam release valve for support.

Grey worked his arm behind the pipes, pulled the gun out, checked the chamber, then raised the pistol. Noble stared down the yawning barrel and watched in slow motion as Grey's finger inched the trigger back.

Sacha Duval lurched around the corner, naked and wielding a large pipe wrench. He stepped up behind Grey and swung. The wrench connected with a meaty thud. Grey staggered forward, but managed to keep his feet.

Duval stood there, too stunned to follow through. His eyes were big as saucers and his mouth hung open. If he'd been smart, he would have kept swinging until Grey went down, but Duval had never been in a fight before.

Grey, one hand cupping the back of his bleeding skull, turned, saw Duval and brought the pistol up. "You son of a—"

Noble tried to pull himself up and realized he was holding a pressure release valve handle. His eyes traced the pipe to the gauge, where he saw a needle edging toward the redline, and then up to the valve. He tightened his grip on the lever and yanked.

A geyser of steam burst from the pipe with a loud whistle. The jet hit Grey in the face. He shrieked, dropped the gun, and sat down hard. Ear-splitting screams reverberated around the engine room.

Duval shuffled back a step, throwing up his hands and turning his face away. He was far enough from the steam that he didn't get burned, but it had been a close call. He put his back to the wall and slid down onto his rear end, shaking with relief.

Noble waited for the head of steam to die off before struggling to his feet.

"I'm blind!" Grey shrieked. "I'm blind!"

Noble reached for the gun.

Grey was writhing on the floor in agony. The steam had liquefied his eyeballs like overcooked eggs and melted the skin of his face. He looked like something from a zombie film. Noble leveled the pistol at that unseeing face and his fingertip turned white on the trigger.

Before Noble could fire the shot that would kill Grey, his thoughts went to Sam. She wouldn't execute a blind man in cold blood. But she wasn't here. She was dead because of Grey. Noble wanted to pull the trigger to satisfy his own need for revenge, but more than that, he wanted to honor Sam's memory. Doubt, loss, and confusion flooded his heart. The gun started to shake. Tears gathered in his eyes and ran down his cheeks. He let go of the trigger, turned the gun around, and hit Grey over the head.

The high-pitched shrieks were cut short and Grey slumped to the floor.

Duval let out a shaky breath and said, "I thought I was going to die."

Noble didn't trust himself to speak. Part of him wanted to put the last bullet through Duval. He stood there, blood dripping from his lacerated palms, holding back a sob of despair.

When Noble didn't say anything, Duval looked up and a shadow of fear passed over his face. "Where's Sam?"

Noble shook his head.

CHAPTER EIGHTY-THREE

Two weeks later, Jaqueline Armstrong boarded *the Yeoman* across from Demens Landing in downtown Saint Pete. Duc waited in the park under the shade of a large oak tree. The mercury in Florida hovered close to sixty-five degrees and locals were bundled up in parkas like the sky was falling. Armstrong stopped at the steps and knocked on the open door.

"Noble," she called. "It's me."

When she didn't get an answer, Jaqueline bent down and stuck her head inside. Noble sat at the galley table, his back against the bulkhead and a beer in one bandaged hand. His eyes were puffy red slits and he was in bad need of a shave. He lifted the bottle to his lips without acknowledging her presence.

Jaqueline stepped down into the galley. The stale reek of old booze and body odor assaulted her nostrils. She tried not to let it show on her face. Her heart was breaking for him. She had chosen Noble because of his feelings for

Gunn. Now Sam was at the bottom of a watery grave and Noble hadn't emerged from his boat in two weeks. Jaqueline had considered counseling but Noble wouldn't go. He wasn't the type. It would be like asking a tiger to turn vegetarian.

"I went to see your mother," Armstrong said. "I hope you don't mind. She's quite a spitfire. She asked about you. I told her you were okay, but you should pay her a visit soon. She deserves to hear from you."

He drank some more beer and made no indication that he had even heard the words coming out of her mouth.

Armstrong said, "You can't blame yourself, Jake."

"The hell I can't."

"Sam made her own decisions," Armstrong told him. "She did the right thing and she's got a star on the wall at Langley."

"That won't bring her back," Noble said.

Armstrong laid a hand on top of his. "You don't have to die with her, Jake. Sam wouldn't want that."

He pulled his hand away, picked up his bottle and swigged. "It was my plan that put her on that boat. I'm the reason she's dead."

Armstrong shook her head. "You and I both know that's not true. Sam would have seen it through with or without you."

"Maybe."

They sat in silence for a while. Finally, Armstrong said, "Any chance you're going to tell me where you stashed Duval?"

Noble shook his head.

"I figured as much."

Noble said nothing.

Armstrong lit a thin cigar while Noble drank. No more words were needed. They were both soldiers, in their own way, who had lost a comrade and the only cure for that was time. Armstrong finished her cigar, went to the door, stopped, and turned back. "Get yourself cleaned up, Noble. I've got work for you."

THE END.

CAN'T WAIT FOR MORE
JAKE NOBLE?

Sign up for the Jake Noble Fan Club and get, SIDE JOBS: Volume 1, The Heist for FREE! This story is available exclusively to my mailing list.

https://williammillerauthor.com/fan-club/

DID YOU ENJOY THE BOOK?

Please take a moment to leave a review on Amazon. Readers depend on reviews when choosing what to read next and authors depend on them to sell books. An honest review is like leaving your waiter a hundred dollar tip. The best part is, it doesn't cost you a dime!

ABOUT THE AUTHOR

I was born and raised in sunny Saint Petersburg, FL on a steady diet of action movies and fantasy novels. After 9/11, I left a career in photography to join the United States Army. Since then, I have travelled the world and done everything from teaching English in China to driving a fork-lift. I studied creative writing at Eckerd College and wrote four hard-boiled mysteries for Delight Games before releasing the first Jake Noble book. When not writing, I can be found indoor rock climbing, playing the guitar, and haunting smoke-filled jazz clubs in downtown Saint Pete. I'm currently at work on another Jake Noble thriller. You can follow me on my website WilliamMillerAuthor.com

f facebook.com/authorwillmiller

🐦 twitter.com/noblemanauthor

📷 instagram.com/wmiller314

Made in the USA
Las Vegas, NV
02 October 2021

31497773R10216